Underneath the Arches

Early on an October morning in London, a team of Flying Squad officers, under the command of the redoubtable Detective Chief Superintendent Tommy Fox, is keeping observation on a repository of stolen property underneath some railway arches in Lambeth.

Two robbers, arriving to lodge the proceeds of yet another robbery, discover – to their horror and to the surprise of the police – that it contains the body of a young woman.

Approaching the investigation in his usual unorthodox way, Fox has to contend not only with the familiar catalogue of villainy but also with two complaints that have been made against him and which are being investigated by the unbending and humourless Commander Willow of the Uniform Branch.

'Porn-brokers', an oil executive who travels frequently between London and Kuwait, big-businessmen, charity workers and a civil servant all come under suspicion. And, in the course of his enquiries, Fox also manages to get rather close to a young female member of the nobility. But then Fox always did have a discerning eye.

Working his unconventional way through the obstacles that seem constantly to be strewn in his path, Fox eventually resolves the mystery of the body that was found Underneath the Arches.

Underneath
the Arches

GRAHAM ISON

LITTLE, BROWN AND COMPANY

A *Little, Brown* Book

First published in Great Britain in 1994 by
Little, Brown and Company

Copyright © Graham Ison 1994

The moral right of the author has been asserted.

A CIP catalogue record for this book is available
from the British Library.

ISBN 0 316 90820 7

Photoset in North Wales by
Derek Doyle & Associates, Mold, Clwyd.
Printed in England by Clays Ltd, St Ives plc

Little, Brown and Company (UK) Limited
Brettenham House
Lancaster Place
London WC2 7EN

Underneath the Arches

ONE

AT JUST AFTER 5.30 A.M., WHEN London was beginning to come to life and a bandit vehicle could meld with the capital's traffic without arousing too much suspicion, a transit van drew up outside a warehouse in Balham and two men in balaclavas got out. They looked around briefly, then opened the wicket door and went in.

Two days previously, Detective Chief Superintendent Thomas Fox of the Flying Squad had made a decision to let the robbery run.

Fox, a firm believer in what the police these days call a hands-on approach – but which his subordinates called interfering – had decided that he was going to oversee the operation in person and had convened a conference of Numbers Three and Four teams to ensure that it all went smoothly.

He would not have allowed the robbery to go ahead had there been any risk of injury to members of the public, but the early-morning theft of video-recorders from a warehouse was not seen as likely to endanger anyone.

Except perhaps the night-watchman and he had been briefed not to put up any resistance. In fact, it had been suggested that he be as co-operative as possible. And he was. Probably because the night-watchman, for one performance only, was to be a detective sergeant called Crozier.

'This heist that's supposed to be coming down the day after tomorrow, Ron,' Fox had said. 'I need a good man to take the night-watchman's place. Someone who can act the part, doesn't get all excited and, indeed, almost appears to

1

be wanting to co-operate.'

'Yes, sir.' Detective Sergeant Ron Crozier had replied in resigned tones. In an unguarded moment when the Scotch was flowing, he had allowed it to become known that he had been an actor before joining the police, twenty-three years previously. Consequently, whenever Fox visualised a role for an ex-actor, it was Crozier who got the job. And Crozier was not pleased. It was not that he foresaw any danger in the assignment but that he might be missing some of the action.

The police could have captured the villains in the act of robbery, but they were anxious to know where the video-recorders were going. Which was why Fox intended to mount an elaborate surveillance.

'There have now been seven of these robberies over the last six weeks.' Fox had addressed himself once more to the conference at large. 'All from warehouses. And these bastards have had off anything from carpets to men's clothing and children's toys. I ask you, children's toys.' Fox made it sound as though innocents' Christmas stockings had been plundered. 'I am told that our great new intelligence-gathering arm,' he had gone on, contriving a sour expression that had brought dutiful laughter from his audience, 'has been working overtime, to say nothing of their divers band of so-called informants, in an attempt to discover who is handling these stolen goods. But to me, as a simple policeman, it appears that these heists are taking place to order, and are selective into the bargain. Only certain items were nicked, almost as if these light-fingered operatives have got a shopping list.'

And that was all that the combined resources of the Flying Squad and the National Criminal Intelligence Service had been able to discover, apart from an unconfirmed snippet from a previously untested inform-ant that there was to be another raid early in the morning, two days hence, on a warehouse in Balham.

Crozier, who had got well into the part, was wearing a grey warehouse coat and spectacles with plain glass lenses. 'Morning, lads,' he said, as if the arrivals were making a

2

routine delivery. 'You're early.'

One of the robbers raised a jemmy in Crozier's direction. 'If you know what's good for you, mate,' he said, 'you'll mind your own business. Don't give us no trouble and we won't give you none. Got it?'

'I'm no hero, mate,' said Crozier, affecting some spurious alarm, 'and I ain't getting me head stove in for the sake of a few quid's-worth of video-recorders.'

'Very sensible,' said the villain and ripped the phone out of its socket. Just to be on the safe side, he followed this up by kicking the socket off the wall and stamping on it.

Very quickly and very efficiently, the two robbers picked out just eight of the higher-priced video-recorders and loaded them into the van. In little more than five minutes, the raid was all over.

Detective Inspector Henry Findlater, sometime head of the Criminal Intelligence Branch surveillance unit, but now a member of the Flying Squad, had been given the responsibility of following the robbers after the raid. When the transit van drove away from the warehouse and out into the main road, two motor-cyclists started to play leap-frog, from time to time changing places with each other, and at other times allowing one of the disreputable looking cars or vans that formed part of Findlater's team to take a turn in keeping their quarry under observation.

Fox, and Detective Inspector Denzil Evans's team of detectives, were eventually directed by radio to a series of arches beneath a railway bridge in the London borough of Lambeth which, for some reason, is always described as being south of the River Thames. In point of fact, it is due east, but this minor geographical discrepancy was of no great interest to the police.

But it was when the robbers arrived at a lock-up beneath those arches that things started to go wrong. For the robbers.

Unaware that at least ten pairs of eyes were watching from various vantage points, one of the robbers tried to open the padlock on the doors to the lock-up while the other swung back the rear door of the transit van. After several attempts, the first robber gave up and jemmied the hasp and eye off the door and he and his accomplice went in.

Seconds later, they came running out, slammed the rear doors of the van and jumped in. Hurriedly starting the engine, and once crashing the gears, the two robbers drove off at high speed.

Parked some way away, Tommy Fox was informed of this minor drama. 'Well don't hang about,' he said to his driver, the lugubrious Swann, 'get to it.' Then he grabbed the handset of the radio and instructed DI Findlater to continue the surveillance. Findlater, in his own vehicle some distance away, sighed. Those had been his instructions anyway.

Swann muttered to himself and swinging the Granada in a U-turn, drove straight to the lock-up.

Fox got out and crossing to the still-open doors, peered in at the cavernous interior. On the bare concrete floor, close to one wall, was the body of a woman. A very dead woman.

Fox was still contemplating this complication to what he regarded as a straightforward robbery when he was joined by DI Evans.

Evans too, stared at the body. 'Bloody hell,' he said.

'Exactly so,' said Fox wearily. 'Why is it, Denzil,' he went on, 'that simple heists always seem to develop some uncalled-for complexity these days? Do these villains do it deliberately?'

'Want them nicked, guv'nor?' asked Evans.

'Oh yes, Denzil, most decidedly.'

'But what about the slaughter, sir?'

'Are you talking of *this* slaughter?' asked Fox, waving a hand at the body, 'or were you employing the criminal vernacular to describe a place where stolen property is secreted?'

'Well, guv, we do want to know where the gear's going, don't we?' As usual, Evans was having trouble keeping up with Fox's rapid changes of plan. He was fairly certain that they were now saddled with a murder, but he could never quite work out Fox's strategy for any given set of circumstances.

4

'Denzil, dear boy,' said Fox patiently, 'you're not suggesting, I hope, that robbery takes precedence over a suspicious death, are you?'

'Well, no, sir.'

'And would you agree with me, Denzil, that this has all the hallmarks of a murder?'

'Yes, sir.' Evans wondered how he had managed, with no effort on his part, to become the butt of another of Fox's little homilies on semantics.

'Then we shall begin. One, send a message to Henry and tell him to make sure that he doesn't lose those two villains. But tell him to "house" them, not to nick 'em . . . not yet. Two, do the usual in respect of this.' Fox pointed at the body and walked back to the Granada. Reaching in through the open window, he took his packet of cigarettes from the top of the dashboard just as Swann was thinking of helping himself to one.

With a sigh, Evans crossed the yard to his own car and proceeded to call out all the people required to record the murder scene. And, with any luck, to provide the investigating officers with as much information as possible to begin their enquiries.

Detective Inspector Henry Findlater wondered how long it was all going to go on. The two villains in the transit van had now slowed to a pace sedate enough not to attract the attention of any traffic policemen who might be about, but in their desire to put as much distance between themselves and the dead body in the lock-up at Lambeth, they had not worried too much about where they were going. Finding themselves eventually in Nine Elms Lane driving south, they carried on until they reached Prince of Wales Drive in Battersea.

With a nonchalance that required a great deal of self-control, they got out of the van, closed the doors and sauntered away. Minutes later, they hailed a taxi.

Fox, hands in the pockets of his light grey cashmere overcoat, watched the team from the forensic science laboratory at work. He had accepted, phlegmatically, that

5

yet another promising operation had been brought to nought by unforeseen circumstances. In this case, a murder.

'Good morning, Mr Fox. A trifle cold this morning, I thought.' The dour Aberdonian tones told Fox that John Harris, the Home Office pathologist, had arrived.

'Morning,' said Fox. 'Got a body for you.'

'Ah! Splendid.' Dr Harris rubbed his hands together in ghoulish anticipation. It was the only emotion that Fox had ever seen him display. 'What sort?'

'Dead,' said Fox, determined that one day he would get a smile from the pathologist.

'No, I meant what sex, age, that sort of thing?'

'I'll tell you what,' said Fox, 'come and have a look. Saves all the explanations, don't you think?'

The dead woman was aged somewhere between twenty-eight and thirty-four, according to Harris, and she had been strangled. Manually. The pathologist knelt down and pointed out the bruise-marks of fingers on one side of her throat, and a deep thumb-mark on the other.

Harris took the temperature of the body and of the lock-up, made inaudible comments to himself about rigor mortis in the shoulder muscles and in the face, and eventually came to the conclusion that death had occurred anything between six and ten hours previously. But, he added with the caution of his profession, more likely ten. He also added that his tentative opinion about the cause of death was subject to the results of a post-mortem examination.

It's a long way from Battersea to Lewisham and the cab fare must have cost an arm and a leg, but the two villains were eventually set down in Brockley Rise where they split up. One went westwards, towards Honor Oak, the other to the east in the direction of Blythe Hill.

The team of watchers took note of the addresses to which they had gone and, having informed Findlater, set up a discreet observation. Findlater sent a message to Fox and waited for further instructions.

He didn't have long to wait. Fox, having overseen the

removal of the unknown woman's body, had returned to Scotland Yard and now sat in an armchair in his office, his feet on a small table, drinking a cup of coffee and perusing *The Times*. And waiting for the arrival of Detective Inspector Jack Gilroy.

Gilroy arrived at the same time as Findlater's message. 'Ah, Jack.' Fox replaced the telephone receiver as Gilroy entered the office. 'Sorry to drag you out.' He glanced at the clock. 'Didn't realise you were late turn today.'

Gilroy ignored the jibe. It was, after all, only eight o'clock. 'Good morning, sir.'

'We've got a problem, Jack.'

'So I understand, guv'nor. The lads in the Squad office have just been filling me in.'

'Denzil's at the mortuary waiting for John Harris to start the day's butchery, and Henry Findlater has just called in to say that he's "housed" these two villains. It will come as no surprise to you, Jack, to learn that they are *habitués* of that vast hinterland of iniquity known as Lewisham. Pop out and nick them, there's a good chap.'

'Right, sir.' Gilroy turned to leave.

'Better take them to Bow Street. It's handy.'

'Not any more it isn't, sir. Bow Street nick's been closed. The court's still there, of course.'

'What?' Fox dropped his unfolded newspaper on the floor, a startled expression on his face. 'What on earth are you talking about, Jack?'

'It's all happening at Charing Cross now, sir.'

Fox shook his head. 'No one tells me anything, Jack. Where in Charing Cross, as a matter of passing interest?'

'The old hospital, sir.' Gilroy knew very well that Fox was aware that the police station had moved, but Fox had obviously decided to be perverse this morning.

'How very apt,' said Fox. 'Oh, and Jack . . .'

'Sir?'

'The van which they abandoned, together with the contents thereof, principally eight high-quality video-recorders, has been removed to Battersea Police Station.'

'Right, guv.'

'Make sure you count the video-recorders, Jack. They're

7

a funny lot down at Battersea.'

By the time that Jack Gilroy had assembled his team and fought his way through the morning rush-hour traffic to Lewisham, it had gone ten o'clock, but Findlater's observation was still in place and he was able to tell Gilroy that the villains were still at home. Using what he believed to be initiative, but what Fox regarded as the norm, Findlater had despatched one of his officers to check on the electoral roll. The officer had drawn a blank. In common with many people, the villains firmly believed that putting one's name down for a vote would almost certainly volunteer them for payment of council tax. Consequently, each of the addresses to which the robbers had been followed was shown in official records as unoccupied. Which came as no surprise to anybody.

Undismayed by this lack of information, Gilroy and his team went first to the house in Honor Oak. Their knock was answered by a small girl with a dirty face, who, with one finger in her mouth, looked shyly round the door at the detectives but said nothing.

'Your daddy at home?' asked Gilroy.

The small girl nodded but still said nothing.

'Who is it, Sharon?' An uncouth female voice bellowed from somewhere in the house.

The small girl ran away towards the voice, leaving the door ajar. Gilroy and Detective Sergeant Buckley followed.

''Ere, who the bloody hell are you?' The woman was standing in the doorway to the kitchen.

'Police,' said Gilroy.

'So? I never invited you in.'

'Didn't have to, missus,' said Gilroy. 'We've got a warrant. Where is he?'

'Oh my Gawd,' said the woman, 'not again.' She walked to the foot of the stairs and was about to shout when Gilroy put a hand on her arm.

'Leave it out,' he said and went upstairs, two at a time and into the front bedroom where he knew, from years of experience, that he would find who he was looking for.

8

'What the bloody hell—?'

'Flying Squad,' said Gilroy. 'And you're nicked.'

'What the bleedin' hell for?' The man swung his feet out of bed and scratched his head.

'How's robbery grab you?'

The second arrest, at Blythe Hill, went much the same as the first. The youth at that house, whose vociferous mother attempted, unsuccessfully, to protect him from the wicked police, was also in bed.

By midday, Gilroy was back at Scotland Yard. 'Both prisoners are now in intensive care at Charing Cross, sir,' he said.

'Hospital?' asked Fox.

Gilroy grinned. 'No, sir. Police station.'

'Shame. Who are they, by the way?'

'One of them is called Sidney Budgeon and the other is Walter Chesney, guv'nor.'

'Splendid work, Jack. I take it that both are known to us? Professionally, of course.'

'Yes, sir. The usual form for blagging and related offences.'

'Good, good,' said Fox. 'Does make life easier when you know who you're talking to. In that case, Jack, I think I shall go and have a chat with these gentlemen. But not before I have a quick audience of the commander. After which I may not wish to see them at all.'

'Really, sir?' Gilroy looked suitably perplexed.

'Yes, indeed, Jack. I have it in mind to unload this murder enquiry onto the local police. Be good experience for them.'

'But there's still the robbery, guv'nor.'

'Indeed there is, Jack.' Fox appeared to have tired of the whole business. 'You can pop down and have a chat to them about that.'

TWO

BUT FOX'S INTERVIEW WITH COMMANDER Alec Myers did not go exactly as he had hoped.

'Well, Tommy, it looks as though you've caught another murder,' said Myers, who had charge of several other branches of the Specialist Operations Department at New Scotland Yard as well as the Flying Squad.

'I was thinking that it might be a good idea if the local CID dealt with that, sir.'

Myers smiled. 'Yes, I thought you might, but the rule is still the same. You found it, you deal with it.'

'But—'

'And apart from anything else, Tommy, it could well form a part of these robberies you're investigating. As an experienced detective officer, you'd have to agree with that, wouldn't you?'

'I suppose there might be an outside possibility, sir,' said Fox reluctantly. It was always the same when ever he tried to avoid what looked like becoming a protracted enquiry. 'But I don't see two low-life villains getting involved in anything that heavy.'

'Maybe,' Myers went on, 'but with your unsurpassable skill as a detective, highly experienced in complex investigations, I imagine that you'll have this one buttoned up in no time at all.' He grinned. 'Keep me posted, Tommy.'

Fox opened the door of Gilroy's office. 'We are going to Charing Cross,' he said tersely.

'Thought we might be, sir,' said Gilroy and received a withering glance from Fox.

'How old are they?'

'Budgeon's thirty-six, sir, and Chesney is twenty-two,' said Gilroy.

'Splendid,' said Fox. 'We shall talk to young Mr Chesney first then.' He glanced at the custody sergeant. 'If you would be so kind, Sergeant.'

Five minutes later, assured that the prisoner had been brought up and placed in the interview room, Fox strode in and looked round. 'You know, Jack,' he said, 'there's no doubt that the architects employed by the Metropolitan Police are starting to get their act together. This is really rather splendid.' He stared at the prisoner. 'Wouldn't you agree?' he asked and smiled.

'I ain't saying nothing.' Walter Chesney was wearing a surly expression, a leather bomber jacket and filthy jeans, and his hair, which was lank and unwashed, came down to his shoulders.

'I was merely saying to my inspector here, that the decor of police stations has improved radically over the last twenty years or so.' Sitting down opposite the prisoner, Fox lit a cigarette and riffled quickly through the man's criminal record. 'Well, Wally, you've not been at it for long . . .' He closed the slim file and pushed it to one side. 'But you've managed to squeeze in a commendable bit of form, I'll give you that.'

'What's this about?'

'What this is about, Wally, dear boy, is an unfortunate incident which occurred earlier today.' Fox paused. 'Oh, Jack,' he said, 'you'd better turn on the apparatus, I suppose.'

'Right, sir.' Gilroy switched on the tape recorder and announced that an interview was being conducted with Walter Chesney by Detective Chief Superintendent Thomas Fox of the Flying Squad in the presence of Detective Inspector Jack Gilroy.

At the mention of Fox's name, Chesney sat upright. He had heard of Fox, and what he had heard did not give him any reason to think that he might shortly walk out of the police station a free man.

Those members of London's loose band of villainry who had not had previous dealings with Fox were inclined to regard him as a dandy, an assumption based upon a sartorial elegance that was impeccable almost to the point of being obsessive. Sometimes called, behind his back, the Beau Brummel of Scotland Yard, he was just as fussy about his spoken English – when he chose to be – even though it was delivered in a rich Cockney accent. But it was a mistake for anyone, policeman or villain, to underestimate him. Those who knew him well knew that he was a hard-nosed detective of the old school. And they also knew that he was the holder of the Queen's Gallantry Medal.

Shortly before Fox had taken command of the Flying Squad, a villain had made the painful mistake of pulling a gun on him. In the interests of law and order – and his own welfare – Fox had walked swiftly across the room and felled the offender with a right hook. He had then stood on the gunman's hand and explained, briefly and in the vernacular, that he was under arrest.

During the resulting trial at the Old Bailey, defence counsel had tried to make capital out of the fact that his client's jaw had been broken in the course of his arrest, and suggested that Fox had used more force than was necessary. This proposition had produced from Fox a response that had gone down in the annals of the Metropolitan Police. 'When a villain draws a gun on an unarmed police officer,' he had said, 'it is my view that the officer may infer that the said villain has abandoned the Queensberry Rules.'

At that point, to the discomfiture of defence counsel, the judge, a former Oxford boxing blue, had glanced up and said, 'I entirely agree.'

'Now where was I?' Fox stared at Chesney for some time. 'Ah, yes. Now, Wally, this morning at about five-thirty, you and Mr Sidney Budgeon, who lives next door to you—'

'No he don't,' said Chesney.

'Oh but he does, dear boy. He is currently occupying the

12

cell adjacent to your own. And is likely to for some time to come I shouldn't wonder.' Fox beamed at the prisoner. 'You and Mr Budgeon took it upon yourselves to steal eight video-recorders from a warehouse in down-town Balham. You then transported these wondrous items of electronic gismo to a lock-up in Lambeth. But at that point, you decided on a radical change of plan. For some reason you took them to Prince of Wales Drive, Battersea, and abandoned them. Now why, I ask myself, should you have done that?'

'I was home in bed.'

'Furthermore,' continued Fox, as though Chesney hadn't spoken, 'you then leaped into a cab and high-tailed it back to Lewisham. And I can produce at least twelve police officers who will happily testify to that fact, when eventually the Crown Prosecution Service can be prevailed upon to arrange for you to be tried at the Old Bailey, or such lesser place as may be decided.'

'Oh!' said Chesney.

'Oh indeed.' Fox stubbed out his cigarette. 'But what is worrying me grievously at this moment is the body.'

'Body?' Chesney's voice rose slightly. He had known instinctively that the sarcastic policeman opposite would get to that sooner or later.

'Dear boy, you couldn't have failed to notice, on the floor of the lock-up, that there was the body of a young lady. A dead body.'

'That weren't nothing to do with us. It was there, like.'

'Indeed it was, Walter, dear boy. The thing that puzzles me, and my officers . . .' He nodded towards Gilroy. 'Is what it was doing there.'

'Dunno!'

'Let's just get this straight then,' said Fox. 'You and Uncle Sid do this blagging and set off for your lock-up in Lambeth. When you get there, you find, to your astonishment, that someone has carelessly left a dead body within. Bit unreasonable that, I thought. And, no doubt, so did you.'

'I'm telling you, we never knew nothing about it.'

'When did you last visit the lock-up, Wally?'

13

'About a week ago.'

'After your last blagging, I suppose,' said Fox. 'When you nicked a quantity of gent's natty suiting.' He held up his hand as Chesney went to say something. 'None of which, I note, seems to have found its way into your wardrobe.' He surveyed Chesney's clothing with an expression of distaste on his face.

'I don't know what you're talking about,' said Chesney. It was unconvincing. When he had embarked on this particular villainous enterprise, he had been assured by the elders and betters of his criminal fraternity that there was no risk. And now, suddenly, he was sitting in a police station facing a very nasty detective who seemed to know all about it. And who kept mentioning a dead body. Wally Chesney was not a happy man.

'What is going to happen now, Walter,' said Fox, 'is that another of my officers will talk to you and you will tell him all about these little heists that you and your nasty little friends have been carrying out. Once that is out of the way, I shall return and talk very seriously to you about this murder with which you and Sidney are involved.'

'Murder?' Chesney whispered the word, but the surprise he tried to convey was unconvincing.

Fox studied the ceiling for some seconds before looking back at Chesney. 'Well, of course it's murder,' he said. 'You don't think she fell over and banged her head on the floor, surely?'

At Fox's request, the custody sergeant removed Chesney to another interview room, there to be interviewed by DI Evans, and brought in Sidney Budgeon.

Budgeon was about five feet seven inches tall, had broad shoulders and a broken nose. He sat down in the chair opposite Fox and took out a packet of cigarettes. 'Got a light, have you?' he asked. 'That bleeding sergeant took mine off of me.'

Fox pushed his lighter across the table. 'Help yourself,' he said.

Budgeon lit his cigarette and handed the lighter back. 'I ain't saying nothing,' he said, exhaling smoke and leaning nonchalantly back in his chair. 'Not without a brief.'

14

'If I were in your position, I think it likely I would adopt the same attitude,' said Fox mildly. 'But there again, as I am Thomas Fox . . . of the Flying Squad the question does not arise.'

Budgeon took a deep breath, coughed on his cigarette, but otherwise remained silent. He too had heard of Fox.

'On the other hand,' Fox continued, 'faced with a murder charge, I think I might try to be as helpful as possible.'

'Murder? What murder?' Budgeon eased himself slowly into an upright position.

Fox sighed. 'Oh dear,' he said, glancing at Gilroy. 'I suppose we've got to go through this farce all over again. I am talking, Sidney, of the dead body which you and young Master Chesney found underneath the arches at about six o'clock this morning.'

'What are you on about?' Budgeon pretended to be quite unperturbed by this statement.

Fox outlined, as briefly as possible, what he had said to Chesney. 'And so you see, Sidney, we know all about it. And at this very moment, young Walter is next door falling over himself to put it all down in writing.'

'Look, guv'nor, I'll square with you.'

'That'll make a change,' murmured Fox.

'We'll have the heist. Ain't got much option, I s'pose.'

'Very realistic,' said Fox.

Budgeon struggled on. 'But the body's not down to us. A bit of honest blagging is one thing, but a topping's definitely not our line of business. It's too risky. Know what I mean?'

'Oh I do, I do indeed,' said Fox warmly. 'So my colleagues and I can count on you for your unstinting assistance, can we?'

'Yeah, well I mean—' Budgeon, somewhat bemused, lapsed into silence.

'Good. Now when did you last visit this lock-up?'

'About a week ago.'

'After the blagging at the stock-room of a high-class gentlemen's outfitters in Tottenham Court Road, you mean?'

'Yeah, that's the one.' Budgeon sighed. If he ever got his hands on the person or persons who had dumped a stiff in the Lambeth lock-up and thereby involved him in his present grief with the Old Bill, he'd make sure they never did such a thing again. There was, after all, a code of ethics among the villainry. Or there was supposed to be.

'You appeared to have some trouble opening the doors this morning,' said Fox mildly as though he were a salesman trying to sell a new set of locks to a nervous householder.

'Yeah, we did. Some bastard had switched the padlock. That wasn't the usual one on there, see. That's why I had to banjo it off.'

'Very unreasonable of somebody,' said Fox. 'And you had not visited this repository of stolen goods during the intervening period?'

'Do what?'

'You hadn't been to the slaughter since the last blagging?'

'No.'

'What happened to the gear that you left there last time, then?' Fox held out his hand and Gilroy gave him a list. 'According to my information, some sixty gents' suits, ditto shirts with French cuffs—' He broke off and glanced at Gilroy. 'What the hell are French cuffs, Jack?' he asked.

'Cuffs which take cuff-links, sir,' said Gilroy.

'Good heavens!' said Fox. 'I thought they all did.' He turned back to Budgeon. 'And fifty silk ties of assorted design.'

'That's a bloody stitch-up,' said Budgeon angrily. 'We never nicked all that. They're trying it on with the insurance. That's bloody dishonest, that is.'

'Good Lord!' said Fox and shook his head slowly. 'Make a note of that, Jack. We'll have to talk to these people. I don't wonder there's a recession if fellows go about fiddling the underwriters like that. Makes you feel sorry for Lloyd's names, doesn't it?' He turned his attention once more to Budgeon. 'And now, Sidney, we come to the important question. If you didn't remove the stolen property from this lock-up in Lambeth, who did?' Fox sat

16

back and lit another cigarette.

'Nothing to say,' said Budgeon.

'Dear me, how unfortunate.' Fox smiled. And waited.

Budgeon shifted uneasily in his chair. 'You can't expect me to grass, can you?'

'Don't see why not,' said Fox. 'It seems to me that whoever took the gear also left a dead body there. And you're the one who got nicked, dear boy. Well, you and the bold Chesney. Think about it.'

There was another longish pause before Budgeon spoke again. 'Will this definitely row me out of this topping, guv?'

Fox pursed his lips. 'I can't make any promises,' he said, 'but let's say it may go some way towards assisting you in your present predicament.'

'I don't want none of this recorded,' said Budgeon.

Fox glanced at the tape recorder. ' Oh, how remiss of me,' he said, 'I quite forgot to switch it on.'

'Harry Dawes,' said Budgeon quietly, as if afraid that he might be overheard by the said Dawes.

'Good grief!' said Fox. 'Don't tell me that old Sliding Dawes is still at it? Better tell me the tale then, Sidney.'

'He's got outlets and that,' said Budgeon, still nervous at having disclosed Dawes' identity. 'But I never seen him as into topping. Not his line.'

'What is his line? Now, I mean.'

'Well, like I said, he's got outlets. He's got all sorts of contacts what wants special gear like. They gives Dawes a bell, and he tells me what's on the list like.'

'And you pop out and do their shopping for them, I suppose.'

'Yeah, well sort of.'

'And who are these mysterious punters, Sidney?'

'Dunno,' said Budgeon. 'You'll have to ask Harry.'

'I shall, Sidney, believe me, I shall.'

'Yeah, I thought you might.' Budgeon looked as unhappy as Chesney had done.

When Fox and Gilroy returned to the Yard, DI Evans was waiting.

'What news from John Harris's carvery, Denzil?'

17

Evans skimmed through a folder of papers he was carrying. 'He confirms the cause as manual strangulation, sir. But he now says that the time of death was at least ten hours prior to the discovery, possibly longer. Something to do with the temperature and . . .' Evans paused.

'And what?'

'And the fact that she was murdered elsewhere and transported to the lock-up subsequently.'

'It would be subsequently if she was murdered somewhere else,' said Fox in an aside to Gilroy.

'It was hypostasis, sir,' said Evans despondently. 'The lividity of the skin indicates that the body was face down to start with but when we found it, it was—'

'Face up. Yes, Denzil, I do know what hypostasis is. Anything else?'

'Yes, sir. Dr Harris found some skin tissue beneath the fingernails of both hands, as if she had tried to tear the attacker's hands away from her neck.'

'Much, is there? I mean enough for DNA testing, if we get lucky?'

'He seems to think so, sir. Anyway, it's been taken to the lab.'

'All that remains for you to tell me now, Denzil, is her name.'

'I don't know, sir.' Evans looked crestfallen.

Fox stared pointedly at the clock over the door of his office. 'Here we are at nearly five o'clock and you still haven't found out who she is, Denzil. That's eleven hours since the body was discovered. Well really, what *have* you been doing?'

'I'm waiting on the lab, sir. We sent all the clothing over there from the mortuary and they're seeing if they can come up with something.'

'Fingerprints, Denzil,' said Fox. 'What about fingerprints?'

'Nothing, guv. She hasn't got a record.'

Fox sniffed. 'Bloody inconsiderate that is,' he said. 'What about teeth?'

'Being done, sir,' said Evans, 'but it's a long business sending details out to all the dentists in London. There are

18

a lot of them.'

'Yes,' said Fox, 'I do know that.'

'And I've got Photographic Branch doing their best to get a decent portrait of her.' Evans hoped that he had covered all the possibilities.

'Yes, well keep chasing them, Denzil. Can't start until we know who she is, can we?'

'What about Harry Dawes, guv'nor?' asked Gilroy. 'Want him brought in?'

Fox took a cigarette out of his case and tapped it thoughtfully on the edge of his desk. 'No, Jack, I think we shall go and talk to him. We won't knock him off. Not yet. If we chat nicely to him, he might think he's in the clear.' He chuckled quietly. 'And that'll be his first mistake, but it will not be his last, Jack. Not by a long chalk.'

THREE

'ON SECOND THOUGHTS, JACK, I think we'll let Sliding Dawes sweat for a while.'

'Pardon?' Until then, Gilroy had been enjoying a drink with Fox in The Old Star public house close to Scotland Yard. But now he put his pint down on the bar and stared. When Fox started acting out of character it worried him.

'Well, it's like this,' Fox went on. 'If we go and see him now, we've got nothing to frighten him with, have we? For a start, we don't know who this bird is whose body we found in his lock-up. Don't even know if he had anything to do with it. Apart from anything else, he's bound to have heard that we've nicked Budgeon and Chesney and if we go steaming in, Dawes will know who grassed on him.' Fox drained his Scotch and looked expectantly at his DI. 'And we might just need Budgeon's assistance. Don't want him duffed up in Brixton do we? Not yet, anyway.'

'What do we do then, guv?'

'We'll get Henry to put a discreet obo on Dawes, Jack, that's what we'll do. Wait and see what happens, if you get my drift. If we leave him alone, he'll think he's in the clear and might do something silly.'

'So what do we do with Budgeon and Chesney, guv? Charge them with warehouse-breaking?'

'Good heavens no, Jack. There's a limit to my generosity. Charge them with robbery. After all, Ron Crozier did say he was threatened with an iron bar, didn't he?'

'And make no mention of Sliding Dawes, guv?'

'Exactly so, Jack.'

*

The arrival of an emissary called Eddie Swinburn at Dawes's villa in Oxford Road, Putney, was witnessed by members of DI Henry Findlater's surveillance team. Being versed in the ways of the police, Swinburn had been cunning enough to arrive late at night and on foot; he knew that the police computer could very quickly identify the owner of a car. The fact that his car was not registered in his name – or in anyone else's – gave him some anonymity, but also left him open to some very nasty questions if any policemen happened to be loitering in the vicinity of Harry Dawes's pad. And in the circumstances, that possibility could not be ruled out.

He had been careful because he knew that Budgeon and Chesney had been arrested and the same source of information had also told him that Tommy Fox had taken a personal interest in the matter. That worried Swinburn, and would also worry Harry Dawes when he heard it.

Dawes's front door opened a fraction and Swinburn oiled his way round it as quickly as possible.

'Eddie? To what do I owe the pleasure?' Dawes was a man of nearly sixty, painfully thin and almost bald. What hair remained was snow-white, and he had a hooked nose and a ragged moustache. Dawes had never married and had never been a front-line villain – even he accepted that he had neither the courage nor the physique for either – but had wielded power in the criminal community for nigh-on three decades. But then fences, or handlers of stolen goods as the law preferred to call them, had always been powerful men.

'I've got a bit of bad news, Harry.'

'Oh?' Dawes carefully fitted a cigarette into an amber holder and reached out for a table lighter. 'You'd better sit down and tell me all about it then, Eddie.' He coughed distressingly as the smoke reached the back of his throat.

'It's Sid Budgeon and Wally Chesney, Harry. They've been nicked.'

'Have they? When?'

'Yesterday morning.'

21

'Oh that is bad news,' said Dawes. 'Better tell me the tale.'

'They done a warehouse down Balham—'

'I heard that was in the wind,' said Dawes.

'And the Old Bill was lying in wait.'

'I see.' Dawes moved across to the mantelpiece and straightened an ornament before facing Swinburn again. 'Well that sounds as though it's all self-contained. I mean, like, it don't sound as though we need to go in for damage limitation, does it?' He flicked ash into a brass ashtray. 'D'you like that phrase, Eddie? Damage limitation is what they do when a spy gets hisself captured. I saw that on the telly. BBC Two, of course.'

'But they didn't get nicked at the warehouse, Harry,' said Swinburn, trying to break the news as gently as possible. 'They got lifted at the lock-up.'

'Now that's not so good,' said Dawes, his mind moving into top gear. 'That's not so good at all.' He crossed to the window and twitching the net curtains slightly, peered out at the deserted street. 'I hope you wasn't followed, Eddie.'

'No, course not, Harry.'

'That's all right then. Well, go on.'

'I'm afraid they got nicked by Tommy Fox and half the bleeding Sweeney.'

'Oh Gawd!' Dawes sat down suddenly in a Rexine-covered armchair that had been in his family for at least half a century. Formerly belonging to his dear departed old mother, it had a particular place in Dawes's affections. In fact, he did most of his thinking in that chair. 'Someone's grassed,' he said eventually.

Swinburn shrugged. 'S'pose so,' he said, trying to sound non-committal.

'There's no suppose about it, Eddie. And I want to know who it is. I mean to say, how else did the filth know where to set up the ambush?'

'It's all a bit dodgy, Harry,' said Swinburn. ''Cos they both got nicked at home, down Lewisham. I reckon the Old Bill followed them from the slaughter.'

'How d'you know all this, Eddie?' Dawes's eyes narrowed suspiciously.

Swinburn detected the danger immediately. 'It weren't nothing to do with me, Harry. I wouldn't grass, you know that. But they was up before the beak at Bow Street this morning and got an eight-day lay down in Brixton. I heard it from a bent screw who Stimkins knows. His missus works in the kitchens there.'

'Who works in the kitchens?' Dawes wanted to get to the bottom of this distressing item of intelligence.

'Fred Stimkins's missus does.'

'How's that then? How can Fred Stimkins's missus get a job in the kitchens at Brixton? Fred's got form.'

Swinburn shrugged. 'Search me,' he said, 'but she does.'

'This is all very disturbing, Eddie. I think we'd better have a drink.' Dawes walked across to a side table and turning to face Swinburn, paused. 'Medium or dry?' he asked.

'Medium or dry what?'

'Sherry, of course,' said Dawes.

Although Dr Susan Gardiner was the fabrics expert at the Metropolitan Police Forensic Science Laboratory, it was the fact that she was a woman that helped to speed up the identification of the female found in the lock-up at Lambeth.

'This is all good quality clothing,' she said to Detective Sergeant Percy Fletcher, indicating the clothes that the dead girl had been wearing, 'but it's the sort of stuff that's available at quite a few outlets. On the other hand, her shoes were very expensive. They certainly cost a lot more than these.' Turning on her stool, she pushed out a black nylon-clad leg from beneath her white coat and waggled a foot in Fletcher's direction.

'Very nice,' said Fletcher enigmatically.

'And they are obtainable only in the London area. They're made by an independent firm out at Harrow. I know that they're sixes, which is just about the most common size, but it's worth trying there before you start gallivanting round the country attempting to track this lot down.' And Susan Gardiner pointed again at the pile of clothing.

Eddie Swinburn left Harry Dawes's house unaware that he was being watched by at least four police officers. He walked confidently down Oxford Road and caught a tube train at East Putney station. Alighting at Earls Court, he made his way into the maze of streets bounded by Cromwell Road and Brompton Road, and disappeared into a large house that was divided into bed-sitting rooms. At least, he thought he had disappeared. In fact, Findlater's men had followed him all the way.

'No trouble at all,' said the manager of the shoe factory in Harrow. He peered into one of the shoes that Fletcher had handed him and jotted down a serial number. 'That number,' he went on, 'will tell me which batch this was. And the records will tell me which retailer took delivery of them.' He looked up and grinned. 'I hope,' he added.

Armed with the address of the shop in the West End of London to which the dead girl's shoes had been supplied, Fletcher continued his enquiries. Obviously the shoes would not have been sold after the date that the body was found, and given that there was very little wear on them, and given also that any shoe which was not a size six could be discounted, Fletcher was fortunate to come out with only three names.

The inverse law of criminal investigation always comes into play in an enquiry of this nature, and it was no surprise to Fletcher to find that the first two addresses were at diametrically-opposed extremes of the Metropolitan Police District. The third, however, was in an expensive block of flats in the Edgware Road.

Fletcher went there first. There was no reply. He travelled to the other two addresses. The women who lived at those addresses were both still alive. And both still had their shoes. Fletcher went back to the address in the Edgware Road.

The hall porter was Polish, but he spoke reasonable English and studied the post-mortem photograph of the dead girl. 'That's her,' he said.

'You're sure?'

'Positive, mister.'

'Good. Have you got a key to her flat?'

'No. Not allowed.'

'Damn!' said Fletcher.

'Yes, sir,' said the hall porter.

'There are times,' said Fox, when Fletcher had delivered his report, 'when I think that the inspectors in this department ought to be sergeants and the sergeants ought to be inspectors.'

Neither Gilroy nor Evans said anything, and Fletcher thought it would be unwise to pass comment on what, to him, seemed an eminently sensible idea.

'What we need now,' Fox continued, 'is a search warrant and a seven-pound key.' Fox always referred to a sledge-hammer as a seven-pound key. 'But it's just possible that Swann, armed with his illegal bunch of twirlers, might do the trick. Get hold of him Denzil, there's a good chap.'

'Yes, sir,' said Evans. 'Where is he, d'you know?'

'Pound to a pinch, he's in the drivers' room with a hand of cards in his grubby paw. Oh, and get hold of Rosie as well. Better still, get Rosie to get Swann. He's terrified of her.'

Detective Sergeant Rosie Webster was a perfectly-proportioned, very tall blonde. And no one argued with her. Always superbly dressed and expensively perfumed, she had frightened quite a few villains – men and women – in her career. And nearly as many policemen.

When the team arrived at the flats in Edgware Road, the complaining Swann got to work on the front door with his 'twirlers', as his bunch of keys was known. Despite the manufacturer's claim that the lock was virtually burglar-proof, Swann effected an entry within three minutes, and the officer in charge of the sledge-hammer put it back in the boot of his car, with a resigned look on his face.

The inside of the flat was elegant. The chairs were of leather, as was the chesterfield, and the carpet had a rich pile. Original paintings graced the walls, one of them a Degas, and several pieces of furniture, according to Fox –

25

who had assumed the guise of an expert in such matters – were genuine and valuable antiques. The remainder was expensive reproduction quite definitely not made out of veneered plywood. 'There's money here,' said Fox approvingly. 'A lot of money.'

Neither Gilroy nor Evans disagreed. The entire interior of the flat indicated substantial wealth.

Fox sat down in one of the armchairs. 'Right lads, get to work,' he said to the fingerprint experts who had come with the Flying Squad officers.

The search went on for almost two hours. Early on, the detectives found sufficient evidence to identify the dead woman as Dawn Mitchell, aged thirty, and Rosie Webster found a framed photograph of her in a theatrical pose, that had clearly been taken by a professional. In a box in a wardrobe, she found dozens of other photographs obviously taken at the same time.

But the one item of property which interested Fox was a little black book. 'This might give us one or two promising leads,' he said, flicking through its pages. He chuckled. 'And even if it doesn't, there are a few people on this list who, I suspect, will not be best pleased to be involved in a murder enquiry.'

There were twenty-seven names in Dawn Mitchell's little black book. Each had a telephone number beside it and, in some cases, an address. And there were at least five nationally-known names among them including a peer of the realm.

'There are three telephones, guv,' said Evans, emerging from Dawn Mitchell's bedroom. 'One in there . . .' He cocked a thumb towards the room he had just left. 'And two in here.'

'So what?' said Fox. 'I've got a phone in my sitting-room and another in my bedroom. The one in my bedroom is for answering the queries of my subordinates who discover, in the middle of the night, that they can't cope,'

'Yes, sir,' said Evans who knew Fox's home telephone number by heart.

'Do a check with British Telecom on the number, Denzil, there's a good fellow,' said Fox.

'But we know who the subscriber is, sir,' Evans looked vaguely mystified.

'Indeed we do, Denzil, but it might just be that the lady in question has her account itemised. In which case it might provide us with some useful information.' Fox sighed.

'Right then, what do we know so far?' asked Fox. he glanced at Gilroy, then back at Evans. 'What about the phone?'

'Ex-directory, sir—' began Evans.

'So are most women who live alone these days,' said Fox. There was a despair in his voice that crime had got that bad.

'And I've got her accounts for the year up to last September, itemised,' continued Evans.

'Good. Get a subscriber check done on all of them, will you.' Fox tapped Dawn Mitchell's address book. 'Looks as though it's time to start asking some questions of her friends and acquaintances.' He moved the book into the centre of his blotter. 'Was there anything on her answerphone tape?'

'One message, sir,' said Evans, 'from a girl called Bunny, inviting her to some party.'

'Oh well,' said Fox and shrugged. 'What about that photograph we found, Jack? Anything on that yet?'

'Yes, sir.' Gilroy flicked open his pocket book. 'There was a set of them, taken about three years ago by a legit West End studio. They supplied a hundred copies of each, to distribute to agencies, one supposes. Seems that Muzz Mitchell was contemplating a career as a model. Doesn't seem to have come to much, though. Most of the prints were in that box that Rosie found in the girl's wardrobe.'

'Well that doesn't get us very far,' said Fox. 'Get hold of Percy Fletcher, Denzil, and tell him to get out and beat on the ground. See what comes up. Neighbours at her block of flats, model agencies, clubs. Perce'll know the sort of thing. Better still, get Rosie to do the model agencies, see if any of them employed the Mitchell girl, or even if she applied to them. And get a few prints run off from that

27

photograph so that we can show them around. Anything else?'

'The fingerprint lads found some marks, but they're still classifying and searching, sir,' said Evans.

'Well chase them up, Denzil.'

'What about Harry Dawes, guv'nor?' asked Gilroy. 'Are we going to give him a spin?'

'D'you know, Jack, I think we might just do that.'

But Detective Sergeant Fletcher drew a blank. It was apparent from the outset that the occupants of the three flats sharing the late Dawn Mitchell's hallway, all foreigners, were even more distrusting of the police than the average member of the indigenous population. They had seen nothing and heard nothing.

And Fletcher's usual West End informants, carefully cultivated over the years during which – and since – he had done duty at West End Central Police Station, yielded nothing either. The name of Dawn Mitchell, they confessed, meant nothing to them.

FOUR

WHEN FOX RETURNED TO SCOTLAND Yard there was a note on his desk telling him to speak to the commander as soon as he got back. Irritably, he screwed it up and threw it into the waste-paper basket before marching down the corridor to Alec Myers's office.

'You wanted to see me, sir?' Fox managed to convey the impression that, heavily involved as he was in a murder enquiry that he shouldn't have been lumbered with anyway, he had little time to respond to Myers's every whim.

'Yes, Tommy. Sit down.'

'I am rather tucked up, sir.'

'This won't take a moment. But there's been a complaint made against you.'

'Well, there's a surprise, guv,' said Fox who had been the subject of so many complaints that he had lost count. 'Who's belly-aching this time?'

'John James Stedman,' said Myers, glancing down at the file on his desk.

'Stedman! That's outrageous,' said Fox. 'That little toe-rag's banged up in Parkhurst doing ten years for armed robbery, with an option for renewal.'

Myers grinned. 'Yes, I know, but he's written to his MP complaining that during the course of a search of his dwelling, you stole two hundred pounds, several compact discs and a quantity of women's clothing.'

'The saucy little bastard,' said Fox, shaking his head.

Myers shrugged. 'Well, Tommy, that's it. Got to go through the motions. Commander Willow of One Area Headquarters has been appointed to investigate.'

29

'Willow?' said Fox. 'Never heard of him.'

'He's a Uniform Branch commander,' said Myers.

'Oh, good.' Fox paused thoughtfully. 'Does that mean I'm off this murder then, guv?'

Alec Myers shut the file and laughed. 'No, Tommy, it doesn't,' he said, 'but try to make yourself available whenever Mr Willow needs you.'

'He'll have to catch me first,' said Fox.

Some four or five days had elapsed since the discovery of Dawn Mitchell's body, and Fox had decided that Harry Dawes could not be left undisturbed any longer. He knew that by now, Dawes would have convinced himself that any fall-out arising from the arrest of Budgeon and Chesney would not be falling in his direction. But he was about to be disabused of that pious hope.

Fox's Ford Granada pulled up outside Dawes's house in Putney. Before they had turned into the street, Fox had ordered Swann to fit the magnetic blue light to the roof and switch it on and, as they stopped, Fox gave the siren a quick burst. So many curtains twitched that there was almost a gale.

Followed by Gilroy, Fox swept up the short path and hammered on the door, pushing it wide as soon as the nervous face of Harry Dawes appeared. 'Well, well, Harry, I didn't believe them.'

'Didn't believe what?'

'My informants told me that you were still alive.' Fox grinned. 'But by the look of you, I'm not so sure that they were right.'

'What d'you want?' asked Dawes, but the sinking feeling in the pit of his stomach told him that he knew exactly what they wanted.

'A little chat, Harry,' said Fox, taking Dawes's elbow and steering him into the sitting-room. 'I must say that you've got some very nosy neighbours.'

'It's all that bleeding noise you made, ain't it? That siren and blue light and all that stuff. That's bleeding harassment, that is.'

'You think *that's* harassment?' asked Fox, shaking his

head slowly as he looked round the room. 'I must say that this is all very tasteful, Harry,' he continued. Apart from Dawes's favourite Rexine-covered chair, there was an uncut-moquette three-piece suite in brown, a large patterned Axminster carpet, and brown velvet curtains. A log fire crackled in a grate that was surrounded by a high mesh guard. On either side were long, highly-polished brass fire-irons, standing to attention. 'Yes, very tasteful indeed.' In fact, Fox thought that the whole ensemble was hideous, but he had greater things in store with which to upset Dawes than a criticism of his furnishings.

'I s'pose there's some reason for your visit, Mr Fox?' asked Dawes nervously.

'Of course, Harry.' Fox settled himself into one of the armchairs and crossed his legs.

A woman appeared in the doorway, carrying a tea-tray. She was about fifty, with grey hair and a wrapover, sleeveless floral overall. 'I've made some tea for your visitors, Mr Dawes,' she said, smiling at Fox and Gilroy.

'Just put it there will you.' Dawes, barely able to disguise his annoyance, indicated a carved Indian table. The last thing he wanted was to encourage Fox to stay any longer than was absolutely necessary. 'This is Mrs Wright, she does for me,' he added.

'Really? Well we have something in common there,' said Fox as Dawes's daily closed the door behind her. He waited until Dawes had poured the tea and handed the cups round before speaking again. 'I've got a bit of a problem, Harry. And as I'm known to be a generous man, I thought I'd share it. Make it your problem too, if you see what I mean.'

'Oh really?' Dawes's hand shook slightly as he stirred his tea. 'Biscuit, Mr Fox?'

'How kind,' said Fox. 'It's about this dead body, you see.'

Dawes spluttered and choked over his tea and Fox nodded knowingly, although he had thought that such things only happened in films. 'What body?' asked Dawes when he had got his breath back. Eddie Swinburn hadn't said anything about a dead body.

'I'm sure you've heard all about it, Harry,' Fox

31

continued. 'I can't believe that your army of snouts hasn't been running down here to Oxford Road to keep you informed.'

Dawes, his composure now somewhat regained, shook his head. 'I don't know nothing about no body,' he said.

'Oh dear. In that case I'll explain. Some four or five days ago . . .' Fox paused. 'No, let's get this right. On the fifteenth of October, last Monday in fact, two of your operatives, namely Mr Budgeon and Mr Chesney, entered your lock-up at Lambeth—'

'I've never heard of them,' said Dawes hurriedly.

Fox ignored him and sipped his tea. 'And to their horror,' he continued, 'they discovered the dead body of a young lady.'

'But—'

'Which,' said Fox, 'must have come as a terrible shock to their respective systems. Particularly at six o'clock in the morning, wouldn't you say, Harry, old thing?'

'Now look here,' said Dawes truculently, 'if you're trying to row me into a topping, you can forget it. I don't know nothing about no dead bodies and I don't know nothing about no lock-up in Lambeth neither.' He reached out unsteadily and put his cup on a table. 'And I ain't never heard of—' He paused. 'Whoever you said they was.'

'Wonderful,' said Fox. 'D'you know, Harry, if you'd gone on the stage in your youth, you'd have made a fortune. And the only time the Old Bill would've knocked on your door would have been to ask for your autograph.'

Dawes stood up, shaking. 'I'm going to have to ask you to leave,' he said. 'This is harassment, that's what it is.'

'Yes,' said Fox mildly, 'you actually mentioned that before. But before we push off, Harry, old dear, we'll just have a look round. Just for old time's sake.'

'Oh no you won't. I ain't invited you.'

Fox produced a sheet of paper from his pocket and waved it gently in Dawes's direction. 'You've seen one of these before, Harry, surely?'

Dawes collapsed into his favourite armchair again. 'This ain't the nineteen-sixties, you know,' he said. 'It don't work like that any more. People's got rights.'

32

'That's true,' said Fox. 'Among which is the right not to have their property stolen, and not to be murdered.'

Fox and Gilroy strolled round the house, but they knew there wouldn't be anything of interest. Harry Dawes had been too long at the game to be caught out that easily. Fox knew that he had another slaughter somewhere, but at the moment he didn't know where. He was hoping that Dawes would be reduced to such a state of panic that he might be tempted to move the vast stock of illicitly-acquired goods that Fox was sure he had.

'I shall telephone my solicitor,' said Dawes with a sudden show of truculent hostility.

'Feel free,' said Fox. 'In fact, use your telephone as often as you like. We haven't got it tapped, Harry.'

Fox knew that the Home Secretary would not grant an intercept warrant for Dawes's phone just to help the police solve a few robberies, but in telling Dawes that his phone was not tapped, Fox was certain that the old villain would think that his every word was being monitored by the police. And that meant that Dawes would have to go out to meet his contacts . . . or that they would have to come to him. Either way, it would suit Fox admirably.

'Mr Fox, I am Commander Willow of One Area Headquarters and this is Sergeant Clarke.' Willow indicated the pale-faced individual beside him. 'And I am investigating a complaint made against you by a Mr John James Stedman of Buckhurst Hill—'

'Parkhurst,' said Fox.

'I beg your pardon?' Willow looked up from his thick file of documents and adjusted his gold-rimmed, half-lensed spectacles slightly. His wife had told him that they gave him an air of authority. Fox thought they made him look a bit of a prat.

'I think you mean Parkhurst.'

'The complainant is serving a sentence of imprisonment in Parkhurst at the moment, Mr Fox, that's true, but he is appealing.'

'Not to me, he's not,' said Fox.

'Yes.' Willow looked uncertainly at Fox before returning

his gaze to his file. 'He alleges, and I quote, that when you executed a search warrant at his premises at 27 Winsome Terrace, Buckhurst Hill, in the County of Essex, a search which resulted in his arrest, you stole the sum of two hundred pounds, seven compact discs—' Willow interrupted himself. 'I have a list of the titles here.' He tapped the file in front of him. 'And two ladies' dresses.'

'He said all that? Couldn't string two words together when I nicked him.'

Willow wrinkled his nose. He did not like the language of the Criminal Investigation Department. 'I understand that his solicitor prepared the complaint,' he said, 'which was sent to the Commissioner by Mr Stedman's MP.' He had hoped that this particular crumb of information might impress Fox, but then he hadn't met Fox before.

'Well I wish you luck with it,' said Fox, 'but I do have a murder to investigate.' He glanced at his watch.

'Be that as it may, Mr Fox, there—'

'And,' added Fox confidentially, 'if you'll take a word of advice from me, you can't trust a word that little bastard says. He'd shop his grandmother for two-penn'orth of cold tea if he thought he could sell it for a profit. He'll probably finish up making a complaint against you.'

'I don't think you appreciate the gravity of this complaint, Mr Fox. Mr Stedman is alleging that you have committed a crime, a serious crime.' Willow was starting to feel out of his depth. Rapidly promoted, he had attended every course at the Police College and had filled one staff appointment after another. His great hope now was to secure a post as a deputy chief constable in some quiet provincial police force. But he was suddenly engulfed by a feeling of misgiving that this complaint wasn't going to be resolved as easily as he had at first thought. 'I think it might be useful, Mr Fox,' he continued, 'if I could start by taking a statement from you setting out the circumstances under which you arrested Mr Stedman.'

'Be very useful indeed, I should think. To you, sir,' said Fox. 'But I'm not making any statements.'

'But—'

'You see, sir,' said Fox helpfully, 'as I am the subject of

34

the complaint, you are obliged to caution me that I need not say anything, but that anything I do say—' He broke off. 'I'm sure you're familiar with the caution, sir, but I have a copy of it here somewhere if you'd like me to find it.' Fox started opening the drawers of his desk.

'Mr Fox,' said Willow with a weariness that hadn't been apparent at the start of the interview, 'I don't want to take too much time over this complaint, and—'

'Neither do I, guv'nor,' said Fox and smiled.

'Well, Denzil, what have you to tell me?'

'I've got the report from Fingerprint Branch, sir,' said Evans.

'Anything interesting in it?'

Evans shrugged. 'Don't know at this stage, sir. Most of the marks were identified as Dawn Mitchell's, but there were others.'

'Whose?'

'We don't know, sir. They're not on record. But there are more of one set than of any of the others.'

'What the hell does that mean, Denzil?'

'There were a lot of prints, all belonging to one person, that were found in the sitting room and the bedroom.'

'Really? How fascinating. But as far as we know, she lived there alone, yes?'

'Yes, sir.'

'Anything else?'

'I think we've identified her, guv'nor.'

'Ah!' said Fox. 'Well get on with it.'

'You're going to like this, guv.' said Evans. 'She appears to be the daughter of Lord Sims. Well, Earl Sims to be strictly accurate.'

'And how do you arrive at Dawn Mitchell being the daughter of someone called Sims? I mean to say, Denzil, it's not as if it were a place name like some peers have, is it?'

'I thought you'd ask that,' said Evans.

'I just did,' said Fox.

'This, sir,' said Evans and laid a letter on Fox's desk.

'What's this then?' Fox picked up the letter and scanned its contents.

'Letter from what looks very much like Dawn's sister, guv. There's a load of grief about their father being worried about her, up here in the Smoke, and how she really ought to get in touch. All that sort of thing. And it's signed "Jane".'

'But I still don't see how you came to the conclusion that—'

'I've been doing some checking, sir.' Evans had an expression of triumph on his face that he had arrived at a solution before Fox. 'And the Yorkshire address on the letter is the address of Lord Sims. According to *Who's Who* and *Burke's Peerage*, his wife is dead, but there is a son, Viscount Swaledale, who is twenty-seven and heir to the earldom, and two daughters, Jane and Dawn. Dawn is thirty years of age and Jane is thirty-five, and divorced.'

Fox handed the letter back. 'You know, Denzil,' he said, 'you're getting quite good at this detecting business.' He stood up and stared out of the window of his office. 'It looks as though we're going to have to go to Yorkshire.' He paused. 'Whereabouts in Yorkshire, Denzil?'

'West of Richmond, sir,' said Evans. 'It's about two hundred and seventy miles from here. On the Dales.'

Fox grinned. 'That'll give Swann something to complain about,' he said. 'And it'll get Pussy Willow off my back.'

'Who's Pussy Willow, sir?' Evans looked puzzled.

'Commander Willow of One Area seems to think that he's investigating a complaint made against me by that little toe-rag Stedman,' said Fox. 'Saucy bastard.'

'Yes, sir,' said Evans, unsure whether Fox was referring to Stedman or Commander Willow.

'Mr Daly, thank you for seeing me,' said Commander Willow. 'This is Sergeant Clarke who is assisting me in my enquiries.'

'Come right on in, gentlemen, and sit yourselves down.' Although Joe Daly was styled the legal attaché at the United States Embassy in London, he was in reality the resident FBI agent and the man to whom all British policemen referred whenever they had matters connected with America. 'Tell me what I can do for you.'

36

'I'm investigating a complaint made by one John James Stedman against Detective Chief Superintendent Thomas Fox of the Flying Squad,' Willow began importantly.

Daly laughed. 'What's Tommy been up to now?' he asked as he placed coffee in front of the two policemen.

'Oh, you know him, do you?' Willow blinked.

'Know him? I should say I do. And so does every God-damned crook in London, I should think. I'll tell you this, Commander . . .' Daly leaned forward slightly and tapped the coffee table with his forefinger. 'The people of this great city ought to be very grateful that they've got men like Tommy Fox protecting them. Yes, sir.'

'Yes, well, er, probably,' said Willow.

'And if this hood Stedman who's stirring up this trouble for him got put inside by Tommy Fox then he oughtn't ever to be let out of the slammer. No, sir. Anyway, I digress. What is it that I can do to help?'

'I'm trying to track down the woman that Stedman was living with,' said Willow, staring at the file now open on his knees. 'Her name's Sandra Nash.'

'A United States citizen, is she?'

'No, but I believe that she left for the States immediately after Stedman's arrest.'

'Is that a fact? Well, Commander, hundreds of people go to America, every day I imagine.'

'I was hoping that there might be some way of finding out where she is now?' Willow didn't sound too hopeful.

Daly laughed, a deep rumbling laugh. 'I'll give it a shot,' he said, 'but visas aren't required any more for ninety days or under.' He drew a notepad towards him. 'Give me a few details and I'll see if I can do anything. But don't hold your breath.'

FIVE

SWANN, HAVING TRIED EVERY TACTIC he knew to avoid driving Fox to Yorkshire, eventually admitted defeat. But he grumbled for the entire journey, muttering to himself and roundly abusing any other motorist who he thought had got in his way . . . which was most of them.

The country seat of the Earl Sims was on a remote part of the Yorkshire Dales, but Fox's first priority was to find a decent inn where he and Gilroy – and Swann – could stay for the night.

The local police station was a stone-built house in the centre of a small village. The sergeant eased himself out of his chair and strolled across to the counter. 'Good afternoon, sir,' he said affably.

'Good afternoon. I'm Detective Chief Superintendent Fox, Metropolitan.'

'Pleased to meet you, sir.' The sergeant glanced briefly at Fox's warrant card, but appeared unmoved by the sudden arrival of a senior Scotland Yard officer. 'What can I do for you gentlemen from London then?' he asked and smiled benevolently.

'Wondered if you could recommend somewhere to stay.'

'Oh aye.' The sergeant ran a hand round his chin. 'Happen you'd like a cup of tea, sir,' he said, 'having come all that way, like.'

'No thanks, sergeant, we're in a bit of a hurry.' Fox had no desire to languish in a Yorkshire police station listening to tales of sheep-stealing and the like.

'Aye, I s'pose so.' The sergeant looked thoughtful and then reeled off the names of a number of bed-and-breakfast establishments in the area, assuming that the

Metropolitan Police were as parsimonious about expenses as his own chief constable.

Fox thanked the sergeant and left, mentally dismissing the information he had been given. After a lengthy search, he and Gilroy eventually lighted upon a country inn with low beams and a crackling log fire.

After dinner, they adjourned to the bar where they had a few drinks and listened to the gossip of the locals who knew, by some arcane grapevine, of the presence of the Scotland Yard officers in their midst. But, try as they might, they did not learn why the London policemen were there.

The following morning, Swann drove Fox and Gilroy for miles across deserted Dales roads until, at almost midday, they reached the Simses' house, a large rambling pile set in grounds that must have amounted to several thousand acres of woodland and grass.

'This is definitely the way to live,' said Fox as he tugged at the wrought-iron bell-pull beside the massive front door and gazed around the gravelled forecourt.

A Filipino dressed in a black alpaca suit answered the door and gazed at Fox for a moment or two before speaking. 'Good afternoon, sir,' he said.

'Good afternoon. I'm Thomas Fox. I've come to see Lady Jane Sims.'

'Please come this way, sir. Her ladyship is expecting you.' The manservant led the way into a large room on one side of the house. On the walls were huge canvases, many of which, Fox thought, must be worth a small fortune. He nodded approvingly and walked across to the large mullioned windows which looked out on to a mulberry tree set in the centre of an immaculate lawn that was bounded by a high ivy-covered brick wall.

'Chief Superintendent Fox?' The woman who entered was tall, nearly as tall as Fox, and her long brown hair was held back from her face by a black velvet bandeau. She wore a scarlet skirt, a sweater of navy blue and stockings to match. She was, Gilroy thought, a classic beauty.

'Yes. Thomas Fox . . . of the Flying Squad. And this is Detective Inspector Gilroy.'

'We spoke on the telephone. I'm Jane Sims.' She held out a hand and Fox was surprised at the firmness of her grip. 'You weren't exactly forthcoming. In fact this is all rather mysterious. Do sit down,' she added, almost as an afterthought, before settling herself into a chair opposite him, and arranging her skirt.

'I wasn't able to say very much, Lady Jane, because I'm not sure of my facts.'

'Oh, that's unusual for a policeman.' There was a twinkle in Jane Sims's eyes and Fox had a feeling that she was mocking him.

'Do you have a sister called Dawn?'

'Yes, what about her?'

'And is she known as Dawn Mitchell, with an address in the Edgware Road?'

'You're beginning to worry me, Mr Fox. Yes, that is correct.'

'In that case, Lady Jane, I'm sorry to have to tell you that she's dead.'

'Oh!' Jane Sims looked sadly at the embroidered screen that stood in a fireplace now made redundant by the efficient central heating. Fox waited until eventually she looked back at him. It was a very direct gaze, and he noticed that her eyes were a deep brown. 'When did this happen?'

'On Sunday or Monday last. That, I'm afraid, is the nearest that the pathologist can get to fixing a time of death.'

'Pathologist?' Jane Sims's eyes narrowed slightly and suddenly she understood why a senior officer from Scotland Yard had come all the way to Yorkshire. 'She was murdered, wasn't she.' It was a statement, not a question.

'Yes. It wasn't until yesterday that we were able to identify her. Well, not until now, in fact. You see, one of my officers found a letter from you to her, but we couldn't be sure until we had spoken to you. Obviously I didn't want to discuss it on the telephone.'

'Obviously.' For a moment Fox thought she was being sarcastic, but then she went on. 'I'm very grateful for your consideration,' she added. 'But I don't know how I'm going to break it to my father. He's seventy, you see. The shock could well kill him. She was the apple of his eye. I'm the one who did it all wrong.'

'Did what all wrong?'

'Married the wrong man.' Jane Sims sounded quite phlegmatic about her admission. She stood up and walked across to an ornate side-table. 'I don't know about you,' she said, 'but I could do with a drink. What would you like?'

'A Scotch, please.'

'And you, Inspector?'

'The same, if I may,' said Gilroy.

Jane Sims poured three stiff measures of whisky and handed the glasses round. 'What can you tell me about Dawn's death?'

Fox was surprised at the woman's constraint, but put it down to her aristocratic breeding and the tradition that families such as hers had developed of keeping a stiff upper lip. 'She was found in a lock-up beneath a railway line in Lambeth.' He saw no point in trying to soften his account of the circumstances under which Dawn Mitchell's body had been discovered. There was no way to do that. 'She had been strangled.'

'My God, how awful.' Jane Sims stared at the fire-screen again and lapsed once more into silence. 'Do you know who killed her?' she asked after a while.

'No,' said Fox. 'I was hoping that you might be able to help.'

'Me? Why me?'

Fox looked at the woman with a level gaze. 'You concluded that she had been murdered before I had mentioned it. Why was that?'

'Because, Mr Fox, I didn't imagine for one moment that a Scotland Yard detective would come all this way to discuss a traffic accident,' said Jane with a half-smile on her face.

Fox waved a hand of dismissal. He had come to the rapid conclusion that this woman was nobody's fool. 'Did you know any of her friends in London?' he asked.

'Why d'you ask that? Do you suspect someone?'

'Not at the moment, but it's where we have to start.'

'I knew hardly any of her friends.'

41

'Did she ever confide in you about boyfriends?' asked Fox.

'Sometimes, but she never seemed to keep one for long. I think she was frightened that she might get too involved.'

'Too involved?'

'Yes. She was thirty last birthday, but she showed no signs of wanting to settle down. Liked the good life too much, I suppose.' Jane toyed absently with a ring on the little finger of her left hand. 'She was always talking about the next party.' There was a pause. 'She wasn't a virgin, you know.'

'I know.'

'Oh yes, I suppose the pathologist . . .'

'Exactly,' said Fox. 'Incidentally, Lady Jane, why did she call herself Dawn Mitchell?'

Jane Sims smiled. 'She had this crazy notion that she wanted to be a model,' she said. 'But I think she imagined that if she used another name, Daddy wouldn't get to hear about it. She thought he might disapprove.'

'And did she have any success?'

'Not really. Not as far as I know, anyway.' Jane crossed to the table and poured more Scotch into her glass before nodding at Fox's drink. 'Another one?'

'Not for the moment, thanks.'

'To be frank, I saw very little of Dawn over the past few years. She'd settled in London and although I've got a flat in Knightsbridge and work in the West End, we had very little to do with each other, apart from talking on the phone. We did that quite often.'

'If she had little success as a model, how did she support herself?'

Jane Sims smiled. 'Daddy paid her an allowance. Quite a substantial allowance, as a matter of fact.'

'D'you know if there was anyone, outside the family, that she was particularly close to?'

Jane shrugged. 'Not that I know of. She was a very attractive girl and whenever I spoke to her, she was always talking about going out to dinner, or to yet another party. She seemed to live a very full social life.'

'Did she come here very often?' asked Fox.

42

'Only very occasionally. Daddy would ring her from time to time, particularly when he was worried about her. Which was quite often. He worried about her terribly. He didn't like her being in London. He thinks it's an awful place.'

'I take it your father doesn't go to London often.'

'Never. He hates it.'

'Not even to the Lords?'

'Not at all. He's got no time for politics.'

'Who's got no time for politics?' The man who had appeared in the doorway was stooped and leaned on a stick. He wore a Harris tweed sports jacket that had seen better days and which now hung on him as though it had been tailored for him when he was more robust. 'Oh, I'm sorry, my dear,' he said, 'I didn't realise you had visitors.'

'Good afternoon, sir,' said Fox as he and Gilroy stood up. The old man hooked his walking stick over his left arm and slowly grasped Fox's outstretched hand.

'Daddy, this is Mr Fox. He's a detective from Scotland Yard. Now come and sit down.' Jane Sims moved quickly to her father's side and gently helped him across to a chair.

'Scotland Yard, eh?' said Lord Sims. 'And what have you been up to, Jane?'

'These gentlemen have brought some bad news, I'm afraid.' Forced by his sudden arrival into telling her father of Dawn's death, Jane knelt down and took one of his hands in her own.

'Oh, what bad news?'

'It's about Dawn, Daddy. I'm afraid she's dead.'

The old man looked at his daughter, his watery blue eyes staring, apparently unable to comprehend what she had just said. 'Dead? What d'you mean?'

Fox and Gilroy sat down again and waited.

'Tell me about my daughter,' said Lord Sims, looking directly at Fox. 'Was it an accident?'

Fox glanced briefly at Jane Sims who nodded. 'Yes, sir,' he said. 'I'm afraid it was.'

'Damned motor cars, I suppose.' The earl shook his head wearily. 'I think I'd better have a glass of brandy, Jane, if you don't mind.'

Jane Sims appeared to be on the verge of cautioning her father about that, but thinking better of it, stood up and poured it for him.

The old man drank it down at a swallow. 'I think I'll go and sit in the study for a while,' he said and easing himself painfully out of his chair, walked slowly out of the room.

'Will he be all right?' asked Fox. He and Gilroy had stood up once more as the earl left the room, and remained standing.

'I hope so. He did the same thing when my mother died. Sat in his study for days, just looking at family photographs.' Jane Sims twisted her hands together in a moment of anguish. It was the first emotion Fox had seen her display. 'Thank you for being so considerate,' she said. 'I think to know that she had been murdered would have been too much for him.'

'But what about the newspapers? There's bound to be a lot of coverage once they discover that a peer's daughter has been murdered.'

'He doesn't read them any more. Hasn't done for years. Never looks at television, either. I think the world's getting too much for him.'

Sensing that there was little more that he could do there, Fox said, 'There's the question of the funeral arrangements.'

'Oh, yes, I suppose so. What happens about that?'

'The inquest will be opened, probably tomorrow. There's no reason why the coroner shouldn't release your sister's body after that. There'll certainly be no police objections.' Fox paused. 'I may need to see you again, Lady Jane,' he said softly.

'Yes, of course.' Jane fumbled in her handbag and produced a card. 'That's my London address,' she said. 'I spend most of my time up there. Please contact me any time you want to.'

'What about your father? Will he be alone here?'

'No. I'll make arrangements for a permanent nurse. Should have done it ages ago, but now that Dawn's gone, he could become quite maudlin. I've been worried about him for some time.' Jane looked at Fox with that same direct gaze. 'There'll be no need for you to contact him, will there?'

Fox shook his head. 'I very much doubt it,' he said, 'Should it be necessary, I'll get in touch with you first.'

'Thank you.' The woman gestured towards the card which Fox still held in his hand. 'My office number's on there as well, should you need it.'

Fox glanced at the slip of pasteboard. 'What business are you in?' he asked.

'I'm an architect,' said Jane Sims and smiled.

'Good Lord!' said Fox.

'And what have you discovered during my absence, Denzil? Anything of world-shattering importance?'

'We've been going through the list, sir,' said Evans.

'What list?' asked Fox, leaning forward on his desk to stub out his cigarette in the ashtray.

'We compiled a list of all Dawn Mitchell's known acquaintances, sir, from the telephone account and from her address book.'

'Go on.'

'A lot of people seemed to know her—'

'I gathered that, Denzil, but is there anyone worth talking about?'

'Most of them met her at parties or at dinner at someone's house.' Evans flicked over a few pages in the file of statements that rested on the corner of Fox's desk. 'The general opinion is that she was a bubbly, happy girl who had everything to live for.'

'Haven't they always,' said Fox.

'Do what, sir?' Evans looked up.

'Every female murder victim under the age of about thirty-five that I've ever come across is described like that, Denzil. Did she have a boyfriend?'

'It doesn't look like it, sir. In fact . . .' Evans broke off while he turned up a statement. 'Yes, here we are. One of the people in the address book, well it's a married couple actually, invited her to dinner about three months ago. They asked her to bring someone with her, but she said that she hadn't got a current boyfriend, so the hosts

45

invited a man to make up the numbers.'

'Name?'

'Jason Hope-Smith, sir,' said Evans.

'Reckons,' said Fox. 'Spoken to him, have you?'

'Haven't been able to yet, sir. He's abroad.'

'Where?'

'Kuwait, sir. He's something to do with oil apparently.'

'And what did the hosts of this splendid dinner party tell you about this chap, Denzil?'

'Only that they'd met him through a friend of their daughter. He's apparently in his thirties, divorced and has problems meeting women in London because he spends so much time travelling.'

'Know the feeling,' said Fox, who was still recovering from his journey to Yorkshire. 'Did he feature in Dawn Mitchell's address book?'

'No, sir.'

'I think we'll go and talk to these party-givers, Denzil. What's their name?'

'Crawley, sir. Mr and Mrs James Crawley.'

SIX

COMMANDER RAYMOND WILLOW SAT IN his office above Edmonton Police Station and stared moodily at the file on his desk. Then, with a gesture of annoyance, he slammed it shut and looked at Sergeant Clarke who was sitting respectfully in an upright chair near the door, poring over his pocket book.

'We are not making any progress with this complaint, skip,' said Willow.

'So it seems, sir,' said Clarke.

'This woman Nash—'

'Stedman's common-law wife, sir?'

'Yes. The American Embassy don't seem to know where she is, or even if she's in the States at all.'

'It's a big place, sir.'

'Yes, Sergeant, I know it's a big place, but until we can get hold of her, we shan't be able to get the full story. Particularly as Mr Fox is being stubborn about making a statement.'

'Well, he is entitled not to make a statement, sir. I mean to say, if he—'

'Don't you start,' said Willow.

. The office that Detective Sergeant Rosie Webster was shown into was cluttered. There were piles of fashion magazines everywhere and a bolt of taffeta leaned drunkenly against a wall. The desk was a rubbish dump of telephones, papers, files and sketches of women's dresses. Behind this desk sat the woman who owned the fashion house. About forty-five, fifty even, she was dressed in jeans and a sweater, and a pair of spectacles hung round

47

her neck on a chain. 'Be with you in a second, darling,' she said, covering the mouthpiece of the telephone with heavily-ringed fingers.

Finishing her conversation, she studied the photograph of Dawn Mitchell through a haze of cigarette smoke. 'She may have applied to us for a job,' she said, 'but sure as hell she never worked here. I always remember our girls. Hundreds of young kids want to be models, but only a few make it. And of that few, only a handful get to the top. God knows why they want to do it. It's a bloody awful job.' She returned the photograph to Rosie Webster with a half-smile of apology. 'Sorry, darling.'

Rosie Webster put the photograph back into her briefcase and ticked another name off her list. 'Twenty-seven,' she said, half to herself. 'I don't know why people do my job either.'

'The grass always looks greener on the other side,' said the couturière. She looked at Rosie's figure. 'I s'pose you don't want a job, do you, darling?'

'I've got one,' said Rosie.

The Crawleys lived in a tall narrow town house in one of the turnings off the Brompton Road. James Crawley was something in television and Constance was a resting actress. A small boy, seven or eight perhaps, whose hair was long enough to make him look like an understudy for Little Lord Fauntleroy, played with a toy car on the floor.

'What a dreadful thing to have happened,' said Constance Crawley. 'I still can't believe it.'

'How well did you know Lady Dawn, Mrs Crawley?' asked Fox.

'*Lady* Dawn?' Constance looked up sharply.

'She was the daughter of Earl Sims,' said Fox, 'although she preferred to be known as Dawn Mitchell.'

'Good heavens, I didn't know that. Your inspector, the one who came the other day, didn't mention that.' Constance glanced at her husband. 'Did you know that, darling?'

'No. No, I didn't. What an extraordinary thing,' said James Crawley in a tired voice.

'It would appear that she was murdered sometime

during the evening of the fourteenth of October,' Fox continued. 'But I am told that she came here for dinner on the fourth of August – a Saturday. Is that right?'

Constance Crawley stood up and crossed the room to a secretaire. For a moment or two, she rummaged among its contents before picking up a slim leather-bound book. 'Ah, here we are,' she said. 'My social diary.' She spent a further second or two riffling through its pages before turning to face Fox once more, the book held open in her hands. 'Absolutely right,' she said.

'And I believe you invited a man called Jason Hope-Smith to make up the numbers?'

'More to balance the sexes really, but yes, that's so.'

'Where does he live, Mrs Crawley?'

Constance Crawley thumbed through her diary again. 'I think he's got a place in Chelsea somewhere,' she said. 'But I've only got a phone number for him. It's a 352 number . . .' She looked up. 'Is that Chelsea?'

'Quite possibly,' said Fox. 'If I may make a note of it, I can find his address.' Denzil Evans had already tried to locate Hope-Smith, but Fox thought that this might be a different address. It was worth a try anyway.

'He's not here very often. In England, I mean.' Constance tossed the book back into her secretaire and, leaving the flap down, walked across the room and sat down again. 'He spends most of his time in the Middle East somewhere. He's in the oil business, I think.' And looking at her husband for confirmation, she asked, 'That's right, Jamie, isn't it?' She glanced at the child on the floor. 'Don't do that, William,' she said, almost automatically.

'Yes,' said James. 'Kuwait, I think.'

'He always rings us whenever he gets back here. Usually spends about four or five weeks in this country and then he's off again. Terrible life, I'd have thought. But he just doesn't have time to make friends, girlfriends I mean, and we take pity on him. I really thought that he and Dawn had hit it off that night.' She put a hand to her mouth, suddenly and theatrically. 'Oh God,' she said, 'you don't think. . .?'

'I don't think anything at the moment,' said Fox. 'I'm just making enquiries. Who else was here, Mrs Crawley?'

49

'Oh dear.' Constance Crawley looked thoughtful but for some reason didn't refer again to her diary. 'Now let me think. Ah yes, there was Freddie and Tessa Hayden – they're always regulars, and good fun – and there was Sheila Thompson and her boyfriend . . .' She looked at her husband again. 'What's he called, Jamie?'

'John Wheeler,' said James Crawley. 'I think. He's the photographer chap, isn't he?'

'That's right. Does portraits of awfully famous people. So he says. Can't say I've ever seen any of his work.' She shrugged. 'But then, there are a lot of frightfully bogus people about these days.'

'Yes,' said Fox and nodded. 'Does he do any fashion stuff?'

'Quite possibly,' said James Crawley. He spoke in a lofty dismissive way as though weary of the nuisance that these mere policemen were making of themselves.

'Anyone else?'

'Yes, there were Tim and Anthea.'

'Who are they?'

'He owns a string of companies, I think. I don't know precisely what he does, but he's quite well off.'

'What's his surname?'

'Oh heavens.' Constance Crawley stared at the opposite wall. 'Jarman, Jardine? Something like that. No, it's Jessop. That's it. Tim and Anthea Jessop.' She looked at Fox, one eyebrow raised. 'Why d'you need to know all this?' she asked.

'To quote Sherlock Holmes,' said James Crawley, looking up from his newspaper, 'when you have eliminated the impossible, whatever remains, however improbable, must be the truth. Is that not so, Inspector?'

'So I'm told,' said Fox, 'and the rank is Chief Superintendent. *Detective* Chief Superintendent.'

A check on Jason Hope-Smith's telephone number proved that he lived in a flat in an old house between King's Road and the Fulham Road. And it was the same address that DI Evans had tried, but this time, Hope-Smith was at home.

'You're lucky to find me,' he said. 'Only got in from Kuwait the day before yesterday and I'm off again on

50

Tuesday.' He pulled the door wide. 'Better come in, but you'll have to excuse the mess. Only use this place as a base really.' And he led Fox and Gilroy into a large sitting room. 'Have a seat. I've just made some tea. Want some?'

'No thanks,' said Fox.

'How can I help you, then?' Hope-Smith returned from his kitchen with a cup of tea and sat down on the settee opposite the two detectives. He seemed quite relaxed and not at all curious about their visit.

'I understand that you knew a Miss Dawn Mitchell.'

'Didn't really know her,' said Hope-Smith. 'Connie Crawley invited me to dinner one evening, back in August I think it was, and Dawn was there. We were the two odd ones out, if you get my meaning. She hadn't got a partner and neither had I. Connie was up to her usual match-making tricks again, I suppose.'

'You'd not seen her before that evening then?'

'No.'

'And afterwards?'

'What about afterwards?'

'Did you see her again?'

'No.' Hope-Smith sipped at his tea. 'What's this about?' he asked.

'Where were you on the night of the fourteenth and fifteenth of October, Mr Hope-Smith?'

Hope-Smith considered the question for only a moment. 'In Kuwait,' he said. 'Why?'

'Because Dawn Mitchell was murdered that night,' said Fox.

'Good God Almighty!' Hope-Smith put his cup and saucer down on the occasional table that separated him from Fox and Gilroy and stared in amazement. 'I didn't see that in the papers.'

'Probably not,' said Fox. 'But you may have seen an account of the murder of Lady Dawn Sims, daughter of Earl Sims.'

'Well, what's that got to do—'

'Same woman,' said Fox, 'but she preferred to be known as Dawn Mitchell.'

'Well, I'm damned.' Hope-Smith shook his head and

51

picked up his tea again. 'Well, I'm damned,' he said once more.

'Let's get back to the dinner party, Mr Hope-Smith. You had never seen this woman before, you say, and you never saw her again. Is that right?'

'Absolutely. But it wasn't for the want of trying.'

'What does that mean?'

'It's bloody difficult, doing the job I do, meeting up with girls. I was married once, but we split up. Got divorced about eight years ago. Since then, I've been going backwards and forwards to Kuwait. Apart from during the Gulf War, of course. Just got out in time and I spent about six or seven months here, waiting for it to get back to normal.'

'You said that you didn't see Dawn Mitchell again, but that it wasn't for the want of trying.'

'Oh yeah, sure. We exchanged telephone numbers and I promised to ring her, take her out to dinner. But each time I tried, I got her wretched answerphone. And she never returned my calls. In the end, I decided that she didn't want to have anything further to do with me. End of story.'

'Did you take her home after the Crawley's dinner party?' asked Fox.

'No, 'fraid not.' Hope-Smith looked wistful. 'All young women these days have got their own cars. They turn up in them and go home in them. Rather puts paid to a kiss and a cuddle in a taxi.'

Fox grinned. 'Yes,' he said, 'I suppose it does. Did you know any of the other people there, apart from the Crawleys, of course?'

'No. Oh, just a minute though. Yes, I'd met Freddie Hayden and his wife, er—'

'Tessa?'

'That's right. Bit of a dragon, she was. But Hayden had an eye for the ladies. Flirted with all of them.'

'And what did his wife think of that?'

'She just smiled. I got the impression that Tessa's quite used to his antics. Seemed to let it wash over her.'

'Can you describe them?' asked Gilroy.

Hope-Smith gazed towards the window, collecting his

52

thoughts. 'He's about fifty, I should think. Tessa's probably middle forties, maybe a bit younger, but she hasn't worn too well. He's got his fingers into all sorts of pies, so I'm told. Big businessman. And he's involved with quite a few charities. There've been whispers that he's in line for a knighthood.'

Rosie Webster tossed her briefcase on to her desk, sat down and lit a cigarette. 'That's twenty-nine bloody fashion houses I've visited now,' she said, 'and nothing.' She kicked off her shoes and, crossing one leg over the other so that her skirt rode up to her thigh, started to massage the sole of one of her feet.

'Hallo,' said Detective Constable Rex Perkins, a recent addition to the ranks of the Flying Squad, 'strip-tease time, is it?'

Very slowly, Rosie put her shoes back on and walked across to the young detective's desk. Leaning menacingly over him, so that he was suddenly aware of her expensive perfume, she flicked his tie over his shoulder and started to undo his shirt buttons, all the time holding his eyes with hers. 'If you think you're up to it, sonny,' she said, 'we can do it right now. Then I shall ring your wife and give her a full report on what I think of your performance which, unless I'm much mistaken, will be abysmal. But I rather think that you're all mouth.' She paused, one long, red fingernail pressing into his chest. 'Well, what about it? Not chickening out, are you?'

Perkins gulped and went bright red. The other members of the Squad who were in the office, and who had stopped to witness Rosie's teasing – they had seen her do it many times before for the benefit of new additions who fancied their chances with her – applauded politely. Perkins grabbed up his files and disappeared out of the door to the accompaniment of raucous laughter.

Rosie sat down at her desk again. 'I shall have to speak to the guv'nor,' she said to the office at large. 'Try and persuade him not to recruit kids.'

Detective Sergeant Percy Fletcher stood up and glanced at the clock over the door. 'Come on, Rosie,' he said, 'I'll buy you a gin across at The Old Star. I reckon you've earned it.'

'Well,' said Fox, 'we're getting nowhere fast. Perce, put yourself about and make a few enquiries, will you?'

'What are you looking for, guv'nor?' asked Fletcher.

'Do a check on this Jason Hope-Smith for a start. I don't fancy him too much. Says he was in Kuwait at the time of Dawn Mitchell's murder. Make sure he was, will you? Too bloody glib for my liking.'

'Right, guv.' Fletcher stood up.

'Haven't finished yet,' said Fox. 'And find out what you can about the other guests at this dinner party. Primarily a pair called Freddie and Tessa Hayden. But softly, softly, mind. I don't want any one of them alerted to our interest.'

Sergeant Clarke looked very pleased with himself as he came through the door of Commander Willow's office. 'I've come up with something, sir,' he said.

'Well I hope it's something good,' said Willow.

'Sandra Nash, sir, Stedman's common-law wife.'

'Well?'

'She was arrested last night for tomming, sir, on West End Central's ground.'

'How did you find that out?'

Sergeant Clarke puffed out his chest. 'Thought it might be a good idea to put her name on the computer, sir, asking for details if she came to notice.' He didn't give a damn about the success or failure of the complaint against Detective Chief Superintendent Fox of the Flying Squad, but Commander Willow was a man who could make recommendations about promotion, and Clarke desperately wanted to be an inspector.

'That was very clever of you, Sergeant,' said Willow. 'And presumably we have an address for this, er, prostitute?

'Of course, sir.'

'Good work, Sergeant. Perhaps you'd make an appointment for us to interview her.' He glanced at the clock. 'Shall we say eleven o'clock tomorrow morning?'

SEVEN

THE PERSONNEL MANAGER OF THE oil company that the police thought employed Jason Hope-Smith, scratched his head. 'He actually works for them out there,' he said, 'rather than for us. Different companies, you see.' He pondered the problem for a moment. 'But I daresay I could find out for you. Is it urgent?'

'Yes,' said Detective Sergeant Fletcher.

'Ah!' The personnel manager clicked down the switch of the intercom. 'Jan, get me the Kuwait office, love.' He leaned back in his chair and waited. 'Should be able to get hold of someone in their personnel department,' he said, 'unless it's a local holiday.'

'Good,' said Fletcher.

A few seconds later the telephone rang and the personnel manager engaged in a lengthy conversation during which there were several pauses, presumably while the person he was talking to referred to his records. Finally, he replaced the receiver. 'According to our people out there,' he said, 'Mr Hope-Smith was in London between the tenth and the seventeenth of October. Does that help at all?'

'Quite possibly,' said Fletcher.

'May I ask what this is all about?' asked the personnel manager.

'No idea,' said Fletcher. 'My guv'nor just told me to make the enquiry. So I did.' He grinned cheerfully, stood up and shook hands, and left.

Lady Jane Sims's first-floor mansion flat was situated in one of the streets behind Harrods of Knightsbridge and although it possessed a lift – the old-fashioned sort with trellis gates – Fox ran up the stairs, two at a time.

Although she had been expecting him, Jane Sims was barefooted and casually dressed in jeans and a sloppy sweater, and her long brown hair was loose round her shoulders. 'Come in,' she said.

The large high-ceilinged sitting-room into which she led Fox had a double set of French doors, across which were drawn long drapes in a material of jazzy design.

Fox stood in the centre of the room and looked around at its expensive furnishings. The flat was a complete contrast to that in which Dawn Sims had lived on the Edgware Road. Where Dawn's had been luxurious and homely, this one was starkly modern, almost barren. His gaze took in the dining table of black glass supported by chromium legs and the six leather and chrome dining chairs tucked neatly beneath it. The armchairs had a functional and uncomfortable look about them which the brightly-coloured scatter cushions did little to soften. Several prints of abstract art adorned the walls and, overall, the flat had the unlived-in air of an office or a showroom, an impression heightened by the drawing-board that stood in one corner.

'You don't like it, do you?' Jane Sims, a whimsical smile on her face, had been standing behind Fox during his critical appraisal of her living-room.

Fox turned. 'On the contrary, Lady Jane,' he said, 'I think it has a unique elegance.'

'Liar,' said Jane, and laughed. 'Do sit down and I'll get you a drink.' She paused at the cocktail cabinet and held a bottle of whisky in the air. 'Scotch, if I remember correctly,' she said, raising one eyebrow.

'Thanks. Just a dash of water. No ice.'

'I should hope not. Nasty American habit, putting ice in Scotch.' Jane walked across the room and handed Fox his drink. Then she sat down on the settee opposite him, crossed her legs and took a sip of her whisky. 'Shall I turn off the music?'

'Not on my account. What is it?'

'It's the music from *Cats*. Have you seen it?'

'No,' said Fox. 'Don't have much time for going to

56

shows. Is it good?'

'I've seen it three times. And I've seen *Phantom* twice. Oh, and *Miss Saigon*. I've seen that twice, too. But then I love Lloyd Webber's stuff. However, Mr Fox, I'm sure you didn't come here to discuss West End shows. How can I help you?'

'Does the name Jason Hope-Smith mean anything to you, Lady Jane?' Fox smoothed a hand across his knee.

'No. Should it?'

'He was a dinner companion of your sister, back in August.'

'I've no doubt she had lots of dinner companions, Mr Fox. What's so special about that one?'

'She was invited to dinner by some friends of hers. The Crawleys, James and Constance.'

Jane Sims shook her head. 'None of those names mean anything to me,' she said, 'but then, as I said the other day, Dawn and I lived separate lives. Whenever we spoke on the phone, she was always chatting away about someone new she'd met. I couldn't keep up with her. She was always bubbling over about somewhere she'd been, or some party she'd been to.' For a moment she looked wistful. 'She lived a very empty life really.'

'So you don't recall Hope-Smith having been mentioned.'

'No, I'm afraid not. But you still haven't told me what was so special about him.'

'Probably nothing,' said Fox, 'but he claimed to have been in Kuwait at the time of Lady Dawn's murder.'

'And now you've discovered that he wasn't, I suppose.'

'How did you know that?'

'I didn't, but that's the implication, surely. You wouldn't be checking up on a dinner companion from last August unless you thought that he'd had something to do with it. After all, you didn't ask me about my movements on the night that Dawn was killed, did you?'

'Didn't have to,' said Fox, determined not to let this woman have it all her own way. 'But I made enquiries and satisfied myself that you were in Yorkshire at the time, and on that particular night you were dining at a local restaurant.'

For a moment or two, Jane appraised him with her keen gaze. Then she smiled. 'Well I'm damned,' she said and stood up. 'You'd better have another drink.' Without waiting for Fox's agreement, she took his glass and poured more Scotch into it.

Fox stood too, and strolled across the room to examine the largest of Jane's abstracts, on the wall opposite the windows. 'What's that a picture of?' he asked.

Jane joined him and, handing him his drink, said, 'You're teasing me, aren't you? You know perfectly well that it's an abstract. It's not supposed to be a picture of anything.'

'Extraordinary,' murmured Fox and sat down.

Jane sat down again too, and placed her own glass on the table beside her. 'I've never really met a detective before,' she said. 'Are they all like you?'

'Good God no,' said Fox.

'No, probably not.' Jane studied Fox for a moment before going on. 'Tell me, Mr Fox, are you anywhere near finding out who murdered my sister?'

'No,' said Fox, 'but the investigation of murder is sometimes very difficult.'

'I imagine it is.'

'But not always—'

'Do you smoke, by the way?'

'Yes, I do.'

'Well please do if you wish. I don't myself, but I'm not one of these people who gets terribly excited if someone else does.' Jane fetched an ashtray from the bottom cupboard of the cocktail cabinet and placed it beside Fox. 'You were saying . . . about investigating murder.'

'Some murders are cleared up almost immediately,' said Fox. 'Particularly what we call domestic murders. But in most cases, I suppose, the victim is known to the murderer.'

'And is this a domestic murder, as you call it?'

'I don't know,' said Fox. 'But possibly Lady Dawn knew her killer. At least, that is the theory I'm working on at the moment.' He crossed his legs and studied the toe of his shoe.

'The thing that's been puzzling me,' said Jane, 'is why

58

her body was found in a lock-up underneath some arches in . . . was it Lambeth, you said?'

'Yes, it was. And it's puzzling me, too.' Fox paused to take a sip of his Scotch. 'Are there any names that your sister may have mentioned that you can remember?'

Jane thought about his question for a while and then shook her head. 'I'm afraid not,' she said. 'Much as I'd like to be able to help, there's nothing relevant that I can think of. I'm sorry.'

'Did your sister ever have a close relationship, Lady Jane? Some time ago even?'

'I do wish you'd call me Jane. I'm not very keen on this title business. It's a bit old-hat these days.' Jane Sims smiled at him. Fox returned the smile and nodded a brief acknowledgement. 'But to answer your question,' Jane went on, 'no, I don't think that there was ever a man in Dawn's life. Not one that she regarded as a future husband, anyway. If she did, she never mentioned it.'

'Never spoke of getting married?'

'No.' Jane Sims looked thoughtful. 'I suppose my own experience may have put her off.'

'Yes, I remember you saying something about marrying the wrong man.' Fox reached across and stubbed out his cigarette.

'It was fifteen years ago, and it was a disaster.'

'Sorry to hear that,' said Fox.

Jane shrugged. 'It's all over now,' she said. 'We got divorced eight years ago, but it was finished well before that. The trouble with being an earl's daughter and living in London – which I was even then – is that most of the men you meet are chinless wonders whose whole life seems to be devoted to playing some stupid game or another, like polo or squash.' She glanced up at the ceiling. 'This one was a complete wastrel. Still, that's life.' She didn't appear to be too upset about her failed marriage, nor did she seem to want to dwell on it.

'Did Lady Dawn ever meet your ex-husband?' asked Fox.

'Yes, of course. She was a bridesmaid. Why d'you ask?'

'It is a failing of mine to ask questions,' said Fox with a grin. 'Policemen hate loose ends.' He glanced at his watch.

'Well,' he said, 'I'd better be on my way.' He placed his empty glass on the table and stood up. 'Thanks for the drink, Jane.'

'It was a pleasure.' Jane Sims stood up too. 'I suppose your wife will be wondering where you've got to,' she said.

'I'm not married,' said Fox. 'Can't afford decent suits *and* a wife. Not on a policeman's pay.'

'That's a shame,' said Jane, and closing the front door behind Fox, stood in thought for a moment or two, her hand still on the night-latch.

'I've come to the conclusion, Mr Hope-Smith, that you're wasting my time,' said Fox.

'Whatever makes you think that?' Hope-Smith looked a little nervous at Fox's sharp opening comment.

'When I was here last, you told me that on the night of the fourteenth and fifteenth of October you were in Kuwait.'

'So I was.'

'Then how d'you account for the fact that the company you work for, having checked with their Kuwait office, told one of my officers that you were in London? From the tenth to the seventeenth to be precise.'

'Oh!' Hope-Smith looked down at the floor, a contrite expression on his face.

'Well?'

'Yes, I was here.'

'Then why did you tell me that you weren't?'

Hope-Smith glanced up, guiltily. 'It's the tax business,' he said.

'What tax business?' Fox was starting to get angry.

'My income in Kuwait is tax-free,' said Hope-Smith, 'but if I spend too long over here, I have to pay some tax to the Inland Revenue. I'm almost over my limit for this year and as the immigration people never stamp your passport, I wasn't going to declare that short stay. Let the blood-suckers think I was still away, you see.'

'Is that so? Well look at it from my point of view, Mr Hope-Smith. You tell a detective chief superintendent from Scotland Yard, who is investigating the murder of a woman whom, on your own admission, you tried several times to contact, that you were out of the country at the time of her murder. Then I find that you were, in fact, here. Now what sort of construction d'you expect me to put on that, eh?'

'Oh Christ!' said Hope-Smith. 'I see what you mean. But I had absolutely nothing to do with her death, Chief Superintendent, I promise you.'

'You'll forgive me for not being convinced, won't you?' said Fox. 'Now then, you can start by accounting for your movements on the night of the fourteenth to the fifteenth of October.' He glanced at Gilroy who made a show of getting out his pocket book.

Hope-Smith ran a hand through his hair. 'I'm not sure,' he said.

'Well you'd better start thinking, pretty damned quick.' Fox pushed his hands into his pockets and leaned back against the mantelshelf.

'I think I stayed in. What day of the week was that?'

'The fourteenth was a Sunday.'

'Yes, I'm pretty certain that I stayed in.'

'Doing what? Watching television perhaps?'

Hope-Smith shook his head. 'No, I rarely watch it. I think I read for a while then had an early night.'

'Is that so?' It was evident that Fox was not going to get any further than that, and in the absence of any proof to the contrary, he would have to accept what Hope-Smith said. But he wasn't going to let him off the hook that easily. 'When are you returning to Kuwait?' he asked.

'Tuesday.' Hope-Smith looked relieved that he would be escaping so soon.

'Well, I can always come out there to see you if necessary. And I shall almost certainly need to see you again.'

That gave Hope-Smith no comfort at all. 'This question of tax,' he said hopefully. 'I suppose you won't need to, well, you know . . .'

'I am a police officer, Mr Hope-Smith, and as far as I can see, you may have made a false declaration to the Inland Revenue. I shall certainly be making a full report to them. Good-day to you.'

'The Jessops went to America at the beginning of October, sir,' said Detective Sergeant Percy Fletcher.

'Hold on, Perce,' said Fox. 'I'm only a simple policeman. I can't keep up with these rapid results you keep pouring into the system. Who are the Jessops?'

'The other two guests at the dinner party, sir.'

'Ah yes, Perce. Gone to America, you say?'

'Yes, sir. Left Gatwick on Air New Zealand flight NZ1 for Los Angeles at 1710 hours on the first of October. Planning to stay until just after Christmas, so their daughter said.' Fletcher paused. 'Don't want someone to pop over there and interview them, I suppose, guv?'

'You suppose correctly, Perce,' said Fox.

'I think I've visited every fashion house and model agency in London, sir,' said Rosie Webster.

'No joy?' asked Fox.

'No, sir. One or two said that Dawn Mitchell might have been to them for jobs, and one said that she might have done some work for them, but they weren't willing to put it in writing.'

'That's life,' said Fox. 'Well, now you've got nothing to do, Rosie, perhaps you'd pop along to St Catherine's House and do a bit of digging on Lady Jane Sims. She was divorced eight years ago, so she said. Find out what you can, will you?'

'I wasn't able to make an appointment, sir,' said Sergeant Clarke. 'It would appear that Sandra Nash is not on the telephone.'

'I can't say that I'm surprised,' said Commander Willow. 'In that case, we shall go to her address. Tell my driver to get the car up, will you.'

'Yes, sir.'

The black Montego turned into Purbeck Terrace, Paddington, and stopped outside Number 54. Willow alighted and looked around. 'Are you sure this is the right place, Sergeant?' he asked.

Clarke referred quickly to his pocket book. 'Yes, sir, this is it.'

'I see.' Willow marched up the crumbling concrete steps and studied the names beside the battery of doorbells. 'Well, there's no one here called Nash,' he said.

'Perhaps she doesn't advertise, sir,' said Clarke but promptly removed the half-smile from his face as Willow scowled at him.

'We'll try this one then.' Willow pressed the bottom bell-push and waited.

Eventually the door opened an inch or two and an attractive black woman of about thirty peered round it. 'What you want?' she asked.

'We're police officers,' said Willow, producing his ornate commander's warrant card.

'Is that so?' The woman looked Willow up and down, appearing to be fascinated by his Marks & Spencer suit. 'You come about them boys selling crack, every night down the street?' She opened the door wide and placed her hands on her hips. 'Because it's about time someone was doing something about it. We're all law-abiding people here, and we don't like having these junkies round here pushing. You know what I mean?'

'Yes, I do, madam,' said Willow, 'but that's not what I'm here about.'

'Well why aren't you? We pay our taxes, just like other folk, and we want something done about it. Now what you going to do?'

'I'll make sure that the local chief superintendent is told,' said Willow, not wanting to get involved in something that, in his view anyway, was not his concern.

'That's what they all say.' The woman wasn't going to give up. 'We been down the station, and the Paddington Residents Defence Association been down the station. And you know what's happened?' Willow opened his mouth to speak, but the woman went on. 'Nothing, that's what's happened. Well it ain't good enough. Why don't you go and arrest these people, eh? You frightened of them, or something?'

'No, madam, not at all, but I am a commander and I am

63

here on a quite different enquiry.'

'Oh, you're a boss cop, eh? Well that's just what we wanted.' The woman leaned backwards, still holding on to the door. 'Henry,' she shouted at the top of her voice. 'Come here, quick. There's a big important policeman here, come to talk about the crack dealers.'

A man of about forty with flecks of grey in his bushy hair, and wearing a bus-driver's uniform, appeared in the hallway of the house. He looked Willow up and down before speaking. 'What are you going to do about this crack, sir?' he asked.

'I've just been trying to explain to your wife—'

The bus driver threw back his head and roared with laughter. 'She's not my wife, sir, she's the woman I live with,' he said.

'Yes, well be that as it may,' said Willow, 'I've told your, er, I've told this lady that I shall arrange for extra policemen to be sent here to deal with the problem. Now then, I am looking for a Miss Sandra Nash, who I believe lives here.'

The bus driver shook his head. 'No one of that name lives here, sir,' he said, and started to list the names of all the people who lived in the house. 'There never been no one called Sandra Nash living here. Black girl, is she?'

'No,' said Sergeant Clarke from behind the commander. 'She's white. And she's a prostitute.'

'A prostitute!' The bus driver's woman screamed the word. 'You come round here and refuse to do anything about the crack dealers and then you say we've got prostitutes in the house.' She took a step nearer Willow. 'I'm going to write to my MP about you, Mister Boss Policeman. I'm going to complain, that's what I'm going to do.' And with that she slammed the door.

'The first thing I want you to do when we get back to Edmonton,' said Willow through clenched teeth, 'is find out what steps the custody officer at West End Central took to verify Sandra Nash's address before he admitted her to bail. And secondly, I want to know when she is due to appear in court. D'you understand, Sergeant?'

'Yes, sir,' said Clarke. He understood only too well.

EIGHT

SOME VERY RICH PEOPLE LIVE in Chiswick which is in west London. But there are also some villains living there. The villains regard the rich people, who live in expensive houses and possess an abundance of luxury items, as fair game and frequently break in to their expensive houses and steal their luxury items. Which is why it took Tessa Hayden some time to open her front door, such opening involving peering through a spy-hole, switching off the intruder alarm in such a way as not to have half the police force turning up, and finally undoing the several locks and bolts with which the front door had been fitted.

'Good afternoon, madam,' said Fox. 'I telephoned earlier. Thomas Fox . . . of the Flying Squad.'

'I'm sorry to have kept you waiting, but it's the burglar alarm.' Tessa Hayden examined Fox's warrant card closely and satisfied herself that it was genuine. At least, she assumed it was genuine, but as she had only seen a police warrant card once before, it was really a piece of play-acting. 'I'm not used to it yet. The nice officer who came round from the police station suggested fitting it – the alarm, I mean – and all the locks and everything.'

'Very wise, madam,' said Fox, wondering what the crime prevention officer got for Christmas from the burglar alarm company. He and Gilroy stepped into the hallway and looked around.

'Come through to the withdrawing room,' said Tessa Hayden, using a term she had read in an up-market magazine as being the correct description for the room where she spent most of her waking hours. She was, as Jason Hope-Smith had said, about forty-five to fifty, and although he had described her as a dragon, Fox actually thought that she had made the best of herself. Given the limitations. And given also that she would always look as though she was about to set off on a day trip to Southend.

Prominent on a grand piano was a framed photograph of Tessa and a man in morning dress, complete with silk top hat, whom, Fox presumed, was Freddie Hayden.

'That was taken at the palace,' said Tessa.

'Crystal Palace?' asked Fox innocently. Gilroy turned away, taking a sudden interest in the view from the French doors.

'Oh no, Buckingham Palace. It was the garden party.' Tessa's condescending tone implied that policemen could not be expected to know about such social events.

'Oh, very nice,' said Fox who had, in fact, been to a garden party at Buckingham Palace only the previous July.

'Mr Hayden and I often go,' said Tessa casually, 'Mr Hayden's connected with one or two charities that you-know-who is interested in.' She whispered the last few words.

'You know who?' Fox repeated innocently.

'Yes, you know.' Tessa continued to whisper. 'Her Majesty,' she said, dropping her voice even further.

'Never!' Fox made a pretence of being manifestly impressed by this revelation. 'Well,' he continued, 'who'd have thought it?'

'Oh yes, Mr Hayden works tirelessly for charity.'

'Is that what he's doing now? He's not in his office.'

'He's gone to Africa. Somalia actually.'

'And when will he be returning, Mrs Hayden?'

'Next week, so he says. About Thursday, I should think.' Tessa Hayden primped at her hair. 'This is quite dreadful about Dawn Mitchell. We called her Dawn, although she was really a lady. A lady in her own right, I mean. She was Lady Dawn Sims, you know.'

'Yes, I did know that,' said Fox. 'But how long have you known it?'

Tessa Hayden looked away. 'Oh, some time,' she said in an offhand way.

'And how did you learn of her death?'

'Connie told me. Er, Mrs Crawley, that is.'

Fox was beginning to tire of this woman's posturing and make-believe. 'I understand that you first met Lady Dawn – or Dawn Mitchell as she would have been known to you – at a dinner party at the Crawleys' last August. Is that correct?'

'Yes, that's right. A lovely girl. Really lovely.'

'And that was the only time you met her?'

'Well . . .' Loathe to admit that she did not hob-nob with the well-to-do all the time, Tessa Hayden appeared to give this question a great deal of thought. 'Yes, now you come to mention it, I suppose it was, but she was one of those terribly warm girls that you felt you'd known all your life.'

'Mr Jason Hope-Smith, whom you will also know. . .?' Fox lifted one eyebrow slightly.

'Er, let me see . . .'

'He's in the oil business. Constance Crawley invited him to make up the numbers. I think he sat opposite Dawn and next to you.'

'Oh yes, of course. A nice young man. I thought that Connie had been ever so clever, matching those two up.'

'I understand that your husband was quite taken with her too, Mrs Hayden.'

There was a brief pause as Tessa Hayden weighed that question but, as is so often the case with women of her sort, she thought she was much more clever than she really was. 'To tell you the truth, he was trying to cultivate her.' Her voice dropped to the conspiratorial whisper she had used when talking about the Queen. 'It was the title, you see. Freddie – that's Mr Hayden – never misses a chance to get a member of the aristocracy involved in his charity work, when he can.'

'I see.' Fox saw only too well. Hope-Smith had said that Hayden had flirted with Dawn Mitchell at the dinner party and Tessa Hayden was now using the girl's title to excuse her husband's philandering. Even though Fox was certain that, at the time, neither she nor her husband had known that Dawn Mitchell was the daughter of an earl. 'What sort of charity work is your husband involved in, Mrs Hayden?'

'You must have seen his shops,' said Tessa. 'They're called Hayden Charity. He made a joke of it and said that Hayden stands for "Help All Your Deprived Emaciated Neighbours".' She smiled and her hands fluttered aimlessly in front of her. 'He's very clever with words, you know.'

'Apparently.' Fox had yet to meet Hayden, but he had already concluded that the man was a bit of a prat.

Harry Dawes was a worried man. The visit of Tommy Fox had frightened the life out of him. The discovery of the body in his lock-up at Lambeth had been unfortunate, to say the least, and the resulting interest that the police were now taking in him – or that he thought they were taking – threatened severely to hamper his operations. But it hadn't stopped him altogether. Convinced that his telephone was being tapped, he was obliged, as Fox had predicted, to use a public telephone to get in touch with his associates, or even to meet them face-to-face. And that was very risky.

Indeed, Fox had not been idle in the matter of the robberies, despite having a murder to investigate, and he had instructed DI Evans to gather as much information as possible about any other warehouse-breakings around the country where a similar method appeared to have been employed.

'There have been seventeen altogether, sir,' said Evans, glancing at a list. 'Over a period of about eight or nine months. And not only warehouses. There've been shop-breakings as well. Rammings, some of them.'

'Saucy bastards,' said Fox. 'What sort of gear have they been having off, Denzil?'

'Clothing mainly, sir. Men's casual wear for the most part. Jeans, sweaters, and trainers. Oh, and tents and camping gear. And quite a lot of women's dresses, too. The other thing that seems to have attracted their attention is electrical stuff. Personal computers, computer games, video-recorders.'

Fox nodded. It was a familiar pattern. 'Where have they been operating?' he asked.

'The furthest north they've been is Birmingham, guv. They hit a couple of places in Chelmsford and Oxford, too. But mainly in London. Well, greater London. Kingston and Croydon seem very popular.'

'Not with me they're not.' Fox shook his head glumly and lit a cigarette. 'They're taking the piss, Denzil,' he said, 'and I'm not having it.'

'No, sir,' said Evans, not quite sure how they were going to stop it.

'What's Henry Findlater up to?' Fox asked suddenly.

'He's still keeping obo on Harry Dawes, sir.' Evans sounded surprised that Fox appeared not to know.

'Good. Tell him to come in and see me.'

'D'you mean you want the obo taken off then, sir?'

'Of course not, Denzil, but he's got a team out there hasn't he?'

'Yes, sir.'

'Well then. Tell him to leave it in place and come in for a chat. It's time we had a conference.'

'Very good, sir,' said Evans. But it wasn't very good at all. Evans didn't much care for Fox's conferences.

'I want every one of Dawes's associates identified,' said Fox, 'and I shall use every man we have, if necessary.' He looked round at the assembled members of the Flying Squad and beamed confidently. 'Henry.'

'Yes, sir?'

'How many visitors has Dawes had since we set up the observation?'

'About four, sir,' said Findlater. 'All identified. But Dawes has been out several times to the public phone box in the Upper Richmond Road. But of course we don't know who he contacted.'

'No, no you wouldn't, Henry.' Fox nodded wisely. 'See you, did he?'

'No, sir, of course not.' Findlater looked hurt.

'Right then, from now on, make sure he knows you're there. It's no good him making calls from public call boxes because we don't know who he's phoning. So we'll let his merry little band of villains go to him.'

'But surely, sir, that'll stop him altogether, won't it? He'll just suspend operations.'

'Exactly, Henry. Keep that going for a week and then we'll withdraw the obo for three or four days.' Fox looked round the room with a triumphant gleam in his eye. 'Then we'll put it back on again . . . discreetly.'

John Wheeler, the photographer who had accompanied Sheila Thompson to the Crawleys' dinner party, looked closely at Fox's face as though assessing its photogenic qualities. 'Yes, I was there.' He grinned. 'This is just like a detective story on television,' he said. 'You know the sort of thing, where someone gets murdered at a country house party and the inspector gets everyone together in the drawing room afterwards and tells them who committed it.'

'Yes,' said Fox, a sour expression on his face. 'There are a lot of plays like that on television. Nevertheless, I am interviewing everyone who attended the Crawleys' dinner party, and I'll be nicking whoever it's down to without gathering you all together at the end.'

Wheeler grinned again and turned off the floodlights in his studio. 'Have a seat,' he said. 'What can I tell you?'

'How well did you know Dawn Mitchell, Mr Wheeler?'

'That was the first time I'd met her. Sheila and I go back a long way and we've been to the Crawleys' for dinner lots of times. But it seems that we're the only regulars.'

'D'you mean that you didn't know anyone else who was there? Apart from the Crawleys, of course?'

'No, I didn't.' Wheeler pulled a packet of cigarettes from his pocket and offered them to Fox and Gilroy. 'There was a boring couple called . . .' He paused to accept a light from Fox and rubbed his hand round his chin. 'Can't remember. Kept banging on about his bloody charity work most of the time.'

'Hayden?'

'That's him. Christ, what a bore. And his wife. Boy, you should have seen her. Talk about mutton dressed as lamb. Wanted me to take a studio portrait of her.'

'And did you?' asked Fox.

Wheeler stood up and walked across to a wooden cabinet with banks of shallow drawers beneath it. 'There,' he said, returning with a proof copy of a photograph. 'That's what you call a work of art.'

Fox examined the picture. Wheeler had actually managed to make Tessa Hayden look attractive and about fifteen years younger. 'You cheated,' he said.

'Too bloody right. I do have a reputation to think about, you know.'

'What about the others?'

'What others?' Wheeler threw the photograph onto a stool and looked back at Fox.

'The others at the party.'

'There was a couple called Jessop. Never found out much about them, except they kept telling everyone that they were going to spend the winter in California. Seemed to be rolling in money. Then there was the bloke that Dawn Mitchell brought with her. Well, I thought that he'd brought her, but I learned afterwards that it was the first time they'd met. He was called Jason. Something to do with oil, so he said. He behaved as though he was about twenty, but I reckon he was nearer forty. Bloody idiot. It was obvious that he fancied Dawn rotten. Tessa had invited him to balance the table.'

'Balance the table?'

Wheeler laughed. 'Yeah, balance the numbers. I didn't mean he was a juggler.'

'No,' said Fox drily. 'I didn't imagine you did. But who told you that he hadn't met Dawn before? Did he?'

'No, Dawn did.'

'That evening?'

'No. We met afterwards.'

'How did that come about?'

'Tessa told everyone that I was a photographer. So suddenly they all discover that they've always wanted their portraits taken.' Wheeler shrugged. 'I suppose you get that sort of thing in your trade?' he said.

'Not really,' said Fox. 'Generally speaking I find that people are not that keen to have their photographs taken by the police.'

71

'That's not what I—' Wheeler broke off, laughing. 'All right,' he said, 'but you know what I mean.'

'How did you come to meet Dawn Mitchell afterwards?' Fox, irritated at having his time wasted in banal chat, persisted.

'She rang me, here at the studio.'

'Did you give her your phone number?'

'Didn't have to. It's in the book, Yellow Pages.'

'What did she want?'

'She was desperate to become a fashion model, and she wanted some photographs taken. Free.'

'And did you oblige?'

'Yes and no.' Wheeler sounded hesitant.

'What's that mean?' asked Fox.

'She said she couldn't afford my fees, but she was prepared to pay in other ways.'

'And did she? Pay in another way.'

For the first time since the interview had started, Wheeler looked embarrassed. 'Yes, but—'

'But what?'

'I wouldn't like Sheila to get to know. We've got a sort of permanent arrangement, if you know what I mean.'

'How long did this go on? Between you and Dawn?'

'I suppose it lasted for about six weeks.'

'And finished when?' Fox glanced sideways at Gilroy and saw that he was taking notes.

'Towards the end of September, I think it must have been.'

'Why?'

Wheeler shrugged. 'Just one of those things, I suppose,' he said.

Fox stood up. 'Do you happen to have any of the photographs you took of Dawn Mitchell, Mr Wheeler?' he asked.

'No,' said Wheeler without hesitation. 'I gave them all to her.'

'You don't keep any proof copies then?'

'Not of private work I do for friends, no.' Wheeler nodded at the print of Mrs Hayden. 'Apart from that one,' he said. 'And I was rather pleased with that.'

'I see,' said Fox. 'Be a bit difficult for the Inland

Revenue to tax some of your payments, I suppose.'

Out in the street, Fox paused with his hand on the door-handle of his car. 'He wasn't the photographer who took the prints we found in her flat, was he, Jack?'

'No, sir.'

'How very strange,' said Fox. 'I wonder why.'

By the afternoon of the second day, Harry Dawes had become aware that the police surveillance on him had been intensified. In fact, he could hardly have avoided noticing. Every time he left his house, two or three men or women, albeit dressed in un-policemanlike garb, had followed him. They walked down the road, seemingly very interested in everything but Harry Dawes. They hung around near the telephone box from which he made his calls, and they walked back to Oxford Road again when he walked back. And whenever Dawes looked out of his sitting-room window, he noticed a dilapidated van with blanked out windows parked in the street or, worse still, a man or a woman just loitering. It got to the point where Dawes even looked with suspicion upon those going about their lawful occasions, like the postman, the milkman and several innocent members of what are called the utilities. And the man who came to read Dawes's meter was subjected to a particularly rigorous grilling.

But Harry Dawes had been jousting with the forces of law and order for too long to be that easily intimidated. The last phone call he had made, knowingly under the watchful eyes of Findlater's team, had been to a trusted lieutenant called Wilkins. Kevin Wilkins had been told to issue instructions to all interested parties that Dawes had suspended operations for the duration of the present emergency.

On the morning of the third day, Harry Dawes, a lifetime of villainous experience behind him, determined to go on the offensive. Putting on his hat and coat, he left the house, pointedly pausing at his gate to look up and down the road. Raising his hat to a road-sweeper whom he firmly believed to be one of Fox's men, he bade him a cheery 'Good Morning' and walked down to Wandsworth Police Station where he made a formal complaint of harassment.

73

NINE

IT WAS A BLACK, FOUR-wheel-drive, cross-country truck with a canvas canopy, a sturdy framework of steel bars protecting its radiator and a towing hook at the back. It would have been more suited to grinding its way over some rough terrain in Yorkshire or Cornwall, or traversing miles of featureless desert in the course of some Cape-to-Cairo expedition. But as it happened, this particular vehicle was moving slowly along a row of shops in Kingston upon Thames. Fourteen miles from London. Or thereabouts.

Just as slowly, the vehicle turned on to the pavement. But then it accelerated, straight through the front of a shop that specialised in hi-fi, television and video. In the quiet of a Tuesday morning – it was 3 a.m. exactly – the noise was terrifying as glass shattered, metal grilles were torn away and glass doors were spread across the interior of the shop together with the cheaper products that had been on display in the windows. But the trio of villains in the truck didn't panic. They knew how much time they had.

Rapidly, two of them leaped from the vehicle, seized four television sets, two video-recorders and a couple of personal computers, and handed them quickly to the third man who had remained in the back of the truck. Calmly, they secured the tailgate and almost sauntered round to climb into the cab. Reversing out of the smashed shop, the wheels of their truck crunching over broken glass, they left a pavement littered with debris and a burglar alarm disturbing the night, and drove off at high speed. A nearby occupant of a flat nearly killed himself leaning out of an upstairs window in an attempt to get the number of the truck. Not that it would have helped if he had. The truck had been stolen.

Three minutes later, at Kingston Police Station, the night duty station officer looked at the message that told him that a unit had been assigned to deal with a ram-raid. Then he stood up, stretched and yawned. In all fairness, there was little else he could do.

At about the same time, in Catford, a shop that supplied expensive computer games to children whose parents couldn't say no, was broken into. As the staff were all at home, safely tucked up in their beds, there was no one to hinder the thieves. So, just for the hell of it, one of them stabbed an inflatable Father Christmas to death.

'Well?' Fox glowered at Denzil Evans as though he was personally responsible for these latest outrages.

'The truck used in the Kingston raid was found abandoned at Esher, sir, which is about—'

'I know where Esher is,' snapped Fox. 'There's a racecourse there. Any witnesses?'

'No, sir. Well, none that's any good.'

'What have the local CID come up with? Anything? Or is it all too much for them?'

'They've had forensics down at the scene and—'

'I take it you mean a scientific examination has been conducted,' said Fox acidly, continuing his battle against the misuse of the word 'forensic'.

'Yes, sir. But they haven't come up with anything.'

'Didn't expect them to, did you, Denzil?' Fox turned to the window and glared at the morning rush hour. 'And the Catford job?'

'They had about two grand's-worth away, guv.'

'It's the same team, Denzil,' said Fox.

'Well, sir—'

'Of course it is, Denzil. Got to be.' Fox turned away from the window and threw the two message flimsies towards his desk. They floated aimlessly past it and into the waste-paper basket. 'I'll not have these bloody people

75

thumbing their noses at me. Understood?'

'Yes, sir,' said Evans. 'By the way, sir, there was a third that we've just heard about.'

'What?' barked Fox.

'A lorry-load of tinned peaches was hijacked near Farnham, sir.'

'Get out,' said Fox.

Commander Thomas, the Director of the Complaints Investigation Bureau of the Metropolitan Police, always made a point of seeing complaints made against senior CID officers. And, for the second time in a month, a complaint against Detective Chief Superintendent Fox of the Flying Squad had dropped on to Thomas's desk in his office high in Tintagel House on Albert Embankment.

Thomas touched the switch on his intercom and spoke to his secretary. 'Get me Commander Willow at One Area Headquarters, please, Sonia,' he said.

Seconds later, Thomas's phone buzzed and he picked up the receiver. 'Raymond?'

'Yes,' said Commander Willow.

'Thomas here.'

'Thomas who?' Willow always played this little game with the man who had got the job that Willow had always wanted.

'John Thomas.'

'Oh, hallo, John.'

'You're dealing with a complaint against Fox of the Squad, I believe,' said Thomas airily, well knowing that to be the case.

'Yes.' Willow spoke curtly. He did not wish to be reminded of it. In fact, he thought that the black woman's threat to complain about him had come to fruition.

'Well there's another one.'

'Is there indeed! Well give it to someone else.'

'I've spoken to the Deputy Commissioner, Raymond,' said Thomas, 'and he agrees that it would be better if you ran the two together. Makes sense, don't you think?'

'No, I don't,' said Willow, 'but if that's what the Deputy wants then so be it.'

'Jolly good. I'll put the papers in the despatch,' said Thomas with an evil smile. He didn't like Willow. Dipping the receiver rest, he tapped out the Deputy Commissioner's direct-line number. 'I've just received another complaint against Detective Chief Superintendent Fox, sir,' he said smoothly. 'I thought it would be a good idea to give it to Ray Willow, as he's already dealing with one against Fox.'

'Good idea,' said the Deputy Commissioner and replaced the receiver, somewhat mystified as to why Thomas had bothered to tell him.

To say that Sheila Thompson was slim was to be polite. She was, in fact, painfully thin. And small-breasted. With short black hair and an elvan face. 'John told me that you'd be coming to see me,' she said.

'Then you'll know what it's about,' said Fox. 'How well did you know Dawn Mitchell?'

'Do take a seat.' Sheila Thompson moved, with feline grace, across to an armchair and sat down. 'I knew her hardly at all,' she said.

'What d'you mean by that?' Fox eased himself into a comfortable armchair and stretched out his legs. Gilroy looked around before sinking into a bean-bag.

'I met her for the first time at the Crawleys' dinner party, as did John.'

Fox sighed inwardly. He detested going through the same routine every time he opened an interview. 'But you saw her again?'

'Oh, yes. I saw her again all right.'

'Miss Thompson, I don't have a great deal of time,' said Fox patiently. 'Could you just explain.'

Sheila surveyed Fox thoughtfully. 'I don't know how much John told you,' she said, 'but he and Dawn Mitchell had a brief fling. Lasted about six weeks, I suppose.'

'Yes, I know.'

Sheila raised her eyebrows. 'Oh, he told you that, did he?'

'Yes, but he seemed to think that you didn't know about it, and he didn't say why it ended.'

Sheila smiled. 'No,' she said, 'I don't suppose he did. Well, it was me who ended it.'

'Really?'

'John and I have had a permanent arrangement for about five years now.' Sheila saw Fox's look of doubt. 'Oh, we don't live together. He's got his place and I've got mine. We prefer it that way. To be frank, we'd drive each other mad if we shared. We've both got terrible tempers.'

'I understand that you're a model, Miss Thompson,' said Fox. Constance Crawley had told him that, but the description could cover a variety of occupations.

'That's right. A clothes-horse.' Sheila smiled. 'And it's not the romantic sort of job that Dawn Mitchell seemed to think it was. It's bloody hard work, and I don't really know way any girl wants to do it.' She shrugged and crossed one leg over the other. 'But it pays well,' she added. 'Once you've got on the circuit.'

'And you have, I take it?'

Sheila nodded. 'Yes, I suppose you could say that. And I can thank John Wheeler for it. He's a superb photographer and he's got contacts. He was the one who got me launched.'

'And that was about five years ago, I suppose?'

Sheila pursed her lips and then laughed. 'Yes,' she said. 'But then Dawn Mitchell tried to muscle in. She used all her feminine wiles and talked John into bed. I imagine she thought that he could do the same for her as he did for me.' She gave an impish grin. 'Professionally speaking, of course.'

'Of course,' murmured Fox and laughed.

'But John realised early on that she hadn't got what it takes. I can't tell you exactly what it does take because it's not easily quantified, but there is some indefinable quality that tells a photographer – and a couturier, I suppose – whether a girl will make a model.'

'And Dawn Mitchell was not a model?'

'No. It's a funny thing. She had all the right measurements and she walked well, but . . .' And with an expressive shrug, Sheila left the rest of the sentence unspoken.

'So why did you end their affair? You'd presumably known about it for sometime.'

'Oh sure. She wasn't the first, and his little affairs were usually quite harmless. I never took much notice. He always came back eventually. You see, John is like most men. Got a good business head on him and you'd have to get up very early in the morning to catch him out. But along comes a pretty girl and flutters her eyelashes at him – or in her case, wiggles her backside – and he falls apart. Men will do the most stupid things when it comes to women.'

'So I've heard,' said Gilroy.

Sheila glanced across the room as if noticing the detective inspector for the first time, and gave him a sexy pout. 'But Dawn Mitchell had ideas for expanding the business,' she continued, looking back at Fox.

'How?'

'Porn.' Sheila spoke in a matter-of-fact way. 'I turned up at the studio one afternoon, unexpectedly. John thought I was doing a photo session, but it had finished early, and there was La Mitchell spread out across a marble-topped table, naked.' She grinned. 'It wasn't really marble-topped,' she said. 'It was marbled Formica, but it looks the part when the prints come out.'

'But lots of photographers do nudes, surely,' said Fox.

'Oh sure. We've all seen the Pirelli calendar, but this little cameo was slightly different. Actually it was *very* different. Explicit is the word, I think.'

'So what happened?'

'I told madam to put her bloody clothes on and get the hell out of it.'

'And what did Mr Wheeler say?'

'He didn't get a chance to say anything,' said Sheila. 'I told him that the one way to wreck his professional reputation was to go down that road. Then I offered him the choice.'

'Of what?'

'Dawn Mitchell or me. I told him that I wasn't playing second fiddle to some whore who wanted to be lusted over by the dirty mackintosh brigade.'

'What did he say to that?' asked Fox.

Sheila Thompson glanced across the room at a vase of

79

gladioli and half smiled before realigning her gaze on Fox. 'He understood the situation,' she said.

'You know, of course, that her real name was Lady Dawn Sims?'

'Yes, so I heard.'

'And it doesn't surprise you that she would want to get involved in that sort of thing?'

'Darling,' said Sheila with a mock upper-class drawl, 'have you never been to a thrash in Mayfair? They're all tarts, deep down.'

'Puts a slightly different slant on the apple of Earl Sims's eye, doesn't it, guv?' said Gilroy on the way back to the Yard.

Fox leaned forward to pick up the handset of his radio as his call-sign came out over the air. 'Comes as no surprise,' he said.

'Commander Willow is here at the factory waiting to interview you, guv,' said the operator in the Flying Squad office at Scotland Yard.

'Sorry,' said Fox, 'your transmission is breaking up. Can't read you.'

Harry Dawes, convinced that his complaint of harassment had resulted in the withdrawal of the police observation on his house, walked down Oxford Road to the underground station. Nevertheless, he took precautions. When the train got to Parsons Green, he alighted. For a moment or two he stared up and down the platform, satisfying himself that all the other passengers who had got off were making for the exit. Then he jumped back on the same train. Harry Dawes was very nimble, despite his age. But it was all to no avail. The surveillance had been lifted temporarily, in accordance with Fox's instructions.

At Gloucester Road, Dawes left the station and walked slowly towards Old Brompton Road. Every so often, he stopped to look in a shop window, using the opportunity to see if he was being followed. Once he went into a newsagent's, bought a paper, then walked back towards Gloucester Road. At the junction, he turned again and retraced his footsteps. Finally, after going down a few side streets and doubling back on himself, he rang the bell marked 'Wilkins' at a large house that had been converted into bed-sitting rooms.

'Well then, Kev,' said Dawes. He kept his overcoat on and stood warming his hands in front of the meagre gas fire which was Kevin Wilkins's only form of heating. 'What's new?'

'The lads done them jobs at Kingston and Catford, Harry,' said Wilkins.

'Yeah, I saw.' Dawes touched the newspaper in his overcoat pocket.

'But they was wondering when they was going to get paid, like.'

'Yeah, well things is a bit difficult at the moment, Kev. I've got the filth breathing down my neck.'

'I s'pose that was because of the body what they found in the lock-up, Harry.'

'You know about that then?'

'Well couldn't hardly be off knowing it, Harry. It's been all over the papers and on the telly.' Wilkins nodded towards a small portable television set that stood on a chest of drawers surrounded by dirty cups and glasses.

'You really ought to clear this place up, Kev,' said Dawes. 'It's a bleeding tip.'

'You know she was the daughter of a lord, Harry, don't you?'

'Course I do. Don't bleeding remind me. You know what happens when one of them gets topped. There's all hell let loose. It's the influence, see, Kev.'

'The influence?'

'Yeah, course. Probably find her old man went to school with the Prime Minister.'

'I thought he went to school down Brixton, Harry. That's what it said when he got the job. Like he was an ordinary sort of geezer. He's always banging on about a classless society.'

'I don't give a toss what they said, Kev.'

'But he never went to no college, Harry, not like all them other toffs.'

'Oh, for Christ's sake stop going on about the bloody Prime Minister, Kev. We've got problems. More problems than what he has. Some bastard has grassed. If I'd known the bloody Sweeney was going to stake the place out, I'd never have put the bloody body there in the first place, would I?'

'Ah, at last.' Commander Willow had camped out in Fox's office awaiting his return. 'You're a very difficult man to get hold of, Mr Fox,' he said.

'I'm investigating a murder, Mr Willow,' said Fox tersely, affording Willow only the minimum of deference to his rank.

'So I understand,' said Willow, 'and that is one of the things I want to talk to you about. I've had a complaint, another complaint, about your harassment of a Mr Harold Dawes of Oxford Road, Putney.'

'Mr Harold Dawes, as you so politely call him, guv, is a dyed-in-the-wool villain,' said Fox. 'One of the best fences south of the river, as a matter of fact, and when I've got enough evidence to screw the little bastard, he'll go down. With any luck, he'll be slopping out his piss-pot in Parkhurst for the next ten years. Alongside your Mr Stedman.'

Willow wrinkled his nose at Fox's coarseness. 'I would remind you, Chief Superintendent,' he said, 'that Mr Dawes has no previous convictions and he cannot see why his every movement should be dogged by teams of Flying Squad officers . . . and nor, for that matter, can I.' He paused. 'Those officers are acting upon your specific directions, are they not, Mr Fox?'

'Yes, they are,' said Fox. He sat down behind his desk and took out his cigarette case. 'Smoke, guv?'

'I don't, thank you.' Willow leaned forward, a look of earnestness on his face. 'I don't think you quite understand the seriousness of your position, Mr Fox,' he said.

'Oh, but I do,' said Fox. 'I've got the murder of an earl's daughter on my plate, and if I don't get a result soon, there are going to be some very nasty questions asked of the Commissioner. In the House of Lords, very likely.

Therefore, sir,' he continued, blowing a column of smoke into the air, 'I shall continue to conduct that enquiry as I think fit until one of two things happens.'

'Two?' queried Willow lamely.

'Yes, sir. Until the Commissioner personally tells me to stop, or until I am removed from the enquiry. Sliding Dawes is the man who keeps the lock-up where the body was found. And if he didn't have something to do with the topping of Dawn Mitchell, then I shall undoubtedly get made commander on the next promotion board.'

'I see,' said Willow, and spent the next thirty seconds trying to work out if he had just been insulted.

TEN

WHEN FOX ARRIVED AT LADY Jane Sims's flat in Knightsbridge, she was wearing black leggings, high-heeled shoes and a thigh-length sloppy sweater. 'Hallo,' she said, 'come in.'

Fox surveyed the girl with an amused expression. 'I'm sorry,' he said, 'I seem to have arrived before you had time to put your skirt on.'

Jane smiled at him. 'In case you haven't noticed,' she said, 'it's the latest fashion.'

'Good heavens,' said Fox as Jane led him into her sitting room.

'Scotch, Thomas?' Jane stood by the cocktail cabinet and waited to see if she would be rebuked for her familiarity, despite having asked Fox, on his last visit, to dispense with her title.

'Thank you.' Fox was secretly pleased that she had used his first name.

'Where is your inspector, incidentally?' Jane handed Fox a glass and sat down on the settee facing him, tucking her feet under her.

'I gave him the evening off,' said Fox. 'More than he deserves, but he's got a wife, so I've heard.'

'Are they all as hard as you in the police force?'

'Good heavens, I'm not hard,' said Fox. 'You should meet some of the others.' He took a sip of whisky. 'And the Commissioner says we've got to call it a service now. The Metropolitan Police *Service*.' He screwed his face into a sour expression.

'Something wrong with your Scotch?' For a moment or two, Jane regarded him with a half-smile. 'I think it's all a

84

big act,' she said. 'I don't think you're nearly as tough as you'd like people to think. Deep down, I'm sure there's a warm, caring personality struggling to get out.'

Fox laughed. 'Yes,' he said, 'that's much the view they hold in Wormwood Scrubs, so they tell me. However, I wanted to talk to you about your sister.'

Jane inclined her head. 'What about her?' She knew that it wasn't a social visit and felt a twinge of regret.

'I've been hearing some conflicting accounts of Lady Dawn.'

'Oh? In what way conflicting?' Jane looked a little apprehensive.

'You'll appreciate that what I'm saying to you is in confidence, Jane.'

'Of course.' A slight frown crossed the girl's face as though Fox had suggested that she just couldn't wait to ring up all her friends and tell them.

'Last time I was here, I mentioned Jason Hope-Smith, the chap who was asked by the Crawleys to partner Dawn at dinner, back in August . . .'

'And I said I didn't know him.'

'Yes, I remember,' said Fox, 'however, when I interviewed him – and I didn't tell you this last time – he said that he had tried to get in touch with Dawn on several occasions after the dinner but failed. He eventually gave up and went back to Kuwait – so he said.'

'I don't imagine that there's anything unusual about that. It is possible for a girl not to fancy a man, you know.'

'Then I saw John Wheeler, a society and fashion photographer—'

'You'll have to forgive me, Thomas, but I haven't heard of any of these people. As I said before, Dawn rarely mentioned her friends to me.'

'Yes, I know,' said Fox, 'but Wheeler claimed to have had an affair with Dawn that lasted about six weeks. Sheila Thompson, Wheeler's girlfriend, said she broke it up. Her story is that she went to Wheeler's studio one day and found him taking pornographic photographs of your sister.'

Jane Sims finished her drink and taking Fox's empty

glass walked across the room and poured out more whisky. 'Am I supposed to be surprised?' she asked over her shoulder.

'Well, aren't you?'

Jane gave Fox his glass back and sat down again. 'Not really, no. She had a good body.'

'You don't see any harm in it, then?'

'No. I'm sorry if that shocks you—'

'It doesn't.'

Jane smiled. 'No, I suppose it wouldn't in your profession. It's not something I'd do myself, but I wouldn't object to posing for one of those tasteful calendars.'

Fox promptly put that distracting thought out of his mind. 'But the other thing that puzzled me was that Dawn asked Wheeler to do some straight fashion plates for her so that she could push them around the agencies in the hope of getting a job.'

'Lots of girls do that, Thomas,' said Jane, 'if they want to be models. I'm told that actresses do the same sort of thing.'

'But Dawn said that she couldn't afford to pay him because she hadn't got any money. The inference I drew from Wheeler, however, was that she was prepared to pay by going to bed with him. And did.' Fox took out his cigarette case. 'D'you mind?'

Jane shook her head. 'No, go ahead,' she said, and fetched an ashtray. She put it down on the table next to Fox and stood looking down at him, holding her whisky. 'D'you think I could have one of those?'

'I thought you didn't smoke.'

'I don't make a habit of it, but once in a while I enjoy one.' Jane leaned forward and waited while Fox held the flame of his lighter to her cigarette. 'I haven't been strictly open with you,' she said as she sat down again. 'But I didn't think it would matter. To be honest, I'd been worried about her.'

'In what way?'

'Daddy cut off her allowance some three months ago.'

'That would explain why she hadn't got any money then. But why did he do that? I got the impression that he thought the world of her.'

'He does, but you don't know him as well as I do. He can

86

be a cantankerous old devil at times, and a bit eccentric, but he did it with the best of motives. He thought that by stopping her money, she would be forced to return home to Yorkshire.'

'I can't imagine that working,' said Fox.

'It didn't. Dawn was thirty, as you know, and you can't treat a woman of that age as though she's still a child. She said that she wasn't going back and that was that.' Jane looked momentarily sad. 'She hated Yorkshire.'

'What was your father's reaction to her refusal to go home?'

'He couldn't believe that she wanted to stay in London. He had convinced himself that it was a terrible place for a young woman and that she was likely to get raped, sooner rather than later. But then he couldn't have coped with present-day London. Dawn and I, of course, never knew it any other way and we accept it as it is. But, as I said when you came to Yorkshire, he hasn't been to London for years and it's not really as bad as he thinks it is. He was in the army during the war and that, I suppose, is where his memories stop, as a young officer living it up in the fleshpots whenever he was home on leave. He met my mother there, you know.' She smiled at some secret recollection. 'In the best traditions of the peerage, he married a chorus girl. Bit of a ladies' man in his youth was my father.'

'Then how did your sister survive, given that she had no success as a model?'

'I tremor to think.' Jane wrapped her arms around herself as though suddenly cold. 'I helped her out when I could, but I keep trying to put the obvious solution out of my mind, Thomas.'

'Which was what?' Fox didn't particularly want to be harsh on this girl, but if she was implying what he thought, it could have a serious bearing on his investigation.

'She met a lot of people in her social life, and although she thought it rather amusing to be plain Dawn Mitchell, she didn't exactly hide the fact that Daddy was an earl. I suppose she found it useful. It certainly helped me in my profession. People think it's rather funny to have their loos designed by someone called Lady Jane. As far as I know, Dawn first started using the name Dawn Mitchell for her modelling career, and that didn't come to anything.' Jane broke off to stub out her half-smoked cigarette. 'But I know, and I'm sure you do too, that models are often regarded in the same way as aspiring actresses. What's it called, the casting-couch syndrome?'

'That might have improved her chances of getting a job,' said Fox, 'but it wouldn't have made her any money . . . not immediately, anyway.'

Jane looked at Fox with her disturbingly direct gaze. 'I don't know whether you're being particularly dense,' she said, 'or whether you're just trying to let me down lightly, but I think she might have made use of her contacts to offer herself to willing partners for money.'

It hadn't been Fox's intention to be considerate – he was wanting Dawn's sister to say what she thought – but now he was brutal. 'Are you suggesting that your sister had turned to prostitution, Jane?'

There was a long pause before Jane spoke again, and when she did, she stared at the carpet. 'I suppose I am,' she said.

'D'you have any proof of that?'

Jane looked at Fox. 'No,' she said. 'It's just a feeling. But if she'd become a high-class call-girl, there wouldn't be any proof, would there? Not if she'd gone to bed with someone and they'd given her money. It's a bit difficult to tell the difference between that and an affair. But perhaps I'm being rather silly.'

'But there must have been a reason for you to think that.' Fox tried, gently, to coax something more out of her.

'Well, she couldn't have lived on fresh air, could she? And I don't think she would have worried too much about the morals of the thing, not if she was prepared to pose for porn photographs. She always did confuse sex with love, and I'm sure that the affair she had with that photographer wasn't her first, or her last.' Jane ran her hands through her hair, pushing it back and holding it briefly at the nape of her neck. 'Oh God!' she said. 'What a thing to think about one's own sister.'

'There's a big difference between having an affair and going on the game,' said Fox coldly. Personally, he didn't think so in this particular case, and the possibility that Dawn might have been a call-girl threw his enquiry wide open. It also reminded him that Denzil Evans's further enquiries into Dawn's address book and telephone bill had not yet produced a result.

Jane drained her glass and stood up. 'Thomas, I don't feel like cooking for myself this evening. Talking to you about Dawn, and facing a truth I didn't want to face, has knocked me over a bit.' She stood in front of him, her arms by her sides, suddenly forlorn and helpless. 'There's an Italian restaurant just round the corner from here. I suppose you wouldn't consider keeping me company over a spaghetti bolognese, would you?'

Commander Willow pushed his way through the crowd that thronged the entrance hall of Marlborough Street Magistrates Court and opened the door to Number One Court.

'Help you, sir?' An elderly constable barred the way.

'Commander Willow, One Area Headquarters,' said Willow in a way which implied that the PC should have known who he was.

'See your warrant card, sir, please.'

Willow fumbled in his pocket and eventually produced the document. 'I'm interested in the case of Sandra Nash, soliciting prostitution,' he said curtly.

The PC glanced at the clipboard in his hand. 'That's right, sir,' he said. 'Answering bail this morning.' He looked up at Willow. 'You a witness, sir?'

Willow glared at the PC and wondered whether he was being facetious. 'No, I'm not. I'm investigating a complaint against police.'

'Jolly good, sir,' said the PC as though he were beyond such things. 'Why not take a seat on counsel benches.'

Two or three ladies of the night appeared before the magistrate and were duly fined, before the court official called Sandra Nash. After a short pause, during which her name was repeated outside the court, more as a formality than in hope of finding her, the PC at the door cried, 'No answer, your worship,' in stentorian tones.

The magistrate, to whom this state of affairs was by no means unusual, nodded. 'Issue a warrant,' he said. 'Next.'

Willow, his face black with rage, stalked out of the courtroom. 'You'd better start making some enquiries, Sergeant,' he said to the hapless Sergeant Clarke. 'And you'd better find some answers.' He swept through the swing doors without a thought for Clarke who was nearly struck in the face by one of them. 'Furthermore,' continued Willow as he crossed the pavement to his car, 'you can tell the custody sergeant at West End Central that I shall want to know what steps he took to verify that bloody woman's address before admitting her to bail.'

'I shall do that this afternoon, sir,' said Clarke, scrambling to get into the car before it drove off.

'Well, make sure you do. Someone's been damned slipshod, Sergeant.'

'Yes, sir.'

'Why have you waited until today?' Willow leaned forward. 'Back to Edmonton, driver.'

'The custody sergeant who dealt with it has been on annual leave, sir. Back late turn today,' said Clarke.

'Is he indeed. Well, get down to West End Central and sort it out.'

'Yes, sir.' Clarke looked miserably out of the car window. 'I see they're putting the Christmas lights up already, sir,' he said, but Willow was reading a file.

'There is a possibility, Denzil,' said Fox, 'that Dawn Sims, alias Mitchell, was on the game, albeit discreetly. How far have you got with that list of names?'

'Working through it, sir, slowly but surely,' said Evans apprehensively.

'Let's make it quickly but surely, shall we?' There was an edge to Fox's voice. He hoped that Dawn Sims hadn't been a prostitute, not only because it would make his enquiry that much easier, but because he had rather taken a liking to Earl Sims. He knew that if it came out that his daughter was a tom, it would probably kill him. And he would rather not have to tell Jane that he'd confirmed it, either.

He reflected on their meal the previous evening. Jane Sims was not as hard and worldly as she pretended to be. Once out of her flat, she had shaken off the gloom that had descended on her and her conversation had been bright and animated. She had talked about everything and anything but her sister in a determined effort to put the whole distressing subject out of her mind. But it hadn't escaped Fox's notice that she was very anxious to learn as much about his personal life as possible. She had consumed more red wine than was probably good for her, and more than one large brandy, and by the time he had escorted her back to her flat she had been just a little unsteady on her feet. She had thanked him for keeping her company and, after the briefest of pauses, had pecked him on the cheek before disappearing indoors.

'I'm PS 27. You wanted to see me?' The sergeant who strolled casually into the Sergeants' Room at West End Central Police Station had exactly twenty-nine years and forty weeks service and allowing for leave due, had only another fifty-six days of police duty between him and his pension, and the general stores in Cornwall that for years he and his wife had screwed and scraped to buy.

'I'm Sergeant Clarke, One Area Headquarters.'

'Are you now,' said PS 27, whose name was Walters. 'Bit off your patch, aren't you, son?' He pulled out a packet of small cigars and without offering it to Clarke, lit one. His worn and shiny uniform strained across his substantial paunch, and there was a pencil stuck behind his right ear.

'I'm assisting Commander Willow in the investigation of a complaint against police,' said Clarke pompously.

'Oh?' Walters's smile vanished from his face. The last thing he wanted to get involved in, in the twilight of his long and undistinguished career, was a complaint. Especially if he was on the receiving end.

'It concerns a Sandra Nash who was charged at this station with soliciting prostitution on Friday the second of November.' Clarke took out his pocket-book and referred to it. 'I've got the charge number here somewhere,' he added.

'What about her?' asked Walters warily, wondering whether it was yet time to call in his Police Federation representative.

'My commander wishes to interview her—'

'Oh, is that all?'

'Not quite,' said Clarke who was still smarting from having been called 'son' by the older sergeant. 'It would appear that her bona fides were not properly checked for bail. And you were the custody sergeant, so I was told.'

Sergeant Walters lumbered to his feet. 'Better get the charge book then, hadn't I?' he said. 'Don't go away, son.'

It was a good five minutes before Walters returned, clutching the large book.

'Any luck?' asked Clarke.

'Depends what you mean by luck,' said Walters. He put the book on the table and started thumbing through its flimsy pages, thinking that it might be better for all and sundry if the entry couldn't be found. 'Here we are. Sandra Nash. Resides at 54 Purbeck Row, Paddington. Address verified from driving licence in the prisoner's possession.' He glanced up. 'That her, is it?'

'Yes, but it's 54 Purbeck *Terrace*, surely?'

Walters swung the book round. 'Look for yourself, old cock.'

Clarke examined the entry closely before looking up at Walters. 'But when I rang up, I was told Purbeck Terrace,' he said. There was an element of agitation in his voice.

'Who d'you speak to?' asked Walters. 'When you rang in.'

Clarke looked at his pocket-book desperately hoping to find something that he knew wasn't there. 'I didn't get his name,' he said.

Walters laughed, slammed the charge book shut and stood up. 'Take a word of advice from an old hand, son,' he said. 'Always get the bloke's number and make a message of it.' Whistling tunelessly, he tucked the charge book under his arm and walked out of the office straight towards the photocopier. He had known official documents to disappear before, particularly where complaints against police were concerned, and he would be much happier once a copy of Sandra Nash's charge sheet was secure in his locker.

ELEVEN

THE SECURITY GUARD SAT IMPORTANTLY behind a battery of telephones and a computer screen at a curved counter in the ornate reception area of Freddie Hayden's office building. 'And what can we do for you, sir?' he asked, with an exuberance that was unmatched by his competence.

'Thomas Fox to see Mr Hayden.' Fox made a habit of never mentioning that he was a police officer when dealing with an officious flunkey like the security guard.

'Have an appointment do we, sir?'

'I have,' said Fox scathingly, 'but I don't know about you.' He had telephoned Hayden earlier that morning and Hayden had made it sound as though he was doing Fox a favour by claiming to rearrange his day's programme.

The chastened security guard ran his finger down a list and then, grabbing at a telephone, tapped out a number. After a brief conversation, he waved an arm towards a bank of lifts. 'Take the lift to the second floor, sir,' he said. 'Mr Hayden's secretary will meet you.'

The woman who was waiting in the second-floor lift lobby exuded efficiency. She was about forty, with immaculate blonde hair and was conservatively dressed in a dark suit with a white blouse. 'Mr Fox?' The woman smiled at Fox and then glanced at Gilroy.

'Yes.'

'If you'd like to come with me, gentlemen, Mr Hayden is waiting.'

The office into which Fox and Gilroy were shown was huge. The thick pile carpet was a light green and stretched from wall to wall, and the desk from behind which Hayden rose was a good ten feet wide. The vertically-slatted blinds were closed to protect the great man from the outside world.

'Mr Fox, Mr Gilroy, how d'you do?' Freddie Hayden was a bluff-looking man with iron-grey hair, and wore a well-cut, and doubtless expensive, suit. Fox reckoned that he was about fifty-two years of age. 'I must say that I was horrified to hear of Lady Dawn's death.' Hayden swept off his gold-rimmed spectacles with his left hand and offered his right to Fox. 'Do come and have a comfortable seat, gentlemen,' he said and led the way to the other side of the office where two leather couches faced each other across a glass-topped occasional table upon which was a glass sculpture of a bird. 'I've asked Toni to arrange for some coffee. I daresay you could do with a cup.'

'Thank you.' Fox sat down at one end of a couch and Gilroy settled himself at the other.

Hayden sat in the centre of the opposite couch and spread his arms along the back. 'I'm a little mystified as to what I can do to assist you,' he said, once his secretary had served the coffee. 'But you may rest assured I shall do all I can to help you catch the loathsome person responsible for this horrendous crime.'

'Oh good,' said Fox. He was not impressed by Hayden's type. He had met too many of them in the past. Professing great support for the police, they would not hesitate to deploy the finest counsel possible if ever they found themselves charged with a motoring offence. Neither would they be reluctant to make the most outrageous allegations against the officer who had summoned them. 'How did you know that Dawn Mitchell was, in fact, Lady Dawn Sims?' he asked by way of opening the important part of the interview.

Hayden wavered only briefly. 'Well, I didn't, to be perfectly honest, Mr Fox,' he said. 'Not at first.' He smiled in a deprecating way and smoothed his hand across his knee. 'But my wife loves that sort of thing.'

'What sort of thing?' Fox grinned. He had detected a trace of Cockney accent lurking deep beneath Hayden's urbane manner.

'Oh, mingling with the aristocracy, you know. But still,

she's likely to be one herself soon.'

'One what?' Fox genuinely wondered what Hayden was driving at.

'I shouldn't be telling you this really, Mr Fox, but if one can't trust the police, well . . .' Hayden stood up and walked across to his desk. Slipping a key from his pocket, he unlocked a drawer and took out a letter. 'There,' he said, 'have a look at that. But,' he added hurriedly, 'I'd be grateful if you kept it to yourself.'

Fox took the letter – it was on notepaper headed Downing Street – which stated that the Prime Minister had it in mind to recommend Mr Frederick Hayden to the Queen for an honour. It went on to say that he should not mention to anyone that he was being considered, but enquired if Mr Hayden would be prepared to accept the honour should the recommendation be acted upon. 'Very good,' said Fox, and returned the letter.

'I've heard, unofficially of course, that the PM has a knighthood in mind,' said Hayden and, obviously deciding that Gilroy's lower rank did not qualify him to read the confidential communication, carefully folded the letter and replaced it in his desk, locking the drawer again and putting the key back in his pocket. 'I don't suppose you've seen one of those before, Mr Fox, eh?' Hayden asked with a chuckle before sitting down again.

'No,' said Fox quietly. No one could ever draw him on his Queen's Gallantry Medal. 'Am I right in understanding that the first time you met Dawn Sims was at the Crawleys'? A dinner party in August, I believe.'

'Yes, that is so. A charming girl.'

'And afterwards? Did you see her again?'

'No, unfortunately not. My wife and I wanted to invite her to dinner, but we could never seem to get hold of her. Tessa left countless messages on Dawn's answerphone, but we never got a response. I'm afraid that we gave up eventually. I suppose she felt that a couple of older people, like ourselves, were not the sort of company she wanted to keep. A shame really. I had hoped to recruit her for my charitable work, you know.'

'Why? What was so special about her?'

Hayden looked surprised at the question. 'Her father's an earl,' he said.

'Yes, I know. But how did you know?'

'To be honest, Mr Fox, I knew, the moment I met her, that she was more than just an aspiring model. One can always tell. I made it my business to find out.'

'How did you do that?'

Hayden smiled. 'I have my contacts,' he said in a way which implied that a network of informants such as his was not available to a mere policeman.

'Yes,' said Fox thoughtfully. He was beginning to tire of the unctuous Hayden. 'And you didn't see her again after the dinner party?'

'No.' Hayden paused. 'I don't know if it's of any use, Mr Fox,' he said, 'but she did ask me if there were any openings for a model in any of my enterprises.'

'She asked you this over dinner, did she?'

'Yes. Yes, she did.'

'And were there any openings?'

'No. Not my line of business, I'm afraid.'

'But you do own a fashion house, Mr Hayden.' Fox looked directly at the magnate. In addition to finding out about Hayden's charity connections, Detective Sergeant Percy Fletcher had spent some time at Companies House in Islington and had provided Fox with a detailed analysis of the companies that Hayden owned. One fact that had caught Fox's eye was Hayden's interest in a *haute couture* fashion house that appeared to be in a good way of business, and which, naturally, employed a string of models.

'How did you know that?' Hayden blurted out, surprised at how much Fox knew about him.

'I have my contacts,' said Fox and, deciding that there was nothing more to be gained by continuing the conversation, stood up. 'Thank you for your time, Mr Hayden.'

'I'm sorry that I can't help further, but do feel free to contact me any time, won't you, if you think I can be of assistance. And I do hope you catch this fellow.' Hayden conducted Fox and Gilroy to the door of his office and opened it. Then he paused. 'You probably know my chief security adviser,' he said. 'Fellow called Hooper. I believe he was one of your top bods.'

'Yes, I've heard of him,' said Fox as he shook hands.

'What d'you make of him, guv'nor?' asked Gilroy as he and Fox rode down in the lift.

'Bogus, Jack. Definitely bogus.'

'He seems to think that he's in the running for a knighthood then, guv.'

'That's what he thinks. But the letter was the usual sort of thing from the Honours Office at Number Ten. But it didn't mention what they had in mind. They never do. I'd laugh like a drain if it was only an MBE, Jack.'

'Who's this Hooper bloke he was on about?'

'Gentleman John Hooper? He was a detective sergeant on the Fraud Squad for most of his service. Good copper was John.'

'Not exactly a top bod then?' said Gilroy as they crossed the reception area.

'Depends how you judge it, Jack,' said Fox. 'When it came to avoiding paying for a round of drinks in the Tank, Gentleman John was unbeatable.'

'Incidentally, did you know they've closed the Tank, guv?' asked Gilroy, speaking of the bar that had, for years, existed on the ground floor of New Scotland Yard. 'Turned it into a health centre apparently.'

Fox stopped suddenly and turned to face Gilroy. 'They've done what, Jack?' he demanded. 'That's outrageous.'

'I suppose you realise, Sergeant,' said Commander Willow, 'that not only have I been made to look a complete fool, but that damned woman at 54 Purbeck Terrace has written a letter to the Commissioner?' He glared out of the window as his car wound its way through the streets of Paddington.

'Is it a formal complaint, sir?' Clarke had mixed feelings about that. Much as he would like to see his pompous commander taken down a peg or two, he knew instinctively that if that happened, the name of Sergeant

Clarke would not be entirely absent from any enquiry into the matter.

'I have resolved it,' said Willow, unwilling to reveal the details of the uncomfortable interview he had been subjected to by the deputy assistant commissioner who had charge of Number One Area. He leaned forward. 'Number fifty-four, driver.'

The house in Purbeck Row was much like the other in Purbeck Terrace, and Willow strode up to the door and rang the only bell.

The man who opened the door was dressed in grubby trousers and a dirty singlet. 'Yeah?'

'Police,' said Willow.

'Oh yeah?' The man looked doubtful.

Willow produced his warrant card. 'I'm looking for a Miss Sandra Nash,' he said.

'Gone,' said the man.

'Gone. Gone where?'

The man shrugged. 'Don't ask me, guv'nor,' he said. 'Upped and left a week or two ago. I've let her room to another lady now.'

'Is that so?' asked Willow suspiciously. 'Would it be possible to see the room that she occupied?' He adopted a slightly more conciliatory tone.

'Yeah,' said the man, not moving, 'if you've got a warrant. But I ain't having nobody poking about in a room what's occupied by someone else. Wouldn't be right, would it?'

'Denzil,' said Fox.

'Sir?' Evans clutched the file containing the results of his enquiries into Dawn Mitchell's friends and acquaintances.

'Find out when Hope-Smith is due back in this country next. I need to talk to him again.'

'Right, sir.' Evans waited, expectantly.

'That's all, Denzil,' said Fox, looking up again.

'I've got the list of Dawn's—'

'Oh, don't bother with that now, Denzil, there's no rush.'

'Very good, sir.' Evans marched back to the office he shared with Jack Gilroy and flung the file on his desk. 'I shall get it right one day, I suppose,' he said.

'Not while you're still on the Squad you won't,' said Gilroy. 'Leastways, not while Tommy Fox is still the guv'nor.'

But Jason Hope-Smith no longer worked for the oil company in Kuwait. And he had moved from his flat in Chelsea.

The grim edifice of Parkhurst Prison stood back from the road between Cowes and Newport on the Isle of Wight. Many of its inmates were serving long sentences for crimes of violence and John James Stedman, who had been given ten years for armed robbery, fitted in well.

Commander Raymond Willow had decided, reluctantly and in the absence of Sandra Nash, that he ought to interview the man who had made the complaint against Fox. He should have done that first of all, of course, but he was not very skilled at investigating complaints against the police and had been postponing the day when he would have to make the uncomfortable journey, by train and ferry, to the prison.

'I am Commander Willow of the Metropolitan Police, and I am investigating the complaint that you made against Detective Chief Superintendent Fox of the Flying Squad,' said Willow as the muscular figure of Stedman was escorted into the interview room. He was about thirty-two and had the surly look of a man who would rob his own grandmother if he thought it would avoid his having to do a day's work.

'Come to tell me it's a whitewash, have you?' asked Stedman as he sprawled into the chair on the opposite side of the table and lit a cigarette.

'Certainly not. I've come to take a statement from you.'

'Oh, what about?' Stedman looked suspiciously at the policeman.

'The allegations that you're making against Mr Fox.'

'That was all in the letter from my MP.'

'Yes, I know, but I need a statement.'

'Why?'

'Because, Stedman—'

'*Mister* Stedman.' The prisoner grinned insolently at Willow.

'Because,' continued Willow, 'you have made an

allegation of a criminal offence. If that is substantiated, then it will go to court.'

Stedman sat up. 'You mean old Fox'll get done?'

'If it is proved that he stole money from you, it is possible that he will be prosecuted,' said Willow stiffly.

'So he might finish up in the nick with me?' Stedman lit another cigarette from the stub of his first. 'Well, there'd be a few in here that'd form a welcoming committee and that's no mistake, I can tell you, copper.'

Willow coughed and shuffled his papers. 'But not unless you are prepared to make a statement.' This, he thought, was his trump card. If Stedman refused, Willow might be able to write off the complaint as having been withdrawn. And that would reduce his report from some twenty or thirty pages to a single sheet.

'Yeah, I'll make a statement,' said Stedman.

'I see.' Willow glanced at Clarke who produced some forms from his briefcase. 'D'you wish to write the statement yourself, or shall I have my sergeant take it down at your dictation?'

'No,' said Stedman, 'he can write it.'

'I must warn you,' said Willow, 'that a false statement may, under certain circumstances, be construed as an offence which carries a penalty of up to two years' imprisonment.'

Stedman scoffed. 'You're terrifying me,' he said.

'Well?'

'It's very simple really. Tommy Fox come round my drum in Buckhurst Hill and give it a spin on a "W"—'

'Just a minute,' said Willow. 'Are you saying that Detective Chief Superintendent Fox visited your premises and executed a search warrant?'

'I just did, didn't I?'

'Yes, but we have to get it in language which a jury will be able to understand.'

'I thought it was s'posed to be my statement, not yours,' said Stedman who was well versed in the matter of statements. 'Tell you what,' he continued with a yawn. 'I'll tell the tale and you write down what you like. If it's kosher, I'll sign it.'

'Perhaps that would be best,' said Willow in his innocence.

'Right. Like I said, Tommy Fox spun me drum and while he was at it, he nicked two hundred notes, seven of me best CDs and a couple of Sandra's dresses. Reckon he's one of them fetishists. What's he do? Take 'em home and sniff 'em?' Stedman leered at the commander.

Willow listened to Stedman's full story and waited while Clarke translated it into written English. 'The titles of the compact discs are as stated in this letter, are they?' He handed Stedman a photostat copy of the letter that Stedman's MP had written to the Commissioner.

'Yeah!' Stedman unwrapped some gum, put it in his mouth and started to chew vigorously.

Willow wrinkled his nose at the smell of spearmint and cast an eye over the statement that Clarke had prepared. Then he passed it across to Stedman. 'Read that,' he said. 'You may alter or add anything you wish before signing it.'

Stedman took the statement and quickly read through it. 'That's about the strength of it,' he said, and taking Clarke's pen, scrawled signatures on those parts of the form that Clarke indicated.

TWELVE

'SO MR HOPE-SMITH'S DONE a runner, has he?' said Fox.

'Looks that way, sir, yes,' said Evans.

'Interesting. I wonder why.'

'Guilty knowledge, sir?' Evans looked hopeful.

'We'll have to ask him. When you find him, Denzil. What have you done so far?'

'I've put his name into the computer, guv, and enquiries are in hand.'

'I should hope so,' said Fox, 'but don't hang about, eh? Have you spoken to the Post Office?'

'The Post Office, sir?'

'Mr Hope-Smith, like everyone else, gets letters, Denzil, does he not?'

'I suppose so, guv.'

'Exactly, Denzil. Therefore, when he moves he would like still to get those letters, and given that there is always a time-lag between moving and telling all your friends – and other interested parties – of your new address, it is always advisable to put in a postal redirection form. Yes? Thus, Denzil, if you speak to the Post Office, they might just tell you where he's gone.'

'Oh, good idea, sir.'

'On the other hand, he might just have disappeared,' said Fox. 'There again, he presumably has a telephone and given that modern people seem unable to survive without telephones these days, a call to British Telecom might give you his new number. And his new number will tell you where he is. Talking of telephones, what about this list of Lady Dawn's friends that you garnered from her address book and her telephone account?'

'I've had all of them checked out, sir.'

'And?'

'Most of them are people she met at parties and the like,' said Evans, 'and have little to say that might help. At least, not at the moment. I've got some of the lads checking their alibis, but most of them seem to be in the clear. But there are three or four who don't fit into that bracket.'

'Such as?'

Evans put a sheet of paper on Fox's desk. 'These are men whose office phone numbers she had in her book, and they appear a few times on the phone bill, too.'

'What sort of business are they in?' Fox leaned forward and glanced at the list.

'There's a solicitor, a company director – owns a string of garages – a television producer and a fairly high-ranking civil servant.' Evans grinned. 'And they're all married, sir.'

'Well, well. And have you been to see them?'

'Not yet, sir. Thought I'd get your views on it first.'

'Very wise, Denzil,' said Fox. 'Very wise. I think we shall go and talk to these chaps. Should be fun, don't you think?'

'Yes, sir, I suppose so,' said Evans hesitantly, not quite sure why Fox thought that it would be amusing. But then Evans's sense of fun rarely accorded with Fox's in circumstances like this.

Fox was fairly certain what sort of relationship had existed between Dawn Mitchell and the four men that Evans had named. He decided to visit the civil servant first on the grounds that he probably had more to lose than the other three by the exposure of what could well turn out to be a sexual scandal. Handled properly, he might be more co-operative if he was promised discretion. Not that a promise of discretion could be guaranteed.

'Mr Barnes?'

'Yes. You must be from the police.' Barnes glanced at the clock and closed the file on his desk, pushing it to one side with an audible sigh. 'But I really don't know how I can help you.' He was in his forties and Fox had been given to understand that he was well in line for greater things. Working on the basis that he had an office to himself, and a secretary, he hadn't done too badly already.

'Indeed. Thomas Fox . . . of the Flying Squad.'

'Oh, really? Isn't that what's called the Sweeney?' Barnes stood up and shook hands. 'Do sit down,' he said.

Fox had already formed the view that Barnes was one of those public servants who regarded the police with thinly-veiled contempt. 'Some people refer to it as the Sweeney, so I'm led to believe,' he said, and without giving Barnes time to relax, hit him with his first question. 'I understand that you knew Dawn Mitchell? Lived in a flat in Edgware Road.'

Barnes sat down, rather suddenly Fox thought, and stared at the detective, the light from his desk-lamp glinting on the lenses of his horn-rimmed spectacles. 'Mitchell, Mitchell?' he said. 'I can't say that the name immediately rings a bell. In what connection, may I ask?'

'Oh, purely a social one,' said Fox airily.

'I'm sorry, Superintendent, but—'

'*Chief* Superintendent,' said Fox. 'Detective Chief Superintendent.'

'Ah yes, of course. But I don't think—'

'She had your telephone number in her address book, Mr Barnes. And it also appeared on her itemised telephone account. It seems that she telephoned you more than once over the last three months.'

'I talk to so many people on the phone, Chief Superintendent, that it's easy to forget just who they all are. This is a very busy department, as I'm sure you'll understand.' Barnes glanced at the clock again.

'And you telephoned her, Mr Barnes. At home.' Fox had no evidence of that whatever, but it was worth a gamble.

'Oh, er—'

'Mr Barnes, shall we stop beating about the bush? My only interest in Dawn Mitchell, or Lady Dawn Sims as she was better known—'

'What?' Barnes was obviously shaken by that revelation.

'I said that she was called Lady Dawn Sims.'

104

'Good God! But I saw something about her in the papers. Hasn't she been murdered?' Barnes had gone quite white. 'I didn't know that Dawn was—'

'I see that you do know her after all, Mr Barnes. As I was saying, my only interest in Dawn Mitchell is that she has been murdered. And my job is to discover her killer.' Fox sat back in his chair and waited patiently.

'Might this all come out? In the papers, I mean. You know what the tabloids are like.' Barnes was suddenly a very worried man.

Fox nodded. 'Yes, indeed I do,' he said. 'But it has all come out, hasn't it? The murder of an earl's daughter is not something that's easily hushed up.'

'That wasn't quite what I meant.'

'Can I save you a bit of time, Mr Barnes?' said Fox, fixing the civil servant with his best interrogation stare. 'You visited Dawn Mitchell on several occasions and had sexual intercourse with her for which you paid.' It was a guess, but not much of one.

Barnes's chin dropped on to his chest. 'Yes,' he said quietly. The bombast had gone.

'Good!' Fox waited until Barnes looked up in surprise at this apparent approval and then went on. 'Now we can get down to the bones of the matter, if you'll excuse the expression. How did you come to meet her?'

'My wife—'

'Oh, you're married are you?' Fox knew that, of course, but thought that he would express some astonishment just for the hell of it.

'Yes, that's the problem.' Barnes was now a very rattled man.

'I can imagine,' said Fox. 'But you were saying . . . about your wife.'

'My wife is very involved in charity work—'

'Which charity would that be?' asked Fox, even though Evans had told him that too.

'The Hayden Trust. I don't know whether you've heard of it.'

'I'm not sure, Mr Barnes.' Fox turned to Evans. 'Have you heard of the Hayden Trust, Denzil?' he asked.

Evans gulped. 'I'm not sure either, sir,' he said.

'No,' said Fox and turned to Barnes again. 'However, Mr Barnes, you say your wife is involved with this, er, Hayden Trust. How is that connected with Dawn Mitchell?'

'Well, not directly, but the Haydens, Freddie and Tessa, invited us to a charity fund-raising dinner, and that's where I met Dawn.'

'And the Haydens were there, presumably.'

'No, they weren't. My wife said that Mr Hayden had gone abroad, something to do with the charity, and that Mrs Hayden was unwell.'

'Really? How interesting. When was this?'

Barnes frowned in thought. 'Early September, I believe. I can't remember the exact date.'

'And it was but a short step from there into Dawn's bed, I take it?'

Barnes looked extremely embarrassed at Fox's pithy assessment of his relationship with the dead girl, but he nodded his head. 'Yes,' he said.

'And how did that come about? Proposition you, did she? Discreetly hand you a price-list and tell you it was all for charity?' Fox found Barnes to be quite an odious character. Slowly, the image of a patronising civil servant was giving way to reveal an immoral little man who cheated on his wife.

'It wasn't like that. We got talking and I told her that my wife and I didn't get on—'

'You mean your wife doesn't understand you?' asked Fox crushingly.

'Exactly,' said Barnes, not realising that Fox was being sarcastic. 'Anyway, Dawn invited me to go round to her flat one evening. We listened to some music and, well, one thing led to another.'

'And how much did she charge you?'

'It wasn't like that.' For once, Barnes's reply was spirited. But unconvincing.

'Are you saying that you didn't give her any money? Incidentally, it's no offence, even if you did.'

'Well, no. I mean, yes, but—'

106

'Which was it? Did you pay her or not?'

'She explained that she was very short of money and I gave her something to tide her over.'

'How much?'

Barnes looked down at his desk and scratched at a mark on its surface. 'A hundred pounds,' he said miserably.

'Where were you on the fourteenth and fifteenth of October, Mr Barnes?' Fox's question was jarring and incisive.

'Er, the. . .' Barnes looked at a calendar and then turned to his diary, fumbling with the pages in his attempt to find the appropriate entry. 'I'm not sure,' he said. 'I'll have to look it up.'

'Perhaps you would do so.'

'Yes, I had a meeting of the steering committee of the—'

'What on a Sunday?'

'Oh, I must have been looking at the wrong day. Er, Sunday—'

'D'you put the social events of a Sunday in your official diary?' asked Fox.

'Well, no, of course not.'

'We don't seem to be getting very far here, do we, Mr Barnes? Where were you on the evening of that day? Sunday the fourteenth of October.'

'At home . . . I suppose.' Barnes was an intelligent man and he knew what was going to come next.

'Who with?'

'My wife.'

'I see.'

'Oh God!' Barnes ran a nervous hand across his forehead. 'What a bloody mess.'

'There is one other thing though,' said Fox.

Barnes looked at Fox, a pathetic look on his face. 'I'll help you with anything I can,' he said. 'Anything at all.'

'How many times, and when, did you visit this woman?'

'Three altogether,' answered Barnes promptly.

'When?'

'Twice in September and once at the beginning of October.'

'And you paid her on each of those occasions?'

107

'Yes.' Barnes's hands were gripped together on his blotter and his fingers intertwined nervously.

'Why did you stop seeing her?'

'I couldn't afford it any more.'

'Was it worth it?'

Barnes looked up, a bitter expression of contempt on his face. 'Yes,' he said. 'She was very special.'

'Thank you, Mr Barnes. We will doubtless be seeing each other again.'

Barnes nodded miserably. He had little doubt of that.

Fox and Evans interviewed the solicitor, the man who owned garages and the television producer. At first, each denied any impropriety, but armed with Barnes's admission, Fox was on stronger ground. Eventually, and very reluctantly, each admitted to having paid Dawn Mitchell for what the newspapers like to call sexual favours. And they all had an unbreakable alibi for the night of the girl's murder.

'I read in the newspaper the other day, Denzil,' said Fox when he and Evans returned to Scotland Yard, 'that something like eighty percent of all married men commit adultery.'

'Really, sir?'

'And probably more than that in the Criminal Investigation Department,' added Fox phlegmatically.

'Yes, sir.' Evans wondered what Fox was driving at now.

'Do you not find it odd, therefore, Denzil, that Barnes and the three others we interviewed, were very reluctant to admit having been over the side, despite my assurance that their replies would be treated in the utmost confidence?'

Evans decided against discussing the exact meaning of his detective chief superintendent's assurances and confined himself to a monosyllabic reply. 'Yes, sir,' he said.

'Mr Fox.' Commander Willow was becoming increasingly apprehensive in his dealings with Fox. 'I have here a statement made by John James Stedman in which he alleges that you stole money and other items from him during the course of a search of his premises—'

'I expect you have,' said Fox.

'In view of the fact that he has made these serious allegations, you are entitled to a copy of his statement, and I now serve that statement upon you.' Willow laid a typewritten copy of Stedman's statement on Fox's desk and glanced at Sergeant Clarke. 'Make a note of the time and date of service, Sergeant,' he said.

Fox picked up the two or three sheets of paper and started to read them, a smile slowly spreading over his face as he did so. Then he laid them down on the desk again. 'You are joking, I hope, guv'nor,' he said.

'I don't find the contents of that statement at all amusing, Mr Fox,' said Willow. 'And if I were in your shoes, I should find it even less so.'

'Are you seriously telling me that Stedman made this statement?'

'Of course. I hope you're not suggesting otherwise.'

'If you ever have the temerity to take this load of garbage to court,' said Fox cheerfully, 'I can tell you that my counsel will make mincemeat of it.' He extended a forefinger towards the top sheet of Stedman's statement. 'According to this, Stedman, who can hardly string two words of English together when he speaks, let alone when he writes, if he can write, says, and I quote, "On Wednesday, the tenth of August last year, at about six a.m., at 27 Winsome Terrace, Buckhurst Hill, in the County of Essex, Detective Chief Superintendent Thomas Fox of the Flying Squad, executed a search warrant on my premises during the course of which—" ' He broke off and laughed. 'Are you saying, Mr Willow, that these are the words used by Stedman? Because I can tell you that he'll not be in the witness box for thirty seconds before ushers start running about the court in a vain attempt to stop the jury from collapsing in helpless laughter.'

Willow looked extremely uncomfortable and shot a malevolent glance at the discomfited Sergeant Clarke. 'Well not exactly, of course, but Stedman's persistent use of the criminal vernacular was such that if Sergeant Clarke hadn't put what he said into plain English, the jury would never have been able to understand it.'

Fox leaned back in his chair with a smile on his face. 'Mr

Willow,' he said, 'one of the things I learned on the junior CID course is that if, for example, an Indian who can only understand Urdu makes a statement, it's no earthly good getting him to sign the English translation because he won't know what he's signing. Therefore, it'll get slung out by the judge.'

'I don't see what that has to do with—'

'And the moment counsel starts to ask Stedman what he meant by some of these big words that your clerk-sergeant—'

'Sergeant Clarke,' said Willow, unaware that Fox was being facetious.

'The moment that Stedman's asked what some of these words mean, you'll find that the statement might just as well have been written in Urdu. If you take my meaning.'

Willow thrust his papers into his briefcase and stood up. 'I shall be seeing you again, Mr Fox,' he said and swept out of the office followed by the hapless Sergeant Clarke who knew, deep down, that he was about to get the blame for this latest fiasco in the saga of Stedman's complaint against Fox.

'I understand that you and your husband knew Dawn Mitchell, Mrs Barnes,' said Fox.

'Yes, that's right.' Patricia Barnes, a rather severe-looking woman who was wearing the minimum of make-up, regarded Fox with a quizzical air.

'I don't know if you are aware but she was in fact Lady Dawn Sims, the daughter of the Earl Sims, and was murdered on the night of the fourteenth of October last.'

'So I believe.' Mrs Barnes did not seem at all surprised at this news and Fox assumed that either Mrs Barnes's husband had come clean or that Tessa Hayden had been on the phone.

'I am making enquiries of everyone who knew her, to discover where they were on the night of her death.'

'Yes, of course,' said Mrs Barnes, who was an avid follower of detective stories on television. 'Well now, let me see.' She walked across to a bureau and opened a drawer. 'My diary,' she said by way of explanation, and after a moment or two, 'I was at home that night.'

'And your husband?'

Mrs Barnes shut the small book with a snap. 'He was out that evening,' she said.

'Have you any idea where he was?'

'No, no idea at all,' said Mrs Barnes. 'I suggest that you ask him yourself.'

'And that,' said Fox, when he and Evans were back in the car, 'just goes to prove that hunches aren't always right.'

'No, sir,' said Evans with a grin.

THIRTEEN

'IT DID CROSS MY MIND that you might have been trying to avoid me,' said Fox as a surprised Hope-Smith opened the door.

Following Fox's advice, Denzil Evans had contacted both the Post Office and British Telecom and found that Jason Hope-Smith had moved only half a mile or so from his old address and was now living in a flat over a shop not far from World's End in the Fulham Road.

'Er, no, not at all,' said Hope-Smith.

'May we come in, or shall we conduct this conversation in the street?'

Hope-Smith opened the door wide. 'I'm still in a bit of a muddle,' he said, leading the way up the narrow stairway and into a cluttered front-room. 'What seems to be the problem?'

'You must have known that I would wish to talk to you again,' said Fox, 'but you didn't let me know where you'd gone.' The fact that Hope-Smith was under no obligation to keep the police advised of his whereabouts was not a consideration as far as Fox was concerned.

'I'm sorry, it never occurred to me. As a matter of fact, I thought I'd answered all your questions.'

'Not quite.' Fox sat down, uninvited, in an armchair.

'Care for a drink?' asked Hope-Smith.

Fox shook his head. 'No thanks.'

'Well then, what can I do for you?' Hope-Smith sat, cross-legged, on the floor in front of a fireplace in which stood an electric fire.

'This dinner party you went to, the one that the Crawleys invited you to. With Dawn Mitchell.'

'Yes?'

'You said, on a previous occasion, that you knew the Haydens, Freddie and Tessa.'

'Yes, that's right.'

'And how did you come to meet them?'

'Same way as I met Dawn. At the Crawleys'. I think it was a Christmas, about two or three years ago. I was in London and my current girlfriend and I were invited by Jimmy and Connie—'

'The Crawleys?'

'Yes. They invited her really. Apparently my girlfriend had been at school with their daughter – something like that – and I got dragged into their Christmas party. Quite a thrash, I can tell you.' Hope-Smith grinned. 'Well, more of an orgy really. Anyway, they took pity on me afer that and whenever I was in London, they'd invite me to dinner or a party or whatever.'

'I see. You told me before that Freddie Hayden was flirting with Dawn.'

'That's right. And with every other woman there.'

'Did the party stay at the dinner table all evening?'

'No, of course not.' Hope-Smith looked slightly puzzled by the question. 'We adjourned to the sitting-room for coffee and brandy,' he said. 'I suppose we must have left at about half-past midnight or thereabouts.'

'D'you recall Dawn asking Freddie Hayden if he had any openings for a model in any of his business enterprises?'

Hope-Smith looked thoughtful for a moment or two before shaking his head. 'No,' he said, 'I can't say that I do, but then it was a large room and we were all circulating. I do remember that Dawn was talking to him at one time, but they were at the other side of the room.'

'Now, Mr Hope-Smith,' said Fox, 'you said that you were at home, alone, on the night of Dawn Mitchell's murder, and you seemed to recall that you had spent the evening reading a book.'

'Yes, I believe so. If that's what I said . . .'

Fox glanced at Gilroy who thumbed through his pocket book. 'Yes, sir, that's exactly what Mr Hope-Smith said.'

'Well, in that case,' said Hope-Smith, 'that's what I did.'

'You will appreciate,' said Fox, taking another gamble, 'that in cases of this nature, we conduct a thorough fingerprint examination of the deceased's premises.'

'Yes, I imagine you do.' Hope-Smith looked up, wondering why Fox was telling him this.

'And you said that you had never visited Dawn's flat. In fact, you claimed not to have seen her again after the dinner party,' said Fox. Hope-Smith remained silent. 'But I'm quite sure you won't mind allowing us to take your fingerprints for elimination purposes, will you?'

'But why?'

'Because you said, first off, that you were out of the country at the time of Dawn Mitchell's murder, but later, when we proved that you were in London, you were unable to state, with any degree of certainty, where you had been – apart from saying that you were at home, reading.'

There was a long pause before Hope-Smith spoke again. 'All right,' he said. 'I did see her again, several times.'

'At her flat?'

'Yes.'

'And did you have sexual intercourse with her?'

Hope-Smith stared at Fox angrily, as though he was about to object to the question. Then he shrugged. 'Yes,' he said, 'I did.'

'So why did you lie when you were first spoken to about it?'

'Because I didn't want to get involved, I suppose, and I knew that I hadn't got an alibi for the night she was killed.'

'Did you murder her?' Fox looked directly at Hope-Smith.

'Christ no!' Hope-Smith looked horrified at the question. 'Why on earth should you think—'

'Mr Hope-Smith, I am investigating a murder and I do not appreciate being obstructed in those enquiries. In fact, I take a rather poor view of people who do so obstruct me. Now then, you saw Dawn Mitchell several times after the dinner party. You went to her flat several times. And you had sexual intercourse with her several times. Right so far?'

'Yes.'

'And did you pay her for going to bed with you?' Fox stared directly at Hope-Smith until he looked away.

'Yes.'

'How much?'

Hope-Smith shrugged his shoulders. 'It wasn't the way you think,' he said.

'And how do I think?'

'You're talking as though Dawn was a prostitute.'

'And wasn't she?' Fox was determined to discomfit the man.

'No, certainly not. She was short of money and I gave her a few pounds from time to time. I felt sorry for her.'

Fox nodded amiably. 'Oh, I see. And what d'you mean by a few pounds, Mr Hope-Smith?'

'A couple of hundred, here and there,' said Hope-Smith miserably.

'Tax-free, of course,' murmured Fox before going on. 'And whose idea was that? Did you take pity on her, or did she suggest that you help with the laundry bills?'

Hope-Smith stood up, his arms rigidly at his sides and his fists rhythmically clenching and unclenching. 'Look,' he said. 'I don't know why you're asking all these questions, but Dawn and I had a good thing going. It was a terrible shock when I heard that she had been killed. But I didn't kill her.'

'What are you doing for a living now?' asked Fox.

'What?' Hope-Smith was clearly thrown by Fox's change of tack.

'I said what are you doing for a living now?'

'Er, nothing, at the moment.'

'I see. Why did you leave your job in Kuwait then?'

'I was made redundant.'

'Really?' Fox stood up. 'How interesting.'

'Well, sir,' said Gilroy as they returned to Fox's car, 'what d'you think?'

'Weak as piss,' said Fox.

'Yes, but is it down to him?'

Fox shrugged. 'Might be,' he said. 'But we'll see, Jack. We'll see.'

115

'We've had the surveillance back on for a week now, sir,' said Detective Inspector Henry Findlater, 'and we've come up with something interesting.'

'Oh, how rewarding,' said Fox. 'Are you going to share this wondrous news with me, or is it a secret?'

Findlater grinned. 'Harry Dawes has acquired himself another slaughter, sir. In Croydon.'

'In Croydon? I said the man had no taste.' Fox walked across to the mirror in his office and adjusted his tie. 'Keep an eye on it, Henry,' he said over his shoulder.

'D'you mean put an observation on the slaughter, sir?' Findlater sounded shocked.

'Of course.' Fox walked across to his wardrobe and put on his overcoat. 'Best way of finding out what the bastards are up to, don't you think?'

'But where will I get the men for that, sir?' Findlater looked desperate.

'Oh, I'm sure you'll manage, Henry. Somehow.'

'Oh, Thomas, it's you.' Lady Jane Sims was dressed in jeans and an old rugby shirt, and her hair was loose and untidy. Her face was pale and she wore no make-up. And she had been crying. 'Come in.' She turned from the door and walked back into her sitting-room, leaving Fox to close the front door.

The man who struggled to get out of the armchair was about twenty-eight years of age. He wore an immaculate suit and Fox immediately warmed to him as being a man who knew how to pick a good tailor.

'This is my brother James,' said Jane and turning to the young man, added, 'This is Thomas, the policeman I was telling you about.'

'How d'you do,' said Fox as he shook hands. 'Thomas Fox . . . of the Flying Squad.'

'Ah! You're the one who's investigating my sister's death.'

'Yes.' Fox glanced at Jane Sims who was dabbing at her eyes with a handkerchief. 'Are you all right, Jane?' he asked.

'No, not really. James has just arrived from Yorkshire. Daddy's dead.'

'I'm sorry to hear that,' said Fox quietly. Although he had met the old man only once, and then briefly, he had taken a liking to him. 'When did it happen?'

'Last night,' said Jane. 'It was a heart attack.'

'I'm afraid that the shock of Dawn's murder was just too much for him,' said James Sims.

'But how did he find out? That it was a murder, I mean.' Fox recalled Jane saying that Earl Sims never read newspapers and didn't watch television.

'It was that damned nurse that we'd hired, I'm afraid,' said Sims. 'Can't blame her really, and she thought she was being kind, but she'd read about it and asked father if he'd seen the latest account in the newspaper.' He shook his head. 'I'm afraid it was just too much for the old boy.'

'So you're the new Earl Sims, I take it?' asked Fox.

James Sims nodded. 'Yes,' he said, 'for what it's worth.' He glanced at his sister who had sat down on the settee and then turned back to Fox. 'I'm most awfully sorry,' he said. 'Very remiss of me, but I haven't offered you a drink.'

Fox waved a deprecating hand. 'I think that Jane's more in need of one than I am,' he said.

'Oh, d'you really think so?' Sims hesitated. 'I always thought that in cases of shock—'

'Yes,' said Fox, 'I know all about that, but if I were you, I'd give her a very large Scotch.'

'Oh, right.' Sims managed a grin. 'Always believe in co-operating with the police,' he said. 'At least in matters of that sort. Same for you?'

'Thanks.' Fox sat down opposite Jane.

'I'm sorry, Thomas. Not being very hospitable, but Daddy and I were very close.'

'Understandable,' said Fox gruffly. He watched as James Sims poured healthy measures of whisky into chunky tumblers

'Was there anything in particular you wanted to see Jane about?' asked Sims. 'Or me for that matter, if you think I can help.'

117

'It's nothing urgent,' said Fox, 'but perhaps you and I could have a chat at some time, just so that I can put you in the picture.'

'Yes, I'd be grateful. I've been in the States for about six weeks, on business . . . and a holiday. Got back to Yorkshire yesterday and walked straight into this lot.' The young man shook his head. 'So I flew down today to break the news to Jane. I thought it would be better than telephoning.' He nodded at his sister, hunched up on the settee, clutching her glass and staring into space. 'As Jane said, she and the guv'nor were very close.'

'I gathered that,' said Fox. He looked at Jane. 'I'll come and see you in perhaps a day or two's time.'

'I'm very grateful to you for keeping Jane informed of what's going on, Mr Fox,' said the new Lord Sims as he shook hands.

Fox paused, briefly. 'What exactly d'you do in the States, Lord Sims?' he asked.

Sims grinned. 'I sell expensive British motor cars to New Yorkers,' he said. 'Or at least, I try to, but the recession doesn't help.'

Jane stood up and, still holding her glass, insisted on seeing Fox to the door. 'Thank you, Thomas dear,' she said and placed a hand on his arm.

Fox nodded briefly. 'My friends call me Tommy,' he said.

It was about six o'clock on Sunday morning and snowing. Not hard, but just enough to leave a thin layer on roads that had, so far, been unsullied by traffic. Huddled in what the police call a nondescript observation van, and cursing the engineers who had installed the inadequate heater, Detective Sergeant Ernest Crabtree and Detective Constable Joe Bellenger were suddenly alerted to the arrival of a Ford Transit van outside the warehouse in Croydon that they had been watching for several days.

'Hallo!' said Bellenger.

'Hallo, Joe,' said Crabtree drily.

The two officers watched as a man got out of the Transit and opened the doors of the warehouse. The van drove in and the doors were closed again. Ten minutes later, the van left the warehouse and drove away.

The police van followed but DS Crabtree, knowing that they would be spotted sooner or later, immediately sent a radio call to DI Findlater and continued to give a running commentary on the Transit's movements until some of Findlater's motor-cyclists reported that they were in place and had taken over the mobile surveillance.

The Transit drove at a sedate speed for several miles until it pulled into a lay-by on the A23 Brighton Road and stopped.

Alerted to this strange turn of events, Findlater and other members of his team moved into position and watched. Over the next thirty minutes or so, half a dozen cars stopped long enough for the driver of each to load a personal computer or a video-recorder into his boot. The registration numbers of the cars were duly noted by the police and, making a snap decision, Findlater detailed some members of his team to follow two of the vehicles.

'And what was the outcome, Henry?' asked Fox.

'Both the cars that were followed finished up at car-boot sales, sir.'

'Different locations?'

'Yes, sir, but both between Croydon and the coast.'

Fox lit a cigarette and nodded thoughtfully. 'Nice one, Henry,' he said.

'D'you want the observation maintained on the warehouse, sir?' asked Findlater.

'Too bloody true I do, Henry,' said Fox.

DI Denzil Evans's enquiries had an interesting result too.

The personnel manager of the oil company repeated what he had previously told DS Fletcher about the Kuwaiti operation being a separate company. Nevertheless, he offered to make a phone call to see what he could find out. 'Hope-Smith wasn't made redundant,' he said when eventually he put the phone down after a lengthy conversation. 'He was kicked out.'

'Did they tell you why?' asked Evans.

'Seems he was running his own little harem out there. And got caught by the police.'

'Could you elaborate on that?'

'Yes, sure.' The personnel manager laughed. 'Apparently, he was living on the outskirts of the city in some huge bungalow, complete with swimming pool . . .' The manager paused. 'And about four nubile young Kuwaiti girls who ministered to his every need, so my opposite number out there tells me. As if that wasn't enough, Hope-Smith was very keen on parties and it seems that he was in the habit of inviting some of his friends to a rave-up every Saturday. Not only were there goings-on in and around the pool with the young Kuwaiti girls but the alcohol was flowing freely as well. And that, inspector, is a flogging job in Kuwait. The management decided that the easiest way out was to make profuse apologies to the government and put Mr Hope-Smith on the next plane to London. I don't think he knows just how lucky he was.'

Fox gave a knowing smile when he received Evans's report. 'Told you he was a prat,' he said.

FOURTEEN

VINCENT CARMODY WAS BY WAY of being Harry Dawes's second-in-command. It was Carmody who had set up the new slaughter – as Dawes's depository of stolen property at Croydon was known in criminal circles – and it was Carmody who had taken over the running of Dawes's operation for the disposal of that property following the intense interest that the Flying Squad had suddenly taken in the ageing fence's activities.

But now that Dawes's complaints had resulted in the removal, or so he thought, of the surveillance team that had, for days, dogged his every move, he felt sure enough of himself to allow Carmody to visit him.

'Well, Vince, and how's it going?' Dawes placed a glass of Manzanilla in front of his lieutenant.

'The stock's moving again, Harry,' said Carmody, taking a hefty swig of his sherry.

Dawes frowned at what he regarded as Carmody's sacrilegious treatment of his best fortified wine. 'Well, that's good news,' he said. 'Where's it going?'

'Car-boot sales have picked up again and one or two market traders are showing an interest. But what with Christmas and the recession—'

'I know, Vince. These is hard times, but what about the other outlet?' Dawes leaned forward, an earnest expression on his face. 'Still taking their usual quota?'

'Yeah. I had to lean on him a bit, like you said, Harry. He wanted out.'

'Did he indeed? Well that bastard owes me, and he'd better not forget it.' Dawes laughed, a grating cackle of a laugh. 'What've you heard, Vince? The Old Bill still

121

sniffing round, are they?'

'Ain't heard nothing, Harry.' Carmody drained his glass.

'Another drop of the Manzanilla, Vince?' Dawes hovered reluctantly with the decanter. 'It's a dry sherry from Sanlucar de Barrameda, you know,' he said, hoping to instil some sense of appreciation into Carmody's palate.

'Is that a fact?' Carmody would much rather have had a pint of lager.

'I put the bubble in for bleeding Fox, you know.'

'Eh?' Carmody sounded apprehensive. It didn't seem like a good idea to upset the filth, particularly when that filth happened to be Tommy Fox, the mention of whose name was usually guaranteed to put the fear of Christ up the average criminal.

'Don't worry, Vince,' said Dawes. 'We're living in a different age now. The law can't just go around stamping all over innocent citizens like they used to. I had a word with my brief and made a complaint of harassment. After all, Vince . . .' Dawes spread his hands expressively and smiled. 'It's not as if I had any form, is it?'

'No, I s'pose not,' said Carmody, aware that with about sixteen previous convictions behind him, he was not in the same happy position as Dawes.

'Well, keep up the good work, Vince,' said Dawes and looked on disapprovingly as Carmody downed his glass of sherry in a single swallow.

Vincent Carmody stepped out into Oxford Road and turned up the collar of his Barbour against the sleeting snow, unaware that two police officers had just been detailed to follow him.

'I have decided,' said Fox, 'that we are going to put the frighteners on the villainry.' His audience of Flying Squad officers looked at him expectantly. 'We are going to spin a few drums.'

There was a collective groan. The prospect of executing search warrants at some unearthly hour on a cold winter's morning did not fill the assembled detectives with a powerful enthusiasm.

'When, guv?' asked Detective Sergeant Crozier.

122

'Tomorrow morning. Bright and early.' Fox beamed at his men before turning his attention to DI Evans. 'Perhaps you'd be so good as to pop round to Bow Street Court and secure a handful of warrants, Denzil.'

'Yes, sir,' said Evans. 'Er, what addresses, guv?'

'Henry Findlater has them.' Fox nodded towards the surveillance DI. 'They are the fruits of his observation. Most of them are persons who appear to specialise in car-boot sales. And particularly in the car-boot sale of stolen property, so it would seem.'

'And where will you be while we're searching these premises, guv?' asked Jack Gilroy, well knowing what Fox's answer would be.

'Oh, I think I'll come along, Jack,' said Fox. 'Join in the fun. At least, with one of the teams.' Even he realised that whatever other attributes he possessed, ubiquity was not one of them.

'Sergeant Clarke?' asked the voice on the telephone.

It was not often that Clarke's wife suggested an early night. In fact, hardly ever, but tonight she had been very affectionate. And then the phone had rung. 'Yes. Who's that?' snapped Clarke.

'It's the custody sergeant at Vine Street.'

'Yes?'

'You've got a marker on the PNC for a Sandra Nash. Says not to be released to bail without reference to you.'

Clarke could not immediately recall why he had put Sandra Nash's name on the Police National Computer. He pushed his wife's hand away and she turned over, complaining. 'What about her?' he asked.

'You tell me, mate. But she's in custody here at Vine Street. Soliciting prostitution.'

'Great!' shouted Clarke into the mouthpiece. His wife muttered something uncomplimentary as one of the children in the next room started crying. 'Hold her until I get there.'

'Yeah, that's all very well, sarge,' said the Vine Street custody sergeant, 'but I've got no reason to hold her just like that. I mean, what's it all about? She wanted for something else, is she?'

'Yes,' said Clarke, swinging himself out of bed and putting his feet on the floor.

'Yes what?' The custody sergeant started to sound exasperated.

'It's in connection with a complaint against police.'

'Oh,' said the custody sergeant, 'that's nice that is. Bloody nice. Well my guv'nor's not going to be too happy holding her on the say-so of some sergeant from One Area Headquarters.'

'There should also have been a marker on the computer that she's wanted on a warrant for non-appearance at Marlborough Street,' said Clarke with a measure of malice. 'Anyway, Commander Willow's the one who wants her, skip, so if you can hold her until the afternoon sitting of the court, he would doubtless appreciate it.'

'Bloody hell, I'd better stand up,' said the custody sergeant. 'What's old Pussy Willow doing getting mixed up with toms then?'

'Don't ask,' said Clarke, and dipping the receiver rest, tapped out the home telephone number of Commander Willow.

At four o'clock the following morning, those members of the Flying Squad who had been nominated to take part in the raids, assembled in the canteen of Cavendish Road Police Station near Clapham Common. The air was thick with cigarette smoke, and the pretty, young West Indian girl behind the counter had been working overtime producing tea, and fending off the good-natured *badinage* of detectives who would rather have spent an hour in bed with her than in searching houses.

'Good morning, gentlemen.' The immaculate figure of Tommy Fox, leaning heavily on his umbrella, appeared in the doorway of the canteen. He was attired, as usual, in his light grey cashmere overcoat and this morning sported a snap-brim trilby that would not have looked out of place in the owners' enclosure at any of the racecourses in England. He lit a cigarette, declined a cup of tea from a passing sycophant and smiled. 'Shall we begin?' he asked.

There was a murmur from the detectives who began standing up.

'Everyone knows where he's going, Jack?' Fox glanced at Gilroy.

'Yes, sir. We've got eight drums to do, all within about ten miles of here.'

'Good,' said Fox. 'The breaking down of doors will commence at 5 a.m. precisely then, gentlemen.' He looked round. 'Ah, Denzil,' he said, catching sight of Evans, 'I shall come with you this morning.'

The assembled members of the Flying Squad breathed a collective sigh of relief. All except for Denzil Evans and his team.

The house that DI Evans had been assigned to search was in a respectable street on the outskirts of Purley. The properties were a mixture of detached and semi-detached houses, and most of the driveways had company cars parked on them.

'Well, the villainry seems to be going up-market,' said Fox as Swann brought the car to a standstill behind the Vauxhall Carlton being used by Evans.

'You can tell they're rich, guv,' said Swann morosely, 'they're still in bed.'

'Stop moaning and give me my umbrella,' said Fox as he got out of the car.

It was still snowing and Evans, quickly surveying the house, sent one of his men round to the back garden before stepping up to the front door and banging loudly on the wooden panel.

'There's a doorbell there, Denzil,' said Fox mildly.

'Might not hear us, guv,' said Evans. He didn't want to be in this place at this time of the morning and had no intention of being felicitous, particularly to the occupants of the house.

After several more knocks on the door and a number of rings on the bell, lights went on, first on the upstairs landing and then in the hall. Finally, the carriage lamp next to the front door spread a pink glow over the waiting detectives and a key was heard turning in the mortise lock. The door was opened, tentatively and on a chain. 'What on

125

earth is it?' asked the young woman whose head appeared in the gap.

'Police,' said Evans, whose keenness to gain access to the premises was now inspired more by the need to escape from the freezing cold outside than a desire to search for stolen property inside. 'Mrs Wilson, is it?'

'How do I know that you're the police?' asked the woman. Evans held up his warrant card and the woman stared at it. 'Well what d'you want?'

'We have a warrant to search these premises, madam, and I must inform you that I am empowered to enter by force if necessary.' Evans blew on his fingers.

Reluctantly, the woman closed the door sufficiently to release the chain and then opened it wide. 'What on earth are you talking about?' she asked, wishing that she had slipped a wrap over her revealing nightdress before coming down the stairs.

'Is your husband at home?' asked Evans.

'If you mean my boyfriend, yes. And he won't be too pleased at being woken up at this hour. What time is it, anyway?'

'Five o'clock,' said Evans, moving into the hall.

'Five o'clock!' The woman marched belligerently to the foot of the stairs. 'Tom, you'd better come down here. It's the police.' She turned back to Evans. 'Well, are you going to explain what the hell this is all about?' she demanded.

'We have reason to believe that there is stolen property on these premises,' said Evans. 'I take it that you're not Mrs Wilson,' he added.

'No. I'm Judith Ransome. Not that it's got anything to do with you.'

'I see. Well, we need to talk to Mr Wilson. Is he coming down?'

'I'm here. And what the bloody hell's this all about?' Wilson, wearing a short dressing gown and smoothing his ruffled hair, came slowly down the stairs.

Evans sighed and went through the whole official rigmarole again.

'Bloody stupid,' said Wilson. 'I'm an estate agent, in a good way of business. What would I be doing with stolen property? I shall be complaining about this. I shall write to my MP. The Home Secretary even.'

Fox hooked his umbrella over his arm and took off his trilby, smoothing the brim with his sleeve. 'You know what you're looking for, Denzil, don't you?' he asked.

'Yes, guv.' Evans needed the helpful assistance of his detective chief superintendent like he needed a hole in the head.

'Are you in charge?' Wilson rounded on Fox, a malevolent glare on his face.

'Indeed.' Fox smiled amiably.

'And who are you?'

'Thomas Fox . . . of the Flying Squad. Detective Chief Superintendent Thomas Fox.'

'Is that so?' Wilson thrust his hands into the pockets of his dressing gown. 'Well, I hope you've got a good reason for disturbing honest people at this time of a morning. I don't wonder the police are losing public support if this is the way you behave.'

'Mr Wilson,' said Fox, appraising the scantily-clad figure of Judith Ransome, 'I never do anything without a good and sufficient reason. It's the way we're trained, you know.'

Wilson followed Fox's gaze. 'Go and put some clothes on,' he said sharply to his girlfriend. 'If you've no objection?' he asked sarcastically, turning back to Fox again.

'Not at all.' Fox smiled and waved a hand of dismissal. 'This car boot sale you went to last Sunday morning, Mr Wilson—'

Wilson's eyes narrowed. 'How did you know about that?' he asked.

'I had my officers follow you.'

'What?' Wilson spat the word and contrived, at the same time, to fill it with the indignation of innocence. 'Is this a police state now then?'

'Alas no,' said Fox.

'Found it, guv.' DS Crozier appeared from upstairs carrying the keyboard of a personal computer. Behind him, DC Tarling struggled with the visual display unit.

'Definitely the one?' asked Fox casually.

'Yes, guv. I've checked the number,' said Crozier.

127

'Splendid. Better take the place apart then.' Fox turned to Wilson. 'This personal computer was stolen from a dealer in Kingston,' he said. 'And you, old son, have got some explaining to do.' He flicked a piece of dust from the crown of his trilby. 'And by the way, you're nicked for the possession of stolen property.'

'What's going on?' A barefooted Judith Ransome reappeared at the foot of the stairs dressed in jeans and a sweat-shirt.

'I've just arrested your boyfriend for possession of stolen property,' said Fox.

'You bloody idiot,' screamed the girl at Wilson, 'I told you it was too chancy.'

'Shut your mouth, you stupid bitch,' said Wilson angrily.

'Oh dear,' said Fox.

Only one of the eight houses that the Flying Squad had set out to search had been unoccupied – and that, it transpired, was because the owners had caught an early flight to the Canaries – but Fox was not too concerned about what he saw as small fry. Three men and one woman had been arrested for possessing stolen property. The remainder, it seemed, had been fortunate enough to dispose of their illicitly obtained goods at the car-boot sales that were now interesting Fox.

Tom Wilson, the man whom Fox had arrested, made a full confession, although he declined to admit more than the one offence. That didn't worry Fox too much because Wilson had put the finger on Harry Dawes with an indecent haste. Well, not Harry Dawes directly, but on Vincent Carmody who, Findlater's team had proved, was the next best thing.

'Are you going to nick Sliding Dawes, guv?' asked Gilroy.

'I think not, Jack,' said Fox. 'I am far from satisfied that we shall derive any benefit from such a course of action. We'll let the bastard sweat for a while.'

FIFTEEN

'I'M COMMANDER WILLOW, ONE AREA Headquarters.'
Willow laid his warrant card on the front-office counter at
Vine Street Police Station where, in pursuance of his
enquiries, as the police are wont to say, he had arranged
to meet Sergeant Clarke and interview Sandra Nash.

'All correct, sir,' said the station officer, unimpressed by
the visitation of a commander from another area. But then
the station officer, having recently failed the promotion
examination to inspector for the third time, was impressed
by very little these days.

'You have a Sandra Nash in custody here, I believe,
Sergeant?'

The station officer turned to a large book that lay open
on his desk. 'We do indeed, sir,' he said. 'Sandra Nash,
soliciting prostitution in Swallow Street last night.' He
looked up. 'And your Sergeant Clarke's in the canteen, sir.
Said he was waiting for you.'

'Perhaps you'd get the custody sergeant to put Sandra
Nash in an interview room,' said Willow. 'Oh, and tell
Sergeant Clarke to meet me there, will you.'

'Yes, sir. Immediately, sir.' There wasn't quite enough
sarcasm in the sergeant's voice to warrant a rebuke.

It was an apprehensive Sandra Nash that was brought
into the interview room by a woman police constable. She
had been arrested for soliciting and had expected to be
released on bail almost immediately. But then the custody
sergeant had told her that she was to be detained
overnight because there was a warrant out for her arrest.
In any event, he had added, she would not be going into
court before half-past two as a senior officer wished to

129

interview her in connection with an important enquiry he was conducting. And that had worried her.

'Are you Sandra Nash?' asked Willow.

'Yeah, s'right.' The girl dropped casually into the chair on the other side of the table from where the commander was sitting, crossed her legs and gazed at her fingernails with a blank and disinterested expression. She was about twenty-eight and wore a short, flared black skirt and a red satin blouse that strained at the buttons. Although she had spent a night in the cells, she had taken pains with her appearance. Her long, black hair was brushed straight and her make-up, although heavy, was freshly applied. 'And I'm losing business being locked up in here an' all,' she said insolently. 'What's it all about anyway?'

'D'you wish me to stay, sir?' asked the WPC who had brought the girl to the interview room.

'No thank you,' said Willow, secure in the knowledge that Sergeant Clarke's presence fulfilled the regulations regarding the interviewing of a female prisoner. He turned his attention back to Sandra Nash. 'I understand that you are the common-law wife of John James Stedman who resided, prior to his arrest—'

'D'you mean was I shacked up with him?'

'Well, yes, I suppose so.'

'Yeah, I was. But we split, when he got nicked.' Sandra was still concerned that she might be in some sort of serious trouble, probably as a result of having been Stedman's live-in lover.

'I am investigating a complaint against police made by Mr Stedman,' said Willow pompously.

'D'you mean you've kept me banged up here for hours on end just for that?' Suddenly, Sandra realised what this was all about. It wasn't she who was in trouble, it was some copper. She relaxed. And decided to have a bit of fun just to get her own back.

'I'm afraid it's unavoidable, madam,' said Willow.

'Oh is it?' Sandra undid the top button of her blouse and smiled impishly at Willow. 'Here, you haven't got a fag have you? I'm dying for a smoke and that cow out there wouldn't give me one.'

'No,' said Willow. 'I don't smoke, and neither does my sergeant.'

'No,' said Sandra thoughtfully. 'I didn't think you would.' She grinned at Clarke. 'I'll bet you still enjoy a screw though, don't you, love,' she said to him. 'You can always pop round my place for a freebie if you feel like it.'

'Madam! I must warn you—' Willow started to go red in the face.

Sandra pushed two fingers down the front of her clearly visible black lace bra and gently rubbed the division between her breasts. 'You don't half turn me on when you get all angry like that,' she said, and wrinkled her nose. Behind the commander's back, Clarke grinned at the girl.

'Were you present at 27 Winsome Terrace, Buckhurst Hill, Essex, on Wednesday, the tenth of—'

'D'you mean when Johnny was nicked?'

Willow glanced up from his sheaf of papers. 'Yes, when Stedman was arrested by Flying Squad officers under the command of Detective Chief Superintendent Fox.'

'Yeah, I was.'

'Yes, well, Stedman has alleged,' continued Willow, hurrying on, 'that on that occasion, Mr Fox stole two hundred pounds in cash, seven compact discs and two dresses.'

'Did he really?' Sandra undid another button and putting her hand inside her bra, moved one of her breasts to a more comfortable position. She smiled wickedly at Clarke who was trying desperately to keep a straight face at this latest affront to his governor's dignity. 'You were saying?' The girl smiled sweetly.

Willow was clearly embarrassed by the prostitute's behaviour. 'Just compose yourself, young woman,' he said sharply.

'That's what I was doing,' said Sandra. 'But hurry it up will you, I'm busting for a pee.'

'I want a statement from you saying exactly what occurred on that occasion, Miss Nash.'

Sandra stood up and, placing her foot on the seat of her

131

chair, pulled up her skirt so that Willow could not avoid being treated to a flash of white thigh. 'This copper come in with a "W" . . .' She smoothed her hands seductively up her black nylon stocking and adjusted the clip of her suspender.

'You mean Mr Fox came with a search warrant?' Willow fixed his gaze on the far wall.

'S'what I just said, weren't it?' Sandra straightened her skirt and sat down again. 'And he searched Johnny's gaff.'

'And did you see him take anything?'

'Yeah, loads of gear. Reckoned it was nicked. And it was.'

'Ah!' said Willow. 'Including, I presume, Stedman's two hundred pounds, the seven compact discs and the two dresses?'

'Nah! I took *them*.' Sandra leaned forward so that Willow was obliged to look away or stare down the front of her blouse.

'I must warn you that anything you say will be taken down—'

'Knickers!' said Sandra and smiled provocatively.

'Young woman, I am trying to conduct an enquiry here.' Willow's temper was beginning to fray quite dramatically.

'They was mine . . . and the two hundred quid was the housekeeping. Johnny give it me right under the copper's nose. He'd just been paid, see. Least, that's what he said.'

Willow moved his chair back a foot or two. 'Let me get this straight,' he said. 'You are saying that Stedman actually gave you the two hundred pounds, and that the seven compact discs and the two dresses were your property?'

'S'right.'

'Why did you go to America, as a matter of interest?' asked Willow.

'Fancied a holiday. Bit of sun and a few men who appreciate a girl like me. Not that it's got bugger-all to do with you.' Sandra Nash pulled the front of her blouse back and forth a few times, wafting some air into her neckline. 'It ain't half hot in here,' she said.

'We do not seem to be getting very far,' said Fox.

'Well, at least we've got a good idea where this stolen gear's going, sir,' replied Gilroy.

132

Fox scoffed. 'A couple of car-boot sales,' he said. 'There's a bloody sight more to it than that. Have a look at the list of stolen property, Jack. There's a hell of a lot of it and you can't tell me that an operator like Harry Dawes is just going to get rid of it at car-boot sales.'

'So what do we do, guv?'

'And we're no nearer to solving the murder of Dawn Sims alias Mitchell, either,' continued Fox, ignoring his detective inspector's question. 'Something will have to be done. If no better reason than that the Commissioner's starting to breathe down my neck.'

'Yes, sir,' said Gilroy. He detected the signs. Any time now, Fox was going to start thrashing about. The irony of it was that he very often managed to solve crimes by doing just that. But God help anyone else who tried it.

Jane Sims seemed to have recovered somewhat from the trauma of her father's death when Fox next called at her flat near Knightsbridge, even though he suspected that her cheerfulness was a little artificial. But that was academic; he was about to put her into sombre mood again.

'I'm sorry about the other day,' said Jane as she handed him a drink. This time she had not asked what he wanted; had just poured Scotch.

'Understandable,' said Fox. 'Your brother gone back to America, has he?'

'Not yet,' said Jane. 'He's still in Yorkshire, sorting things out, but he'll be going back soon, I think.'

'Funeral go all right?'

'As well as such things can go, I suppose.' Jane shivered slightly. 'The Yorkshire Dales are pretty inhospitable at the best of times, but it poured with rain all the time we were at the cemetery.' She took a sip of her whisky. 'What was it you wanted to see me about the other day, Tommy?' she asked, hoping to steer him away from the subject of her father's death.

Fox took out his cigarette case and offered it to her, but she shook her head. He noticed that the ashtray now appeared to have a permanent place on the coffee table.

'I'm afraid that your sister—' He broke off, wondering how best to put it. But then he decided that Jane was likely to be irritated by anything other than directness. 'It seems that Dawn had become a call-girl, more or less,' he said.

'What d'you mean, more or less?'

'We have now traced at least five men who have admitted to paying her for sexual intercourse.'

'Oh no!' Jane ran a hand through her hair. 'I was hoping that it wasn't true when you suggested the possibility the other day. D'you think that one of them killed her?'

'The five we've seen were a pretty gutless lot,' said Fox. 'Not that that's any guide, of course. But if they were clients then there are almost certain to have been others who we have yet to trace.'

'D'you think you'll be able to find them?'

'I hope so. We've all sorts of enquiries going on at the moment. But we need a slice of luck.'

Jane smiled at that. 'I thought you were all terribly professional,' she said. 'Isn't that the sort of thing that only happens in books?'

'Don't you believe it.' Fox grinned at her. 'We just need that one break, that's all.'

Jane leaned forward, her elbows on her knees and her face cupped in her hands. 'Do you honestly believe that you're going to find Dawn's killer?'

Fox had grave doubts. He knew that the clear-up rate for murder in London was higher than for most other crime, but he was afraid that the killing of Dawn Sims might just fall into the twenty per cent of unsolved cases that lay on the books to haunt the officers of his Department. 'Of course we shall, Jane,' he said.

'What sort of men were they? The ones that Dawn—' Jane broke off, unable to put into words what her sister had been doing before she was murdered.

Fox wondered why she wanted to know. 'A pretty sleazy bunch.'

'I don't doubt that, but what were they?'

'A civil servant, a bloke who owns a string of garages, someone in television—'

'And where did she do this? Did she meet them in some

crummy hotel room, or what?' Jane was obviously intent on extracting all the sordid details.

'As far as we knew, she entertained them in her own flat in Edgware Road.'

'My God, how sordid it all sounds.' Jane felt in the pocket of her jeans and pulled out a handkerchief. Some loose change fell on to the edge of the sofa on which she was sitting and scattered on the floor. Snuffling and dabbing at her eyes, she stood up. 'Let me get you another drink, Tommy,' she said and, taking his glass, turned quickly so that Fox should not see that she was crying.

Fox wisely ignored her distress and gathering up the coins from the carpet, placed them on the coffee table. 'I thought the nobility never carried money,' he said.

Barnes, the civil servant who had reluctantly admitted to being one of Dawn Sims's clients, was not happy to see Fox again.

And Fox was not happy at having his time wasted. 'Mr Barnes, you're buggering me about,' he said.

Barnes blinked. 'I'm not sure that I—'

'It's this simple, Mr Barnes. I am investigating a murder and I do not appreciate people like you telling me lies.'

'I thought I was very open with you,' said Barnes, making a vain attempt to preserve some of his dignity. As a senior civil servant, he was unaccustomed to people abusing him in his own office.

'You may have thought that you were being open, but I know you weren't. When Mr Evans and I saw you last, you told us that on the night of the fourteenth and fifteenth of October, the night of Dawn Sims's murder, you were at home with your wife.'

'That's right.'

'Your wife has told us that you were not at home. Furthermore, she said that she didn't know where you were.'

'You've spoken to my wife?' Barnes was unable to keep the dismay from his voice.

'In a murder enquiry, Mr Barnes, we talk to whomsoever we please.' Fox paused. 'Well?'

'I was at home. I swear I was. I don't know why my wife

135

should have told you that I wasn't. It doesn't make any sense at all.' Barnes picked up a slip of paper from his desk and glanced at it briefly before screwing it up and throwing it into his waste-paper basket.

'In that case,' said Fox, 'I'll have to talk to her again, won't I?'

'Must you?' Barnes looked desperately at the detective.

'Yes,' said Fox coldly. 'I must.'

'Thought you might be interested to see these, guv'nor,' said Detective Sergeant Percy Fletcher. He spread a number of glossy photographs on Fox's desk.

'Where did you get those from, Perce?'

'I was doing the rounds of the porn shops, guv, beating on the ground, like you said. And I came across these. They're photographs of the original photographs, so the experts tell me.'

'What does that mean?' Fox lined up the six black and white half-plates in front of him and continued to study them. 'Pretty graphic, aren't they, even for Soho.'

'I tried tracing them, but it was hopeless, guv,' said Fletcher. 'It seems that they photograph the original prints and then run hundreds off the new negatives. It's a licence to print money. My snout picked them up from another supplier who got them from a bloke in a pub. If I'd gone on long enough, I'd've finished up in Portobello Road market most likely.'

Fox nodded. He knew the futility of trying to trace the origin of pornographic photographs. 'Should have asked me first, Perce. I happen to know who took these lurid snaps of Lady Dawn Sims.'

'Recognise them?' Fox slung the photographs of Dawn Sims on to a bench in John Wheeler's studio.

The so-called society photographer put his head in his hands and groaned. 'Bloody hell,' he said. 'Where did you get those from?'

'On sale in some sleazy sex-shop in darkest Soho,' said Fox. 'But someone's stolen your copyright. I should sue if I were you.'

'Very funny,' said Wheeler, shuffling the photographs into a neat pile and handing them back to Fox. 'I suppose you're going to do me for that.' He had an expression of resignation on his face.

'What for?'

'Well, they don't leave much to the imagination, do they. I mean, there's no doubt they're obscene.'

'Strange to relate,' said Fox airily, 'it's no offence to take pictures like these.' He waved the bunch of prints in the air. 'If it was, there'd be a few husbands convicted of photographing their wives and girlfriends. Which is all you did, really, given that you were screwing her at the time.' Wheeler went to say something, but Fox carried on. 'The offence subsists in selling such material, but quite frankly, the police are on a hiding to nothing if they waste their time trying to prove that anything is obscene these days.'

'I didn't sell them,' said Wheeler wearily. 'I wouldn't have flogged pictures of a girl I was having an affair with, would I? At least, not pictures like those.'

'So how did they reach what is loosely known as the open market?' asked Fox. 'Who did you give them to?'

'I gave Dawn the only copies that were made,' said Wheeler. 'I even destroyed the negs. You can turn this place upside down if you want to.'

'No thanks,' said Fox. 'I thought that's what had happened. I just wanted to be sure.'

'Sheila won't be getting to hear about this, will she?' asked Wheeler imploringly. He knew that if his lover, Sheila Thompson, learned of the existence of the photographs, she'd leave him.

'Not unless you tell her,' said Fox cheerily.

SIXTEEN

WHEN DICK AND MAISIE ELWELL and their two teenaged children got home after spending Christmas with Dick's parents in Scotland, they had an unpleasant shock. Their house had been burgled. The only good thing about it all was that the Elwells had been the victims of professional thieves. Admittedly, the drawers had all been emptied and the contents of cupboards and wardrobes strewn about, but there was no graffiti and none of the other gratuitous vandalism that is, all too often, present in this age of social decay.

The television was gone, along with the video-recorder, the new hi-fi, several valuable pieces of Mrs Elwell's jewellery, Dick Elwell's personal computer, a power drill, a food processor, five small silver cups that Dick Elwell had won at his golf club, and a stack of popular CDs from the bedroom of Trudy Elwell, the Elwells' seventeen-year old daughter. Not surprisingly, Dick Elwells' collection of opera CDs had been left.

Fortunately for the police who arrived from nearby Sutton Police Station, Dick Elwell was a meticulous man. The serial number of every item of stolen property that possessed one had been recorded by him and was handed to the police when they arrived.

The police made sympathetic noises, promised to send a scenes-of-crime officer, and added the break-in at the Elwell's home to the list, knowing that there was a less than one-in-ten chance of the thieves ever being arrested.

'There've been two more warehouse-breakings that seem to have Sliding Dawes's handwriting on them, guv,' said Gilroy.

'Wonderful,' said Fox, tossing a file into his out-tray. 'What is it this time?'

'A place out at Dagenham, sir. Suppliers of camping equipment and the like.'

'Bloody hell,' said Fox.

'I've got the list here,' continued Gilroy. 'Jeans, sweaters, tents and groundsheets.' He shot a quick glance at Fox. 'And tommy-cookers, sir.'

'What?' Fox looked sharply at his inspector.

'They're a sort of spirit stove that you can cook on when you go camping, so I believe, sir,' said Gilroy.

'I do not go camping, Jack,' said Fox. 'Unless there's a hotel with at least three stars, I don't go at all. What about the other place?'

'Food wholesalers, sir. Dried foods mainly. Rice, flour, curry powder, dried milk, pulses, sugar and salt. That sort of thing.'

'What the hell's Dawes up to, Jack? Is he going to make the biggest curry in the world and get himself into the *Guinness Book of Records*?'

'Maybe, sir,' said Gilroy with a grin.

'Well I've got news for him,' said Fox irritably. 'He's going into the record books all right, for the most counts on one indictment ever seen at the Old Bailey, if I've got anything to do with it.'

'What are we going to do, sir? Spin his slaughter at Croydon?'

'Did the lads on obo there see this gear arrive?'

'No, sir.'

'Well then, how do we know it's down to Dawes?'

Gilroy paused. 'I think he's rumbled the surveillance, guv'nor. And I think he's got another slaughter somewhere.'

Fox nodded gloomily and idly unwound a paper clip. 'I've got a nagging suspicion that you might be right, Jack,' he said.

'D'you want to spin the slaughter at Croydon then, guv?'

'Don't see that we've much option, Jack. I'm not having that weaselly little bastard thumbing his nose at me any longer. Do the business, Jack, will you.'

'Yes, sir,' said Gilroy and went off to get a search warrant for Dawes's warehouse at Croydon.

'Vince, what news?' Dawes ushered Vincent Carmody into the sitting-room of his house in Oxford Road, Putney, and poured sherry.

'It's going well, Harry,' said Carmody, settling himself on the settee. He knew better than to sit in Dawes's favourite Rexine-covered armchair. 'We've got the new slaughter set up down Hounslow and it's all legit.'

'What d'you mean, all legit?' Dawes paused in the act of handing Carmody a glass of sherry. 'How can it be legit?'

'I mean we done like what you said, Harry. It's a company. Carmody Trading Ltd. There's a sign over the door and we've even got a van with it on the side. All registered up Companies House. I done what you said and saw your mouthpiece. He done all the necessary.'

'I like it, Vince. Yes, I definitely like it,' said Dawes. 'It'll take more than bleeding Tommy Fox to work that one out.'

'Yeah, well I hope so,' said Carmody. He didn't share Dawes's views that Fox could be that easily deluded.

It was Detective Sergeant Rosie Webster who was credited with finding the first crack in the Dawn Sims murder case. But it was Fox, needless to say, who pushed a case-opener into that crack and levered it apart.

'I've just had a bell from Property Index, sir.'

'How nice,' said Fox. 'And?'

Rosie studied the piece of paper in her hand. 'There was a burglary-dwelling reported yesterday on Sutton's ground. A Mr and Mrs Elwell.'

'Bloody hell, Rosie. Do we have to be wearied with rubbish like that?'

Rosie smiled at her boss. 'Ah, but you'll like this, sir,' she said. 'Mr Elwell had his second-hand personal computer nicked.'

'Poor chap,' said Fox.

'But he'd kept the serial number.'

'Good for him.'

'And it was one of those nicked in the ram raid at Kingston, a month or two back.'

Fox leaned forward, suddenly interested. 'Where did he get it from, Rosie? A car-boot sale?'

'No, sir.' Rosie laid the piece of paper on Fox's desk and planted a finger on it. 'That's where he got it from, sir.'

Fox studied the information that his detective sergeant had put before him and chuckled. Then he sat back in his chair. 'What's the time, Rosie?'

Rosie turned and looked at the clock over Fox's door. 'Just gone midday, sir,' she said.

'Splendid,' said Fox. 'In that case, my girl, I shall give you a Scotch.' And he walked across to his drinks cabinet.

Fox tapped out Gilroy's extension number and waited. 'Have you got the search warrant for Sliding Dawes's slaughter at Croydon yet, Jack?' he asked when his DI answered.

'Yes, sir. Got it in front of me.'

'Good,' said Fox. 'Well, tear it up and send Ron Crozier to see me.'

Gilroy replaced the receiver and stood up. 'D'you know, Denzil,' he said to Evans, 'it never used to be like this on the Squad before Tommy Fox arrived.'

'Helps to brighten the day though, doesn't it, Jack,' said Evans who had been fortunate enough, of late, to avoid most of the flak.

'They tell me that you used to be an actor, Ron,' said Fox, grinning at Detective Sergeant Crozier.

'Yes, sir.' Crozier sighed inwardly. Whenever there was some dodgy plan that Fox wanted to put into action, his opening gambit was always the same. Fox knew damned well that he'd once been an actor. It was only a few weeks back that he'd had to take the part of a storeman.

'Splendid. Now, you'd better sit down and listen carefully to what I want you to do.'

'Yes, sir.'

'Rosie Webster came up with a useful gem of information this morning. A gentleman by the name of

141

Richard Elwell, Esquire, a burgess of the Borough of Sutton, had his drum done over during the Christmas break and the thief or thieves made away with, among other things, his second-hand personal computer.'

'I see, sir,' said Crozier.

'Ah, but you don't, Ron, not yet,' said Fox. 'The assiduous Mr Elwell had made a note of the PC's serial number and also, happily, recalled where he had acquired it. Namely, a charity shop being run under the auspices of the Hayden Trust. But the said PC was among those stolen in the recent ram-raid at Kingston.' He sat back and linked his fingers together. 'There, Ron, how does that grab you?'

'Where did they get it from, sir? The charity shop, I mean.'

'Don't know, Ron,' said Fox airily. 'But you're going to find out.'

'Oh, right, sir.' Crozier made to stand up.

'Where're you going, Ron?'

'To make enquiries at this charity shop, sir.'

'No, no, Ron. You miss my drift. You don't need to be an actor for that sort of enquiry.'

'Oh!' Crozier relaxed again. He should have known that there would be more to it than that.

'Given that the head of the Hayden Trust is a Mr Freddie Hayden who also happened to know the late Lady Dawn Sims whose body was found in Sliding Dawes's lock-up at Lambeth, I should like you to conduct enquiries of a more arcane nature.'

'Thought you might, sir,' said Crozier.

'Very perceptive of you, Ron. Now, what I want you to do is to get a job with Hayden Trust, unpaid only if absolutely necessary, and find out what goes down there.'

Crozier was completely bemused. 'But, sir,' he said, 'is there any evidence to link the theft of a personal computer in Sutton with the death of Lady Dawn Sims?'

'None whatsoever,' said Fox. 'Until you find some.' And then he outlined precisely what he had in mind for Crozier.

'Would that be Gentleman John Hooper by any chance?'

Freddie Hayden's chief security officer thought that he knew the voice on the telephone but, like all old coppers, didn't show out beyond admitting that he was indeed called Hooper.

'Tommy Fox here, John.'

'Hallo, guv. How are you?'

'Very well, John.'

'What can I do for you?'

'Thought I'd buy you a lunch, John.'

Hooper was immediately on the defensive. He knew that there was rarely such a thing as a free lunch, but when the head of the Flying Squad offered one, there was definitely a catch in it. 'What's the score?' he asked.

'Thought it'd give us a chance to talk over old times, John, swap a few yarns. You know the sort of thing.'

'Yeah, I do,' said Hooper suspiciously. 'Where and when?'

Detective Sergeant Ron Crozier was wearing a second-hand Marks & Spencer suit that he had picked up at a jumble sale. It was not a very good fit, but that was intentional. He wore a shirt, originally white, with frayed collar and cuffs, a nondescript tie that looked as though it should mean something, and a pair of black shoes that needed repairing.

The grey-haired woman who looked up as he entered her office, was about fifty-five, and was dressed in a grey skirt and red blouse. She wore spectacles with blue frames and had the air of a woman who was doing good works and wanted everyone to know that she was. 'Yes?' she said in a rather peremptory tone.

'I was wondering if you wanted any help,' said Crozier in his most conciliatory voice.

'Help? What sort of help?' The woman appraised Crozier with a critical eye.

'I wanted to do some charity work,' said Crozier, adding the word 'ma'am' after a short interval.

Somewhat mollified by this respectful approach, the woman invited Crozier to take a seat. 'Well, now,' she said, 'we'll have to see. Have you done anything like this before?'

'No, but I've heard about the Hayden Trust and I think

143

it's doing very good work.' Crozier leaned forward confidentially. 'To be perfectly honest, ma'am,' he said, 'I'm out of work and it's driving me mad sitting around at home all day doing nothing but watch the telly. So I thought to myself, there are lots of people worse off than you, and if you can't afford to give money, at least you can give them your time.' He grinned. 'What I've got a lot of lately.'

'Well, I must say,' said the woman, her animosity ebbing by the minute, 'that that is a very public-spirited attitude.' She shuffled a few papers. 'We wouldn't be able to pay you anything, not wages, I mean. . .' Crozier looked slightly disappointed. 'But we could probably run to the occasional meal and a few expenses. Legitimate expenses, of course,' she added hurriedly.

'That's all right,' said Crozier. 'I wasn't looking for a job, not as such. I have got the dole money, after all.'

The woman opened a small card index that rested on the corner of her desk and skimmed through it. Then she plucked out a card. 'Now we do need some help at our depot at Epsom. I'm afraid it's rather heavy work, packing and loading. That sort of thing. And taking relief supplies to either Heathrow or Gatwick Airports.' She glanced briefly at Crozier over the top of her spectacles. 'The trouble is, very few people want to get involved in the aspects of our project that entail hard work. They all imagine that it consists of charity balls at the Grosvenor House and that sort of thing. But the real workers are the people who hump the stuff around. They're the true backbone of our organisation.' She preened herself slightly as though struck by some invisible ray of self-righteousness.

'Suits me,' said Crozier.

'Splendid. When can you start, Mr, er—'

'Crozier. And I can start as soon as you like.'

John Hooper sat down opposite Fox in the restaurant just off the Strand that Fox had selected for their meeting.

'John, nice to see you,' said Fox. 'What are you drinking?'

'Seeing it's you, guv, a large brandy,' said Hooper.

The menus came and went and during the meal, Hooper and Fox discussed old colleagues, old cases and old senior officers. The conversation was much the same as that conducted between any two policemen of mature years and service.

When the brandy came, Fox got to the crux of his meeting. 'Met your boss the other day, John,' he said.

'Yeah, he told me,' said Hooper. 'Something to do with a murder, he said.'

'That's right, John. Lady Dawn Sims.'

Hooper nodded. 'He wanted to know about you.'

Fox grinned. 'Oh, and what did he want to know?'

'What sort of copper you were, whether you were straight. All that sort of thing.'

'I hope you advised him accordingly, John.'

Hooper drained his brandy and looked hopeful. 'Course I did. What was it that instructor used to say at the training school? Blue uniforms are thicker than pound notes.'

'Did he really? Can't say I've ever heard that before.' Ordering two more brandies, Fox offered Hooper his cigarette case and then got to the point. 'The Hayden Trust, John.'

'What about it?'

'This is strictly between you and me, you'll understand.'

Hooper looked offended. 'Like I said, blue uniforms are—'

Fox held up his hand. 'Yes, all right, John, point taken. A personal computer that was nicked from a dwelling house in Sutton over Christmas was bought second-hand from one of your Freddie's charity shops.'

Hooper shrugged. 'People are always donating stuff to charity,' he said. 'Bring it in by the van-load sometimes. It's inevitable that some of the gear's nicked. But charities don't look gift horses in the mouth.'

'I know all that, John, but your guv'nor knew Dawn Sims. Dawn Sims's body was found in Harry Dawes's slaughter at Lambeth—'

'Don't tell me that Sliding Dawes is still at it,' said Hooper.

145

'And some,' said Fox. 'And that computer almost certainly came from a ram-raid in Kingston a couple of months ago, the proceeds of which were fenced by Dawes.'

'Ah!' said Hooper.

'Beginning to see light at the end of the tunnel, John?'

'Yeah, I think so. Have you made enquiries at the shop?' Hooper paused. 'Not that it would do any good. They don't keep records of where the stuff comes from. They'll take anything that's brought in without even asking who you are. That afternoon it's in the window, next day it's gone.'

'I know all about that,' said Fox. 'But I'm just wondering if it went direct from Dawes to the charity shop.'

'Could've done, I suppose.' Hooper was beginning to get confused by Fox, but he was not the first old policeman to whom it had happened. 'What are you driving at?'

'I don't know really,' said Fox with uncharacteristic candour, 'but I've put Ron Crozier in, under cover.'

'Who's Ron Crozier?'

'He's a DS on the Squad.'

Hooper shook his head. 'Know the name,' he said, which is what most policemen say when they have never heard of someone. 'What's he doing anyway?'

'Working at the Hayden Trust depot at Epsom.'

'No, I mean what's he hoping to find out?'

'It's just a hunch, John, but I've got a feeling about your Freddie Hayden.'

'Soon to be "Sir" Freddie,' said Hooper.

'How did you know that?' asked Fox. 'I thought it was supposed to be Top Secret.'

'It is,' said Hooper, 'but everyone in the organisation knows about it.'

Fox's eyes narrowed. 'You haven't been giving his secretary a seeing-to, have you, John?'

'Chance'd be a fine thing,' said Hooper. 'Anyway, she's being looked after by one of the directors.' He grinned. 'So, what d'you want me to do about your man Crozier?'

'How close d'you get to Hayden?'

'In and out of his office all the time,' said Hooper. 'He

146

relies on me to keep him informed about what's going on in the organisation.'

'Like what?' asked Fox.

'Like who's fiddling their expenses. Like who's got a new house with a bigger mortgage than his salary. Like who's screwing whose wife.'

'You're the hatchet-man then?'

'No, he doesn't sack them,' said Hooper. 'Just threatens them and they work harder and become dedicated company men.'

Fox laughed. 'And what's he got on you, John?'

'Leave it out,' said Hooper. 'You know me. Always played away from home.'

'What I want you to do then, John, is to tell Hayden that you've done a bit of checking on this Ron Crozier down at the Epsom depot because you thought you recognised him. Something like that. Then tell him that he's got form and that he's only just come out from doing a five-stretch for thieving . . . and that's why he can't get a job. There'll be papers in the Scrubs to back it up, just in case he knows someone and wants collateral.'

'What's the point of all that?' asked Hooper.

'It's what I call beating on the ground,' said Fox. 'Sometimes, something comes up.'

SEVENTEEN

STILL READING THE FILE IN front of him, Denzil Evans
lifted the receiver of the telephone. 'DI Evans,' he said
absently. But suddenly he concentrated on what was being
said to him by the detective chief inspector at Chelsea
Police Station. 'And when was this, guv?' he asked, starting
to scribble furiously on a notepad.

A few minutes later, Evans tapped on Fox's door.

'Ah, Denzil.'

'Just had a call from the DCI at Chelsea, sir,' said Evans.
'Jason Hope-Smith has been arrested.'

'Good gracious,' said Fox. 'What's he been up to?'

'There's been an allegation of rape made against him,
sir.'

'That's very interesting, Denzil. What are the ins and
outs?' Fox grinned. 'If you'll excuse an apt phrase. You'd
better sit down,' he added, 'before you get too excited.'

Evans perched on the edge of the chair in front of Fox's
desk and consulted his notes. 'The alleged victim is a girl
called Trixie Harper, sir. A single woman, aged
twenty-nine. She lives in the flat above Hope-Smith. Seems
that they had become friendly since he moved in and last
night he took her out to dinner at some Chelsea
restaurant. When they got back, he invited her in for
coffee. Miss Harper alleges that Hope-Smith then attacked
her and raped her.'

'Early complaint?' asked Fox, using policeman's shorthand to query whether the girl had reported the matter
immediately.

'Instant, sir, so it seems. Miss Harper fled screaming into
the street wearing nothing more than a towel. She was

taken care of by the driver of a passing bus who probably thought his luck had changed.'

'And when was Hope-Smith arrested, Denzil?'

'Two o'clock this morning, sir. Denies the allegation, naturally—'

'Naturally,' murmured Fox.

'And was bailed to reappear at Chelsea nick thirty days hence, or sooner if required.'

'Bailed?' said Fox angrily. 'Why wasn't the little bastard charged?'

'Conflict of evidence, guv.' Evans looked at his notes again. 'Appears that when Miss Harper was examined by the divisional surgeon, he only found evidence of rather vigorous sexual intercourse. There were no signs of scratches or bruising to her body that would indicate an assault or a struggle and her clothes were not damaged at all. The implication is that she undressed voluntarily and—'

'And then changed her mind when it was too late,' said Fox with a sigh. 'Well, Denzil, that's a woman's prerogative, but it's going to make it bloody difficult to get him down. Just have to hope that he gets an all-woman jury,' he added, 'if the bloody Crown Prosecution Service deigns to charge him.'

'Think that puts him any nearer the Dawn Sims topping, guv?'

'I'd like to think so, Denzil,' said Fox. 'From what the people in Kuwait said, he's certainly a bloke who likes his crumpet, but then so do a lot of other men.'

'Are you going to interview him again, sir?'

Fox pondered that problem for a moment. 'Not until I've spoken to the DCI at Chelsea,' he said. 'Don't want to bugger up his job for him but I think that I'll get Henry Findlater to keep an eye on Hope-Smith so long as the DCI at Chelsea doesn't object. Have his passport off him, did they?'

'Yes, sir, they did,' said Evans.

'I've done the enquiry on Lady Jane Sims's ex, sir,' said Rosie Webster, laying the search form on Fox's desk.

Fox glanced at it. 'Piers!' he said. 'What sort of first

name's that?' He tossed the form to one side. 'Anything of interest, Rosie?'

'More or less as she said, sir.'

'Reckons,' said Fox and sniffed.

'They were married fifteen years ago and divorced seven years later on the grounds of having lived apart for more than three years.'

'Yes,' said Fox, 'that's what she said.'

'He was five years older than Lady Jane, sir, and was an officer in the Guards at the time. Shortly after they were married, he left the army. Apparently, his colonel advised him against pursuing a military career on the grounds that he was bloody useless.' Rosie looked up and smiled. 'So he became a futures-broker or something of the sort, but went bankrupt at about the time they split up.'

'How the hell did you find all that out, Rosie?' asked Fox. 'That wasn't in the records at St Catherine's House.'

'No, sir,' said Rosie and smiled again. 'But I'm friendly with a major in his old regiment and I wheedled it out of him.'

'Always did think you'd got influential friends,' said Fox. Certainly Rosie Webster's clothes and her expensive perfume implied that there were one or two wealthy men among her coterie of admirers. But that came as no surprise to Fox. Nor to anyone else.

'D'you want this information filed in the incident room, sir?'

'No, it's not relevant to the enquiry. You can leave it with me.' Later, Fox took the results of Rosie's enquiry into the incident room and put it through the shredder.

The Hayden Trust Charity depot at Epsom was like a huge Aladdin's Cave. Great wooden racks groaned under the weight of clothing, medical supplies, dried food and tents. In fact, everything that could be used for the relief of suffering, famine and sickness in far-off countries was there.

The supervisor of this vast emporium was a man called Alec Tinsley. Now into his fifties, he had spent most of his life in the army as a quartermaster. But none of his military mannerisms had been left behind with his uniform. 'My name's Mr Tinsley,' he said, 'and I'm in charge of this lot. What I say goes. Get that into your head and we'll get on famously. Understood, Crozier?' His attitude was not influenced by the fact that Crozier was an unpaid volunteer.

'Yes, Mr Tinsley.'

'Right, now what d'you know about stores? Anything?'

'Not a lot, no.'

'Right, then we'll have to teach you, I suppose.' Tinsley sighed at the unfairness of a world that, all his life it seemed, had foisted people upon him who knew nothing about their jobs. 'I'm going to put you in the section that handles dried foods. I know exactly what's there, so don't go nicking nothing. There's no perks here, my lad. Understood?'

'Yes, Mr Tinsley,' said Crozier once more.

'Right then. When we get supplies coming in—'

'Where do they come from, Mr Tinsley?'

Tinsley gazed reflectively at Crozier. 'I don't see as how it's got anything to do with you,' he said, 'but various public-spirited commercial organisations around the country donate supplies and deliver them here. Some sort of tax fiddle, I suppose.' Tinsley was unwilling to accept that some people did things out of the goodness of their heart. 'Other stuff's bought with the donations what people make to the Hayden Trust.' He sniffed and fingered his moustache. 'And that's all you need to know, cocky.'

'Oh, right.'

'When this gear arrives, your job is to check it in and make sure it gets put in the right place. Then when we makes up loads, ready for air-lifting to some distant shore, you puts it together. Understood?'

'Yes, Mr Tinsley.'

'Right then.' Tinsley slipped his pen into the top pocket of his grey warehouse coat and marched back to his office in the corner of the huge warehouse.

Freddie Hayden's secretary, Toni, replaced the receiver and glanced up at John Hooper. 'He's on the phone to New York,' she said curtly. She didn't like the chief security officer and, although in her privileged position, she could afford to be a little frosty towards him, there was a limit to how far she could go. The indirect cause of her animosity – and her caution – was the affair that she was having with one of the married directors. She was convinced that Hooper had learned of it and had passed the information on to Freddie Hayden. What was not in doubt, was the change in Hayden's attitude towards her. Over the last six months or so, he had been hinting that she should be more than just his secretary, and occasionally put his hand on her breast or her bottom and made indecent suggestions. She did not relish the idea of going to bed with Hayden, but that, she thought, would probably be the price she would have to pay to safeguard her own and her lover's job. She glanced at the indicator panel on her desk and saw that the light had gone out. 'He's finished,' she said.

'Morning, sir,' said Hooper breezily as he closed Hayden's office door.

'Good morning, John. And how are you this morning?'

'Fine, sir, thank you.' Hooper had no time whatsoever for Hayden. He had met too many men of his type during his police service, but Hooper needed the job. In addition to a good salary, he had a company car, free medical insurance and a free pension to add to his police pension when he eventually retired. 'I've come across a disturbing bit of news, sir.'

'Oh dear. You'd better come and sit down, John. Help yourself to some coffee.' Hayden waved a hand towards the sideboard and sat down on one of the two settees. 'And what is this distressing intelligence?'

'I was having a look round down at Epsom, sir—'

'Oh?' Hayden tensed slightly. 'Is there some trouble down there?'

'Well, no, not as such, sir, but I came across a face.'

'Aha! Did you now? A tea-leaf?' Hayden enjoyed listening to Hooper's criminal slang and attempted to emulate it, though usually without much success.

'No, there's no thieving going on, sir, but I saw this fellow who's been taken on as storeman. Name of Crozier.'

'What about him, John?'

'Just came out of the Scrubs. Did a handful.'

'A handful?' Hayden leaned forward eagerly.

'Five years, sir. Aggravated burglary.' Hooper leaned back nonchalantly. 'I have my sources, of course, sir, and I learn that he's got a string of previous convictions for dishonesty.'

'What's he doing at Epsom then?' Hayden frowned. 'Who took him on? What are we paying him?'

'Apparently he wandered into the Trust's head office and volunteered his services,' said Hooper. 'Reckoned he couldn't get a job and wanted something to occupy his mind while he was on the dole.'

'A burglar, you say?' Hayden looked reflectively at the glass sculpture on the coffee table.

'That's right, sir,' said Hooper. He could see that any minute now, Fox's under-cover man was going to be dismissed, but he couldn't work out the detective chief superintendent's ploy. Nevertheless, Hooper had his own position to think about. 'Want me to give him the big E, sir?' he asked tentatively.

'No, leave it with me. Some heads are going to roll over this one, John.' Hayden stood up, a frown on his face. 'Don't these people ever check with you before they take on staff?'

'Usually, sir,' said Hooper. 'Especially since that last memo you sent out.'

'Oh, Tommy!' Lady Jane Sims pushed her hair out of her eyes with the back of her hand. 'How good to see you. Come in. I was just getting myself some supper. Will you join me?' As usual, she was dressed in jeans and an old rugby shirt.

'No thanks,' said Fox. 'I grabbed a quick sandwich earlier on.'

Jane tutted as she led Fox into the sitting-room. 'You single men are all the same,' she said. 'You should take more care of yourself. Sit down and I'll get you a drink.'

'Don't let your supper spoil. In fact, I won't stay, but I was passing and I thought I'd just drop in to see how you were.'

'Of course you'll stay . . . if you don't mind watching me

eat, that is.' Jane handed him a tumbler of whisky and walked through into the kitchen.

'I saw your brother the other day,' said Fox.

'Oh, what about?' shouted Jane from the kitchen.

'Just to put him in the picture. He rang me at the Yard and we went for a drink at his club.'

'How boring. I hate gentlemen's clubs. Is he all right?'

'Yes.' Fox was surprised that the new Earl Sims appeared not to have been in touch with his sister.

'He rings me from time to time, but I'm never quite sure where he's ringing from.' Jane came back into the sitting-room with a plate of pasta and a glass of wine. 'Be a dear and push one of those tables over, Tommy.' She nodded towards a nest of occasional tables. 'How did he take the news of Dawn's behaviour?' She glanced quickly at Fox, wondering whether he had told her brother more than he had told her.

'He was a bit upset by it, naturally,' said Fox. 'But fairly phlegmatic.'

'What does that mean?'

'That there was nothing that could be done now. But I got the impression that he wished that he had kept a closer eye on her when she was alive. Apparently, he didn't know anything about her allowance having been cut off by your father.'

'Yes, that's all very well,' said Jane, 'but if he stayed in one place for five minutes, I'd've known how to get in touch with him.' And then, seeming to realise that it was not the done thing to criticise her brother to a comparative stranger she changed the subject. 'Are you any nearer finding her killer?' She took a forkful of pasta as though not really interested in the answer.

'Still got a lot of irons in the fire,' said Fox. The law regarding sexual offences prevented him from telling the girl about Hope-Smith's arrest.

'You're keeping something from me,' said Jane, looking up with a wry smile.

'No I'm not. It's just that there are so many things going on, that to tell you about them would merely confuse you.'

Jane stared at Fox for a moment or two and then took a sip of wine. 'What's that lovely expression you policemen

154

use? You are hopeful of an early arrest?'

Fox grinned. 'Yes, something like that.' He wished it were true. 'By the way, Jane, I've got a couple of tickets for *Starlight Express*. I don't know if you're interested, but you did say you liked Lloyd Webber's stuff . . .'

'Oh, how super.' Jane's face lit up. 'You shouldn't have.'

Fox waved a deprecating hand. 'We get free tickets at the Yard from time to time,' he said.

'Don't spoil it,' said Jane and stood up to get Fox another drink.

Alan Wadman, the detective chief inspector at Chelsea, stood up and shook hands. 'Hallo guv'nor,' he said. 'Come to talk about Hope-Smith?'

'Yes.' Fox peered at Wadman's notice board before sitting down. 'What's happening?'

'Doesn't look promising, guv. I don't think we've got a chance of getting a result here. The girl, Trixie Harper, is adamant that she was raped and the divisional surgeon confirms that sexual intercourse took place. But Hope-Smith, in his statement under caution, claims that she was willing. He said that she undressed voluntarily and willingly engaged in sexual intercourse. However, there's no denying the evidence of the bus driver that he saw her, wearing just a towel, in the street outside the premises or that she was screaming her head off.'

'Are the CPS going to give it a run?' asked Fox.

Wadman laughed. 'There's no telling with that lot,' he said. 'Still banging on about the fifty-per cent rule.'

Fox nodded moodily. He was familiar with the policy that the Crown Prosecution Service would only go to court with a case in which they thought they had a more than even chance of getting a conviction. 'Well, I know what I'd've done, before they set up that comic opera outfit,' he said. 'I'd've put him on the sheet and let him try and talk his way out of it.'

'That's what I'm hoping to persuade them to do,' said Wadman, but he didn't sound too confident of succeeding. 'How's your murder enquiry going, guv?'

'It's not,' said Fox.

155

EIGHTEEN

'MRS PATRICIA BARNES?'

'Yes.'

'I am Detective Sergeant Rosie Webster of the Flying Squad.'

'What d'you want?' The woman peered at Rosie suspiciously, apparently unable to comprehend that the tall elegant blonde on her doorstep could possibly be a police officer.

'May I come in?' Rosie inclined her head and gave the woman one of her most fetching smiles.

'Oh, yes, I suppose so.' Mrs Barnes stood back to admit Rosie and showed her in to the sitting-room.

'My detective chief superintendent came to see you the other day—'

'Well someone did. Is this about the murder of that wretched girl?' Mrs Barnes was clearly puzzled by this second visit from the police within eight days.

'It is, Mrs Barnes, yes.'

'Well, I don't see what that's got to do with us.'

'But you knew her, Mrs Barnes, didn't you?'

'Yes. I told the policeman that.'

'You also told Mr Fox that your husband hadn't been at home on the night of the fourteenth of October, the night of Lady Dawn Sims's murder.'

'Did I?' Patricia Barnes looked blankly at the electric fire and its twinkling artificial logs.

'This is a serious matter, Mrs Barnes,' said Rosie. 'And if your husband was not here on that night, he may be arrested.' She was getting a little tired of Mrs Barnes's

156

apparent indifference to the gravity of the police enquiries.

'Arrested?' Suddenly Patricia Barnes shook off her apathy and concentrated on what Rosie was saying. 'Why on earth should he be arrested?' She seemed quite shocked at the possibility.

'We are interviewing everyone who knew Lady Dawn and who is unable to account for their movements on the night she was killed. Your husband claimed to have been with you on the fourteenth of October, but you told Mr Fox that he wasn't here. That does tend to make us suspicious.' Rose waited patiently to see what Mrs Barnes would say to that.

'He was here.'

'Are you sure?'

'Positive.'

'Then why did you tell Mr Fox that he wasn't?'

'Miss, er—'

'Webster.'

'It is Miss, is it?'

'Yes, that's right.'

'I thought that career women always liked to be called Muzz.'

'Not all of us,' said Rosie and smiled.

'Then you probably won't understand what it's like to have a husband who's a womaniser, my dear.'

'How d'you know that he is?' asked Rosie, who knew all about womanising men.

Mrs Barnes looked at Rosie with a pitiful smile. 'You can always tell,' she said. 'A sudden improvement in their appearance, an excess of after-shave, and an evasiveness when you ask them where they're going or where they've been.' She shook her head at the futility of it all. 'And Harry, because of his job, always shelters behind the Official Secrets Act.'

'Does he do work of national importance then?' Fox had told Rosie that if Barnes were to rush down to Fleet Street and give them the entire contents of his filing cabinets, they would probably throw it all away.

'I doubt it,' said Mrs Barnes in resigned tones. 'But he is

a womaniser, and I knew the moment he set eyes on Dawn that he wouldn't be able to resist her. The one thing that puzzles me is that she bothered with him. Harry's just a dowdy little civil servant, but she was a good-looking girl. There must have been dozens of young men who would have taken her fancy.'

'And that's why you told Mr Fox that he hadn't been here that night, was it? A sort of revenge.'

Patricia Barnes nodded and stared at the fire again. 'Yes, my dear,' she said eventually. 'I realise that I shouldn't have done it, but I thought I'd teach him a lesson. Worry him for a change, the way he worries me with his philandering.'

'I see,' said Rosie. 'I take it that you're prepared to make a statement, saying that he was here that night, then?'

'If that's what you want, yes. Will this get me into trouble?'

'I shouldn't think so.' Rosie smiled and took a statement form from her briefcase. There was no way that the Crown Prosecution Service would consider a case of wasting police time. And she knew that Fox wouldn't even ask them when he had heard the reasons for Mrs Barnes's original lie.

Gentleman John Hooper stopped his car near a phone box in Greenford and rang Tommy Fox. He had been a policeman for too long to make confidential calls from his office. 'I've put the bubble in for your man Crozier,' he said when eventually he was connected to the head of the Flying Squad.

'Well done, John. And what did the great man have to say to that?'

'Said he'd deal with it personally, guv,' said Hooper.

'Did he now? That's interesting. Tell me, John, as an old Fraud Squad officer, what d'you think about the state of health of Hayden's companies?'

Hooper thought about the question for a moment. 'Well,' he said eventually, 'I haven't been able to examine the books – he doesn't trust me that much – but let me put it this way. If I had some spare cash, I wouldn't invest it in

Hayden. Nothing concrete mind, just a gut feeling.'

'Thanks, John. I owe you one,' said Fox and replaced the receiver.

Commander Raymond Willow was in a foul mood. The train from Waterloo had been late and the ferry crossing to the Isle of Wight choppy. And the sarcastic sneer on John James Stedman's face as he was brought into the interview room at Parkhurst Prison did nothing to improve that mood.

'I have interviewed Miss Sandra Nash. . .' began Willow.

'Oh good. So you found her.'

'It is not good, Stedman. Your complaint was a pack of lies, wasn't it?'

'How d'you reckon that then?' Stedman lit a cigarette and leaned back in his chair. His whole attitude was one of disdainful nonchalance.

'Because Miss Nash stated to me that you gave her the two hundred pounds that you allege Detective Chief Superintendent Fox stole from you, and she further states that the seven compact discs and the two dresses were her property anyway.'

'Yeah, that's right,' said Stedman and looking past Willow, grinned at Sergeant Clarke who was perched uncomfortably on a hard chair some feet behind his commander.

'So you made a false statement to me?' Willow leaned forward in what he believed to be a menacing attitude.

'S'right.'

'You do realise that in certain circumstances, that could be construed as an offence, I suppose?'

'Tell you what,' said Stedman. 'When I've done me ten years' bird, come back and talk to me about it again.'

'Why did you tell these falsehoods then?' asked Willow.

'I'll tell you why, copper,' said Stedman, leaning forward with an earnest expression on his face. 'That slag I was living with reckoned she was going to stand by me, so I give her two Cs to tide her over like. And that was the last I saw of the little cow. She never come and see me when I was on remand down Brixton. And she never showed up at the trial neither.'

'What's that got to—'

'So I thought I'd flush her out. I knew you geezers would track her down and that's all I wanted. So now you can tell me where the little bitch is.'

Willow smiled triumphantly at Stedman. 'I'm afraid I can't do that, *Mister* Stedman,' he said. 'It's confidential information.'

'But that's bleedin' outrageous. She nicked two hundred quid off of me.'

'No she didn't,' said Willow. 'You gave it to her and doubtless the officers in whose presence you did so will testify to that fact.'

'You sure you're a copper?' asked Stedman and glanced at Clarke. 'Don't half talk posh, your guv'nor, don't he?' he said, and looking back at Willow, added, 'Well, in that case, you can bugger off, squire.'

Fox listened carefully to Rosie Webster's report of her interview with Harry Barnes's wife. 'She has a point there,' he said eventually.

'What's that, sir?'

'Why should a girl as attractive as Dawn Sims be interested in a bloke like Barnes. You've not seen him, of course, Rosie.'

'No, sir.'

'Well, he's not exactly good-looking.' Fox shook his head. 'There's more to this than meets the eye,' he added.

'Crozier!' Alec Tinsley, the overseer of the Hayden Trust's depot at Epsom, stepped out of his office and bellowed across the warehouse. 'Come in here a minute.'

'Yes, Mr Tinsley,' Detective Sergeant Ron Crozier crossed to the glass-walled cubicle that Tinsley dignified with the term 'office' and closed the door behind him.

'I've got a special job for you, Crozier. Take the van, the blue Commer, and go to this address.' Tinsley handed Crozier a slip of paper. 'There's some stores to be picked up and brought back here. Got it?'

'Yes, Mr Tinsley.'

'Good. Now there's just one thing, Crozier. Some of the gear what you'll see down there has come from suppliers who don't want their shareholders to know that they're contributing to charity, see? So mum's the word. Don't tell no one.'

'D'you mean it's a bit dodgy?'

'What d'you mean, dodgy?'

Crozier shrugged. 'Well, you know, a bit iffy like.'

'No, it's not a bit iffy like,' said Tinsley, 'not that you've got any room to talk about things being iffy, Crozier.'

'What's that s'posed to mean?'

'I know all about you, my son. Nothing goes on around here without Alec Tinsley getting to hear about it, I can tell you. Done a bit of time, have we?'

Crozier introduced a defensive and downtrodden whine into his voice. 'We all make mistakes, Mr Tinsley,' he said.

'I wouldn't call doing five years for burgling a house and beating up the occupants making a mistake, my son. I'd call it downright deliberate.' Tinsley fixed Crozier with a condescending stare. 'But play your cards right, Crozier, and keep your trap shut, and who knows? You might even finish with a nice little bonus in your pocket. But not one that the DSS'd know about, either. And just remember this. You might be a bloody villain, but you don't frighten me. Expert in unarmed combat when I was in the army, I was.'

'When d'you want this stuff collected, Mr Tinsley?'

'No time like the present, lad. And one other thing . . .'

'What?'

'Your little secret's safe with me. But if that bastard Hooper gets to hear about you then so will Mr Hayden. And that'll be good-bye Crozier.'

'Who's Hooper, Mr Tinsley?'

Tinsley lowered his voice. 'He's an ex-copper who tells Mr Hayden everything what goes on. You want to watch him and keep your lip buttoned if he ever comes poking around. Got it?'

'Bloody filth,' said Crozier and spat on the warehouse floor.

'The complaint made against you by John James Stedman has in effect been withdrawn, Mr Fox,' said Willow stiffly.

'Thought it might be,' said Fox cheerfully. 'Going to do him for wasting police time, guv?'

Willow ignored that jibe. 'Well, after interviewing Miss Sandra Nash—'

'The scrubber he was living with, you mean?'

'Exactly so,' said Willow. 'It seems that Stedman gave the two hundred pounds to her.'

'Yes, I know. I saw him do it.'

'Oh!'

'And the fact that he did was noted in both the property register and in Detective Inspector Evans's pocket-book. Did you examine the property register by any chance?' asked Fox with a smile.

Willow glanced at Sergeant Clarke who shook his head. 'We haven't actually got around to that yet,' said the commander.

'Pity,' said Fox. 'Might have saved you a bit of time if you'd done that first . . . sir.'

'But,' said Willow, determined not to be outdone, 'there still remains the complaint against you which was made by Mr Harold Dawes. A complaint of harassment, you may recall.'

'I do indeed, sir,' said Fox. 'A malicious and unwarranted complaint if ever there was one.'

'Yes, well be that as it may, I have to tell you that I intend now to pursue that complaint.'

'Really?' said Fox. 'That'll be interesting for you.'

'Come in, Tommy.' Dick Campbell, the Deputy Assistant Commissioner, Specialist Operations, put down the evening paper and indicated a chair. 'Problems?'

'Only one, sir,' said Fox. 'And it's called Willow, a commander on One Area.'

'What's he been doing to upset you?'

'This murder of Lady Dawn Sims, sir—'

'Oh, yes, how's it going?'

'Slowly,' said Fox. 'But you may recall that the body was found in one of Sliding Dawes's slaughters.'

Campbell nodded. 'In Balham, wasn't it?'

'Lambeth, sir.'

'Well, how does Commander Willow feature in all this?'

'I've had an obo on Dawes for some time now, sir, and I'm convinced that he's tied into this topping somehow. I'm not sure how, but there's something there. Anyway, Dawes, cunning bastard, made a formal complaint of harassment. Objected to the obo apparently.'

'Well, how did he know it was there? Your blokes losing their grip or something?' Campbell smiled. He knew that that would not be the case, but he couldn't resist baiting Tommy Fox when rarely the opportunity arose.

'It was deliberate, sir. To put the frighteners on Dawes. Then I took it off and put it back on again a couple of days later, discreetly. So that he'd think it'd gone altogether.'

'What's the problem then, Tommy?'

'The problem is that Commander Willow was appointed to investigate the complaint and he's going to go steaming down to Putney to take statements, just when I reckon that everything's about to come on top. And if he does, it'll throw the cat among the pigeons. Frankly, I don't care how many statements he takes, but I'd rather he did it in Brixton, after I've nicked Dawes.'

Campbell laughed. 'I think you'd better have a Scotch to soothe your nerves, Tommy,' he said and waved a hand towards his cocktail cabinet. 'Help yourself, and pour one for me while you're at it. Be back in a moment.'

DAC Campbell went to the office next door, received a nod of approval from the Assistant Commissioner's secretary and tapped lightly on Peter Frobisher's door.

After Campbell had left, the AC telephoned the Deputy Commissioner who in turn telephoned Commander John Thomas, the director of the Complaints Investigation Bureau at Tintagel House.

Following a short conversation with the Deputy, Thomas telephoned Commander Willow at One Area Headquarters. 'Thomas here,' he said.

'Thomas who?' asked Willow.

'John Thomas at CIB. I believe you've got an outstanding complaint against Detective Chief Superintendent Fox of SO8, Raymond?'

'Yes,' said Willow guardedly. He was beginning to get paranoic regarding anything connected with Fox. 'What about it?'

'Put it on hold until you hear from me again, Raymond, there's a good chap. Deputy Commissioner's directions.'

'The Crown Prosecution Service bloke's been on about Budgeon and Chesney, guv,' said Gilroy.

'Who the hell are they?' asked Fox.

'The two we nicked the morning we discovered Dawn Sims's body in the lock-up at Lambeth, sir.'

'Oh yes. I'd forgotten about them, Jack. Put them on the sheet for robbery, didn't we?'

'The CPS solicitor wants to know when we'll be ready to go for trial. He says the beak's getting a bit touchy about constant remands in custody.'

'Daresay he is,' said Fox with a yawn and looked thoughtfully at the ceiling. 'Tell him that other arrests connected with that case are imminent and it would be prejudicial to try those two at this stage. You know the form, Jack. Tell him something like that.'

'And are they, sir?'

'Are they what?'

'Are other arrests imminent, sir?'

'Well they are, but not that imminent, Jack. I'm going to the theatre tonight, so crime will have to wait.' Fox took a clothes brush out of his wardrobe and handed it to Gilroy. 'Just have a flick round the back of my collar, Jack, there's a good fellow,' he said.

NINETEEN

CROZIER WAS SURPRISED AT THE modest size of the warehouse that accommodated the firm of Carmody Trading Ltd at Hounslow, the address which Tinsley had given him. He drove on to the forecourt and was met by Vincent Carmody who told him to drive round to the rear of the premises.

'I've been told to ask for Mr Carmody,' said Crozier when he got out of the van. He had recognised Carmody immediately from one of the many surveillance photographs which Henry Findlater's team had taken, and which now adorned the walls of the Flying Squad incident room.

'That's me. Who are you?'

'Ron Crozier. Mr Tinsley's sent me to collect some gear for the Hayden Trust.'

Carmody looked Crozier up and down for a moment or two. 'Ain't I seen you somewhere before?' he asked.

'Dunno,' said Crozier. 'It's possible, I suppose.'

'Yeah!' Carmody rubbed his chin thoughtfully. 'Anyway, back your van in here,' he said and opened a set of double doors.

Two men started loading Crozier's van the moment he had switched off the engine. Boxes of clothing – jeans and sweaters according to the labels – were put swiftly on board. A few sacks of rice and half a dozen tents were followed by two crates of fell boots and about six large cardboard containers which bore no indication of their contents.

'Right, off you go,' said Carmody, 'and no poking about in your cargo on the way.'

'Don't you want a signature or nothing?' asked Crozier.

'No, mate. We trust you.' Carmody twisted his face into an evil grin and moved closer to Crozier. 'And the next thing I'm doing is ringing Alec Tinsley to tell him exactly what you're taking away from here. So if you're thinking of nicking anything, forget it.'

'I'm not into nicking,' said Crozier.

'Not much,' said Carmody. 'I've just sussed you out. Weren't you in the Scrubs?'

'So what?' Crozier knew that details of his false prison record must have been passed to Carmody by Tinsley. 'But you weren't. Leastways, not at the same time.' Fox had ensured that none of the petty criminals working for Dawes had been in Wormwood Scrubs prison at the time that Crozier was supposed to have been there.

Carmody grinned. 'See you around,' he said.

'Good morning, sir,' said Commander John Thomas.

'Good morning, John,' said the Deputy Commissioner, looking up from *The Times* as the head of the Complaints Investigation Bureau entered his office.

'I need a direction, sir,' said Thomas officiously. 'I've received a complaint from a prisoner at Parkhurst prison.'

The Deputy Commissioner folded his newspaper. 'What about?'

'It's a complaint against Ray Willow, sir. It comes from a John James Stedman, serving ten years for robbery.' Thomas glanced briefly at the file in his hand. 'He complains that Commander Willow failed properly to investigate a complaint of theft that had been made by Stedman against Detective Chief Superintendent Fox of the Flying Squad.'

The Deputy Commissioner groaned. 'D'you know, John,' he said in a tired voice, 'I think that the Metropolitan Police will eventually sink under the weight of all the paper it generates. I reckon we use half a dozen rain forests a year all by ourselves.'

'Yes, sir,' said Thomas. 'But I need you to nominate a deputy assistant commissioner to investigate the complaint.'

The Deputy Commissioner held out a hand for the file. Quickly perusing it, he handed it back. 'Give it to Dick Campbell,' he said. 'He'll make a thorough job of that load of rubbish.'

'I hope you're satisfied,' said Harry Barnes as Fox and Evans entered his office.

'Yes thank you,' said Fox, deliberately treating Barnes's outburst as though it had been spoken without sarcasm.

'I've broken up with my wife, you know.'

'Have you? Well that's hardly the fault of the police, is it, Mr Barnes?'

Barnes glared at the two officers. 'Was there something in particular you wanted?' he asked.

'Were you being blackmailed by Dawn Sims?' asked Fox.

Barnes looked up in alarm. 'Why should you think that?' He fiddled nervously with a ball-point pen, making repeated clicking noises as he pressed its knob up and down.

'Well, were you?'

Barnes dropped the pen into a pot on his desk and, recovering some of his self-confidence, asked, 'Are you satisfied that I had nothing to do with the death of this woman?'

Fox recognised Barnes's attempt to deflect the question. 'I take it that you were being blackmailed then,' he said.

For a few brief moments, Barnes studied the surface of his desk. 'Yes.' He spoke softly without looking up.

'How was she blackmailing you, Mr Barnes?'

Barnes looked up, his stare a combination of both resolve to stand his ground and loathing for this policeman who had forced him to face the unpalatable truth. 'I'm sorry,' he said, 'but I'm not prepared to discuss my relationship with her any further.'

'You may have to do so in court,' said Fox.

'Then you'll have to subpoena me,' said Barnes with a flash of grim determination.

'It's Ron Crozier, guv,' said Crozier. He had waited until he had arrived home before telephoning Fox.

'How's it going, Ron?'

'I picked up a load of gear from Vince Carmody's slaughter today, guv. Which means Harry Dawes's slaughter, of course.'

'Nice one, Ron. Tell me about it.'

'They're at it, guv,' said Crozier, 'and the Hayden Trust seems to be well involved.' He went on to tell Fox that Dawes's right-hand man was now operating as Carmody Trading Ltd and described all that he had seen in the warehouse at Hounslow.

'D'you want me to hang in there?'

'For the time being, Ron,' said Fox. 'You don't think they've sussed you out, do you?'

'No, sir, definitely not.'

'Right, Ron. Keep it up for another day while we sort out what to do next.' There was a pause. 'Any indication of when you're doing the next run?'

'No, sir, but I could try and give you a bell.'

'That'd be good, Ron,' said Fox, 'but don't put yourself on offer.' He paused. 'Better still, don't bother. I'll switch Mr Findlater and his team to cover both the depot at Epsom and Carmody's place at Hounslow.' There was a chuckle. 'Don't be surprised if you get nicked in the next day or so, Ron.'

'Well, if *you're* going to nick me, I'd better ring my brief now, guv,' said Crozier.

'Saucy bastard,' said Fox.

It had gone midday the following day before Fox was able to get hold of Detective Inspector Evans. 'Where the hell have you been, Denzil?' he asked.

'Court, sir,' said Evans.

'Good God!' said Fox. 'What with?'

'The three men and the woman we nicked the morning we did those raids, sir.'

'What are you talking about, Denzil?'

'You remember when Henry Findlater's lot saw cars picking up gear from a Transit van, sir, in a lay-by on the A23, south of Croydon somewhere?' began Evans patiently, 'as a result of which we raided a number of drums. You came with me when we nicked Tom Wilson for handling a stolen personal computer . . .'

'Vaguely,' said Fox.

'He had a girlfriend called Judith Ransome who was wearing a see-through nightdress, guv.'

'Oh yes, of course I remember, Denzil. How did you get on?'

'All went down, sir. Fined two hundred and fifty pounds each.'

'Bloody hell,' said Fox. 'I sometimes wonder why we bother.'

Evans looked apologetic on behalf of the judiciary. 'Was there something you wanted to see me about, sir?'

'Yes, Denzil. Believe it or believe it not, the Crown Prosecution Service has decided not to charge Hope-Smith with rape.'

'Doesn't surprise me, sir,' said Evans. 'The evidence was a bit thin.'

Fox gave his DI a sour look. 'What's that got to do with it?' he said and lit a cigarette. 'The victim, Denzil, or the ex-victim, I suppose we should say . . .'

'Trixie Harper, sir.'

'Yes. What d'you know about her?'

'Only that since she made the allegation, she's moved, sir.'

'Where to? Any idea?'

'Not offhand, guv, but I'm sure that Mr Wadman at Chelsea will have it.'

'Find out where she's gone to, Denzil. I've a feeling that a little chat with that young lady might be beneficial to our enquiries. Use my phone.'

To Evans, that proposal appeared to be another Tommy Fox shot in the dark, but he telephoned Chelsea and found that Trixie Harper had moved to Holland Park. 'When d'you want to see her, sir?' he asked.

Fox stood up. 'Now, Denzil,' he said.

It was a medium sort of girl who opened the door. She was of medium height, medium build and had medium-length brown hair. And she wore a midi-length dress.

'Miss Harper?'

'Yes.' The girl gave the two policemen a curious look.

'We're police officers,' said Fox. 'We'd like to have a word with you if we may.'

'Oh, not again,' said Trixie Harper. 'I thought that was all over and done with.' She led the way into a bed-sitting room which the landlord had the temerity to describe as a studio flat, and sat down.

'I'm awfully sorry to trouble you,' said Fox, seating himself opposite the girl. 'I'm Thomas Fox ... of the Flying Squad.' He waved a hand towards Evans who looked extremely uncomfortable perched on the edge of a divan. 'And that is Detective Inspector Evans.'

'Have you come to tell me why you're not taking action against that bloody man Hope-Smith?'

'Alas no,' said Fox. 'That case was nothing to do with me. The police at Chelsea were dealing with that.'

'Where are you from then?'

'New Scotland Yard,' said Fox, 'but I would rather like to talk to you about Hope-Smith, Miss Harper.'

'Why?'

'I am investigating the murder of Lady Dawn Sims and—'

'D'you think he might have done it? Well, it doesn't surprise me.' Trixie Harper's face took on a vengeful expression.

'At the moment, I don't know who was responsible for her death,' said Fox, 'but Hope-Smith certainly knew her.' He paused. 'Intimately.'

'I'll bet he did, the bastard.'

'Miss Harper, I have read the statement you made to the woman officer at Chelsea and I have no wish to dwell on that unpleasant incident, but is there anything else that you can tell me about Jason Hope-Smith? How long have you known him, for instance?'

'Only since he moved into the flat below mine.' Trixie Harper gave that some thought. 'A matter of weeks really,' she added.

'And that was the first time he had taken you out, was it? The night that he—'

'The night that he screwed me, you mean?' The girl smiled at Fox.

'Er, yes, that's one way of putting it, I suppose.' Fox was somewhat taken aback by Trixie's response. It wasn't at all the sort of reaction he had expected from a woman who had alleged that she had been raped. He glanced across at Evans. 'Put your pocket-book away, Denzil,' he said, and turned back to the girl. 'Miss Harper, I don't care what you said at the police station, and I'm not bothered what you said in your statement, but I do want to learn as much as I can about Hope-Smith.'

Trixie Harper looked from Fox to Evans and then back to Fox. 'He suggested that I went on the game,' she said.

'What made him suggest that?'

'I'm a stripper,' said the girl bluntly. 'But I'm hoping to be an actress one day.'

'Did he know that?' Fox had noticed that the girl's occupation had been shown on her statement as 'artiste', and some inner feeling had prompted him to bring Evans with him instead of Rosie Webster. Many women were quite happy to tell men things that they wouldn't want a female officer to hear.

'Yes.'

'How did he find that out?'

'I told him.' Trixie crossed her legs and gave Fox a half-smile.

'When?'

'About the second time I met him, I suppose. We arrived at the front door at the same time one night. It must have been just after midnight, I think, and I'd just got out of a taxi. I'd done a cabaret in a West End club which finished late.' Trixie sighed. 'But then they usually do,' she said. 'Anyway, he asked me what I'd been doing and I told him.'

'And presumably that made him think—'

'That I was an easy lay? Yes. Most men make that mistake. Just because you take your clothes off for a living, they seem to think that you're willing to jump into bed with them at the drop of a hat.'

'And you weren't, of course.'

171

'I was actually.' Trixie looked directly at Fox and smiled. 'So he didn't rape you at all.'

'You did say you didn't care what I'd said at the police station, didn't you?'

'I did.'

'A couple of weeks later, he invited me out to dinner. We both had a lot to drink. I suppose I must have had nearly a whole bottle of wine at the restaurant, and then we had some brandy with our coffee when we got back to Jason's flat. He asked me to do a strip for him, a sort of personal cabaret—'

'Just like that?'

'Yes. Well, I reckoned he'd paid for it. It was a very good dinner.' Trixie smiled, as though aware that everything in life had to be paid for. 'So I finished up sitting on his lap, naked, with him pawing me. I suppose you could say he'd paid for that too.'

'And Hope-Smith was fully dressed all this time, was he?'

'Yes. But it didn't take him long to get his clothes off.' Trixie smiled again. 'And then he suggested we went in to the bedroom. I must admit that I quite fancied him, up to that point.'

'What happened to change your mind, Miss Harper?'

'We'd spent about an hour screwing,' said Trixie in matter-of-fact tones, 'and we were lying there smoking a cigarette . . .' She paused to take a packet of cigarettes from a side table and offered one to Fox. 'And that's when he came up with this outrageous suggestion,' she continued, puffing smoke into the air.

'That you should become a prostitute?'

'Yah!' Trixie uttered the word with an upper-class drawl. 'He gave me some sob-story about being unemployed. He said that he could set me up in a decent apartment and arrange for some high-class clients. And that we could split the proceeds fifty-fifty.'

'What did you say to that?' asked Fox.

'I more or less told him to sod off, but he persisted, saying that it would be easy money. I said it might be for him, but I'd be the one on my back doing all the bloody work. He just laughed. So I thought I'd teach him a lesson. I grabbed a towel and went downstairs and out into the street. Then I started screaming my head off.'

'I see.' Fox had taken an instant dislike to Hope-Smith the moment he had met him and he was quite amused at the way Trixie Harper had sorted him out. But he was a police officer and couldn't really condone the false statement to the police that she had been raped by him. 'So the whole of your story to the police at Chelsea was a fabrication?'

'You did say that you didn't care what I'd said to them, didn't you?' Trixie inclined her head and smiled.

'Yes, I did . . .'

Fox must have sounded dubious. 'Actually I've just made all that up,' said Trixie and looked out of the window, an impish expression on her face.

Fox grinned. 'I shan't say anything to the Chelsea police, Miss Harper,' he said. 'It appears that no harm's been done, apart from giving Mr Hope-Smith an uncomfortable few days.' He knew that the Crown Prosecution Service would not consider proceedings on the grounds that the girl would undoubtedly change her story again at court. And apart from anything else, there would be an outcry that a girl who was *possibly* a victim of rape was being harried by the police. 'And did you see him again, after all this?'

'Only the once. We met on the stairs two days later. He threatened to beat me up if I didn't tell the police the truth.'

'Did you tell the police at Chelsea that he'd threatened you?'

'No. After all, he was right, wasn't he? I just upped and left. Moved in here.' A look of concern crossed Trixie's face. 'You won't tell him where I'm living, will you?'

Fox smiled and shook his head. 'Of course not,' he said.

'What d'you make of all that, guv'nor?' asked Evans on the way back to the Yard.

'I reckon the thing that really upset her was Hope-Smith's suggestion about the financial arrangements,' said Fox. 'Offering her only half of what she earned falls into my definition of a diabolical bloody liberty.'

Dick Campbell's secretary laid a sealed envelope on his desk. It was addressed to the Deputy Assistant Commissioner, Specialist Operations, and carried the injunction that it should only be opened by him.

'Just arrived from Commander Thomas of CIB, sir,' said the girl.

'Ah, that'll be the result of that ridiculous complaint against Tommy Fox, I suppose,' said Campbell and ripped open the envelope. For a few moments, he stared in disbelief at the latest entry on the minute sheet of the file that the envelope had contained, and then slung the file on the desk. 'I don't bloody believe it,' he said. 'Brenda, find out the times of trains and ferries to the Isle of Wight, will you?'

TWENTY

FOX HAD SENT FOR DI Findlater and instructed him to mount a surveillance on the Hayden Trust depot at Epsom and the premises of Carmody Trading Ltd at Hounslow. As usual, Findlater had mildly complained that he hadn't enough men, but that had had no impact whatsoever on Fox. Next Fox had sent DI Evans to Bow Street magistrates court to get search warrants in respect of the same two warehouses.

That done, he sat back and thought about his visit to the theatre with Jane Sims. When he had collected her from her flat – and later in the crush bar when he had bought her a drink – she had been bubbling over with excitement at seeing *Starlight Express* and had told him that she couldn't remember the last time that she had had an evening out. But her outfit of grey skirt and jumper, grey stockings and flat grey shoes had caused Fox to raise an eyebrow at what he considered to be her 'county' uniform. And he determined that he would have to persuade her, albeit gently, to make more of her attractive figure. The only relief to her greyness had been a white blouse, the collar of which peeped out over the neckline of her jumper.

'Denzil,' said Fox, when Evans returned from court, 'I think we'll pay Hope-Smith a visit. Rattle his bars for him a bit.'

Hope-Smith was not at all pleased to see Fox. After his recent experience at the hands of the police at Chelsea, he had, in fact, taken a violent dislike to detectives. With a bare minimum of civility, he invited Fox and Evans into his

175

sitting-room. 'Well,' he said truculently, 'and what d'you want this time?'

'The photographs of Dawn Sims,' said Fox. Evans shuddered inwardly.

'Er, what photographs?' The direct approach had obviously unnerved Hope-Smith. 'I don't know what you're talking about.'

'I'm talking about the obscene photographs that Dawn Sims gave you. Photographs of herself which can only be described, at best, as provocative.' Fox fixed Hope-Smith with a steely glare.

'How did you know I'd got them?' Hope-Smith's shoulders sagged with resignation as he walked across to a bureau and unlocked it. From an inner drawer, he withdrew copies of the six photographs that had been taken by John Wheeler, and handed them to Fox.

'I didn't,' said Fox and grinned. Evans breathed a sigh of relief. He didn't mind his governor taking risks, but he knew that Fox would always expect him to back him up. 'How many clients did you procure for Dawn Sims, as a matter of interest?' asked Fox, and Evans's breathing seized up once more.

'What makes you think—'

'Because she wasn't the last girl you suggested should go on the game to support you, was she?'

'Have you been talking to that damned stripper, Trixie what's-her-name?'

'Who's she?'

'She's the bloody woman who made that spurious allegation that I'd raped her,' said Hope-Smith.

'Oh, did you suggest that she turned to prostitution as well, then?' Fox gazed mildly at the unemployed oil man.

'You know bloody well I did,' said Hope-Smith angrily.

'Just answer the question,' said Fox. 'How many clients did you procure for Dawn Sims?'

'Look, I don't have to—'

'There is but a whisker between me talking to you here and conveying you to the nearest nick and continuing our conversation there,' said Fox. 'You haven't forgotten, I hope, that I am investigating the murder of Dawn Sims and right now, Jason dear boy, you are well and truly in the frame.'

'But I—'

'Because you knew her, you falsely claimed to be out of the country when she was murdered, you've been fiddling your income tax, you're in possession of obscene photographs of the murdered woman and you have attempted to turn other young women to prostitution so that you could live off their immoral earnings. And, on top of all that, you got the sack for running a brothel in Kuwait.' The last was a wild guess, but from what Evans had told Fox, it was probably nearer the truth than the story of the parties that Hope-Smith had organised.

White-faced, Hope-Smith sank into a chair. 'How the hell d'you know all that?' he gasped.

'Because I'm a detective,' said Fox. 'A very senior detective with a lifetime's experience of hunting down the unrighteous, most of whom, I may say, make you seem like a rank amateur. Now are you going to answer the question, or am I going to nick you for murder?' He leaned back in his chair and waited.

'Oh Christ!' said Hope-Smith, running his hands through his hair. 'I seem to have got into a load of bother here, don't I?'

'And I've only just begun, dear boy,' said Fox mildly.

'It was her idea.'

'Who are we talking about now?'

'Dawn.' Hope-Smith gestured towards the photographs resting on the coffee table. 'She gave me those. Her old man cut off her allowance, you see, and she was desperate for money. She wanted to see if I could sell them. She said she had lots of copies.'

'And did you?'

'One or two, but we didn't get much for them. Pictures like that are dirt cheap in Soho. After all, you can buy the same sort of thing in almost any corner-shop newsagent's now.'

'So you suggested that she went on the game, is that it?' Fox went on relentlessly.

Hope-Smith put his elbows on his knees and pressed his

head between his hands. Then he looked up. 'It was her idea,' he said, 'but she didn't know where to start.'

'So you pointed her in the right direction, I suppose?'

'More or less, yes. I said that I could find some high-class clients who'd be willing to pay for her services. She'd got a good flat, you see.'

'So I saw,' said Fox drily.

'And I started to make contacts for her.'

'Crummy little civil servants like Harry Barnes, you mean?'

Hope-Smith looked at Fox with an air of desperation on his face. 'I can't remember the names,' he said.

'Well you'd better start remembering,' said Fox. 'Because they're all murder suspects, along with you.'

'I didn't kill her,' said Hope-Smith. 'She was a lovely girl.'

'So lovely that you were willing to send her out on the streets,' said Fox. That was a deliberate exaggeration; there was some difference between entertaining clients in a cosy flat and working a King's Cross beat. 'How many clients did you introduce to her?'

'About six, I think.'

'You think? And who were they?'

'I honestly can't remember their—'

'Oh come now, Mr Hope-Smith. Where did you find these men?'

'West End clubs mainly.'

'How did you approach them? Go touting round the tables, did you?'

'No. If I met someone who looked as though he'd got some money and was on the lookout for a good time, I'd offer to put him in touch with Dawn. And I'd suggest that he gave her a gift.' Hope-Smith gave Fox an imploring look, willing him to believe what he was saying. 'They all knew what giving her a gift meant.'

'Did you suggest an amount?'

Hope-Smith nodded miserably. 'Depended on what I thought they could afford,' he said. 'But it was usually upwards of two or three hundred pounds. I remember on one occasion I met an Arab I'd known in Kuwait who was

178

over here on a business trip. I suggested to him that the price was a thousand. He didn't argue. We had champagne that night.'

Fox stood up. 'You're just a stinking little pimp really, aren't you, Smith?' he said, intentionally omitting the first half of Hope-Smith's hyphenated name.

'I'm not happy about Hope-Smith,' said Fox, when he and Evans had returned to the Yard. 'He's a lying little toad.'

'Are you going to nick him, guv?' asked Evans.

'No, Denzil. At least not yet. He's getting over-confident. Thinks he's got away with it, you see.'

'Got away with what, sir?'

'I don't know, Denzil,' said Fox. 'That's the problem. But he's been up to more than he's admitted, that's for sure.'

'Supposing he does a runner, guv?' said Evans. 'After all, he's disappeared before.'

'You can't run away from a name like Jason Hope-Smith,' said Fox.

'So you're John James Stedman,' said DAC Campbell as he gazed at the piece of human detritus that lounged in the chair of the interview room at Parkhurst Prison.

'Yeah, that's right.'

'Good. Well perhaps you'd care to explain what that load of toffee's all about.' Campbell threw Stedman's letter of complaint on the table.

'It's a complaint. About that other copper what come down here and—'

'I can read, and I can also read what the law says about wasting police time,' said Campbell nastily. 'It seems to me that you're just sitting here in Parkhurst whiling away your time by making false complaints that have no foundation whatever.'

'So what you going to do? Have me up in court and get me fined? Cos I ain't got no money.' Stedman gave Campbell a surly grin.

'That's it exactly,' said Campbell. 'Except that it won't be a fine. They'll just tack a bit on the end of your ten years. Then I'll have a word with a friend of mine in the Prison

Department at the Home Office and get you moved to Barlinnie.' The fact that the prison most hated by the criminal fraternity was in Scotland, and not therefore administered by the Home Office, was a factor that did not lessen the impact of Campbell's empty threat. He knew that Stedman wouldn't know much about the internal workings of Her Majesty's Government.

'Now look—' Stedman sat up, an anxious look on his face.

'I take it you wish to withdraw this complaint?' asked Campbell.

'Well, if you think that'd be best . . .' said a worried Stedman.

Campbell grinned. 'I think it would, friend,' he said. 'And I don't suppose that we'll be hearing from you again, will we?' It wasn't really a question.

Crozier drove the blue Commer van out of the Hayden Trust depot at Epsom and on to the main road. After he had driven half a mile, he glanced in the driving mirror and was pleased to see one of Henry Findlater's motor-cyclists on his tail. Fortunately for the arrangements that Fox needed to put in hand, the traffic was heavy and it took Crozier nearly two hours to reach Carmody's warehouse at Hounslow.

Once again, Carmody appeared on the forecourt and supervised the loading of Crozier's van with a mixture of stores that was much the same as before.

But then it all started to go wrong. For Carmody. As Crozier got back into the driving seat, two Vauxhall Carltons swept round the rear of the premises and blocked the exit. The next moment, the warehouse was teeming with Flying Squad officers, led by DI Evans, who had paused only long enough to send a radio message to Fox saying that the raid had begun.

'Here, what the bloody hell—?' began Carmody, but in his heart, he knew what was happening. He had experienced this sort of thing before. Many times.

'Flying Squad,' said Evans tersely, 'and we have a warrant to search these premises.' He waved a printed form under Carmody's nose.

180

'You won't find sod-all here, copper,' said Carmody. It was a show of bravado. He knew fine that there was enough evidence in the warehouse to send him back to prison once more. For a substantial stretch.

'If that's the case,' said Evans, 'you've got nothing to worry about. Righto, lads, get to it,' he added to his team.

Straightaway, the members of Evans's group of detectives fanned out all over the warehouse, examining its stock and taking careful note of serial numbers, batch numbers and any other data that they hoped would identify the contents of the heavily-laden shelves as stolen property.

After an hour of feverish activity, Evans turned to Carmody and his four assistants. 'You're nicked,' he said. 'Possession of stolen property.' And he threw in a caution, just for good measure. Evans was a careful policeman.

Fox had not needed to tell Detective Inspector Gilroy how to position his cars to prevent any escape from the Hayden Trust depot and now, with Gilroy beside him, he strolled nonchalantly into the small office in the corner of the warehouse.

'Who the bloody hell are you?' asked Tinsley. He was bristling with rage at this incursion into his domain. An incursion that had occurred without his consent. Tinsley was very proprietorial when it came to the supervision of the Epsom depot.

'Thomas Fox . . . of the Flying Squad.' Fox smiled disconcertingly at the depot overseer. 'And you I take it are Alec Tinsley, company quartermaster sergeant – retired?'

Ignoring Fox for a moment, Tinsley strode to the doors of the warehouse and glared at the Flying Squad cars and the group of detectives who were waiting to be unleashed. Then he turned back to Fox. 'What's the meaning of this?' he demanded truculently.

'The meaning of this, old dear, is that I am about to execute a search warrant in respect of these premises in my unending quest for stolen property.'

'Oh, are you? I suppose you know who owns this set-up,

181

do you?' Tinsley waved an arm as if to encompass the entire warehouse, and then thrust his hand into the pockets of his grey warehouse coat.

'Mr Frederick Hayden, according to my usually trustworthy informants,' said Fox.

'That's right,' said Tinsley, 'and he ain't going to be best pleased when he hears about this.'

'I think that goes without saying,' said Fox, and turning to Gilroy, added, 'You may begin, Jack.'

'Mr Hayden's got friends in high places,' said Tinsley, 'and he can bring influence to bear.'

'Is that a fact?' said Fox as he watched Gilroy's team of detectives setting about a thorough search of the warehouse stock. 'Tell me, Alec old thing, just to save us a lot of time and trouble – both of us, that is – perhaps you'd be so good as to tell me where you keep the gear that Carmody sends you.'

'Who?'

Fox sighed. 'Oh well,' he said. 'We can do it the hard way, if that's what you want.'

An hour later, when Gilroy's men had found ample evidence that the warehouse contained huge quantities of stolen property, Swann, Fox's driver, ambled in. 'Mr Evans is on the radio, guv,' he said. 'Wants a word.'

'Got five bodies, guv,' said Evans once Fox had made contact with him. 'Where d'you want them?'

'Take them to Charing Cross nick, Denzil. I rather like that place. It's got couth.'

'How did you get on, guv?' asked Evans.

'Splendidly, Denzil dear boy,' said Fox. 'I've got about six prisoners to add to the collection, including the odious Mr Tinsley.'

The arrival of Detective Chief Superintendent Fox and eleven prisoners at Charing Cross Police Station did nothing to improve the mood of the custody sergeant. Out of Fox's hearing, he mumbled about the arrests not having been taken to the nearest police station, and went on to complain about the job not being the same as when he had joined it some twenty years previously.

Despite that, the prisoners were duly processed and placed in the cells until Fox decided that he felt like questioning them. 'Let me see your list, Denzil,' he said, having taken over half the CID office. And he settled himself at the desk of an ousted detective sergeant and started to peruse the details of the stolen property that Evans had found in Carmody's slaughter. And where it remained, under guard, until arrangements could be made for its transfer to the bulk property store of the Metropolitan Police.

'Enjoy your trip to the Isle of Wight, sir?' asked DAC Campbell's secretary.

'Yes and no,' said Campbell. 'Bring your book in, Brenda. I want to dictate a report. A short report.'

Brenda sat down in a chair opposite Dick Campbell's desk and crossed her legs. Then she opened her shorthand notebook and waited, pencil poised.

'I refer to the Deputy Commissioner's minute and to the complaint, at 1A hereon, made by John James Stedman. . .' Campbell glanced up. 'Stick his CRO number in there, Brenda.' The girl nodded. '. . . a prisoner serving ten years in Parkhurst Prison for robbery. I have this day interviewed Stedman who, after a short discussion, expressed the wish to withdraw his complaint.' He handed the file to his secretary. 'Date it today and I'll sign it before I go home,' he said.

'What's the plan of campaign, sir?' asked Gilroy.

'I think we'll have Vincent Carmody out of his nice warm cell and give him a bit of a talking to,' said Fox. 'And if his answers come up to snuff, I daresay that you and I will be taking a trip to Putney there to lay hands on Sliding Dawes.' Fox rubbed his hands together. 'I've been waiting for this day for a long time, Jack,' he added.

'But supposing he doesn't grass on Dawes, sir?' asked Gilroy.

Fox shook his head in bewilderment. 'Jack, you're such a pessimist,' he said. 'I can't understand why you never became an accountant.'

TWENTY ONE

FOX CAST AN EAGER GLANCE at Vincent Carmody as
though he were some rare specimen of biological interest
that he had been allowed to examine. 'Fancy you getting
yourself captured again.'

'I want my brief,' said Carmody. It was the standard
response of any villain the moment he reached the
interview stage. Particularly when it was Tommy Fox
doing the interviewing.

Fox nodded. 'Daresay you do,' he said. 'In fact, I'd go
further. Right now, you are in desperate need of legal
advice.'

'Well then?'

'But first,' said Fox, 'we'll have a little chat.'

'I want to make a phone call,' said Carmody. 'It's my
right.'

'Yes, I think you're probably correct there, Vince. Just
jot the number down on this piece of paper and I'll ensure
that one of my officers puts you in touch with your chosen
subscriber forthwith.'

Carmody took Fox's pencil and scribbled down a
number. Then he leaned back, a triumphant sneer on his
face, convinced that the Metropolitan Police had, indeed,
changed its ways.

Fox examined the slip of paper and roared with
laughter. 'You are joking, aren't you, Vince?' he said.

'Why? What's wrong with that?'

'Only that it happens to be Sliding Dawes's phone
number, old son. And if you think I'm letting you warn
him that he's about to be nicked, you've got another think
coming.'

'How d'you know that?' Carmody looked unhappy.

Fox shook his head. 'Mind you, ' he said, 'I'm not sure that Dawes'd be charged even if we did nick him.' He turned to Gilroy. 'There's really no evidence to link Harry Dawes with this particular bit of villainy, is there, Jack? I reckon that our Vincent's been going it alone.' He turned to face Carmody again. 'This little lot is firmly down to you, isn't it, Vincent, old son?'

'No, it bleedin' ain't,' said Carmody and then stopped, realising that he had just fallen into the trap that Fox had set for him.

'All in all, Vince . . .' Fox continued as though Carmody had not butted in. '. . . I think the worse thing you could do is to tell Harry you've been nicked. He might think that you're trying to take over his business. Apart from anything else, it'd spoil his holiday.'

'What holiday?' Carmody gave Fox a suspicious glance.

'Oh, didn't you know?' said Fox as he started to weave his latest piece of fiction. 'Off to the South of France is our Harry. Said something about needing to winter in the sunshine. Well, at his age, I suppose it's essential. Nice to get away from the fog and frost of London. The cold plays havoc with old bones, you know.'

'You're not going to let him do a runner, are you?' Carmody appeared appalled at the prospect that the police seemed prepared to let Dawes escape.

'Has he committed some crime then?' asked Fox airily, and gave Carmody an enquiring glance that did little to comfort him.

'I ain't saying nothing.' Carmody lapsed into a moody silence, aware of the dangers of informing on the likes of Harry Dawes.

'All right then.' Fox stood up. 'Put him down, Jack,' he said, 'and we'll have a chat with Mr Tinsley, well-known old soldier and co-conspirator with our Vincent here.'

Carmody was about to protest at this latest allegation of Fox's, but changed his mind and allowed himself to be led back to his cell.

Alec Tinsley was bristling with indignation when he was brought into the interview room. Divested of his warehouse coat when he was arrested, he was now attired in a brown chalk-striped suit with wide lapels and wide-bottomed trousers.

Fox surveyed this latest affront to his concept of sartorial elegance with a frown. 'I didn't realise they were still handing out demob suits,' he said. 'Or is that an exhibit on loan from the Imperial War Museum?'

'I'm pissed off with the way I'm being treated here,' said Tinsley. 'I know my rights. Twenty-five years I spent in the army, and I know what's what.'

'Quartermaster sergeant, weren't you?' asked Fox, lighting himself a cigarette.

'That's right.'

'Mmm!' said Fox. 'Didn't get far in twenty-five years, did you? I met a general the other day with that amount of service.'

'I want Mr Hayden to be informed,' said Tinsley. 'He'll have one of his lawyers down here in no time at all.'

'I wouldn't bank on that, old son. I think he's already taken the view that you've besmirched the reputation of his charity.' Fox lowered his voice. 'And I have reason to believe that there are things in the offing for Mr Hayden that might well be prejudiced if it became known that some of his employees were at it.'

'What's that mean?'

'If you don't know,' said Fox, 'I'm afraid that I'm not at liberty to divulge that information. However, suffice it to say that not only does Mr Hayden deny that you work for him, he claims never to have heard of you.' That was another of Fox's fabrications. He had no intention of speaking to Freddie Hayden until the eleven prisoners that were locked up at Charing Cross had been interviewed. 'Let me put the facts to you plainly, Alec, old sport. My officers and I examined the stock of the warehouse that you look after, and a substantial quantity of that stock was the proceeds of several robberies that have taken place over the last few months. And as you are in charge of it, it's down to you.'

But Tinsley's twenty-five years in the army had taught him one thing: when things go wrong, blame someone else. 'I didn't know nothing about that,' he said. 'But it might interest you to know that a bloke what was taken on recently, name of Crozier, has just come out of prison. Done five years for burglary.'

'Yes, I know about him,' said Fox. 'He's one of my detective sergeants and the only nicking he's done is of blokes like you.'

'What?' Tinsley was clearly outraged at this deception. 'I don't believe it.'

Fox stood up. 'I don't know why I'm wasting my time talking to you,' he said. 'There's ample evidence to charge you with handling stolen property, and that's what I intend to charge you with. For starters.'

'Hold on,' said Tinsley. 'I ain't having this on my own. There's others.'

Fox sat down again. 'Now that, Alec, seems to me to be the most sensible thing you've said since arriving at this wonderful police station.' He paused. 'Well?'

'One of the directors organised it all. I never knew that this gear was bent.'

Fox nodded amiably. 'I suppose, Alec, old fruit, that with your vast experience of accounting for military stores, you can spot a fiddle a mile off?'

'Too bloody right I can,' said Tinsley.

'Funny you missed this one then.' Fox cast a despairing glance at Gilroy before looking back at Tinsley. 'Who is this director then?'

For a moment or two, Tinsley remained silent. Then, reaffirming his earlier decision that if he was going down, one or two others would join him, he said, 'His name's Skinner, Peter Skinner.'

'And where does he fit in?' asked Fox.

'He's a trustee of the charity. And he's a director of one of Hayden's companies.' Tinsley now adopted a whining tone. 'I was only doing what he told me. He said that some of the donors to the charity didn't want to be identified and we had to collect the stuff through an intermediate.'

'I think you mean intermediary,' murmured Fox. 'And where will I find this Mr Skinner, Alec, old friend?'

'He's at head office. Same place as Mr Hayden.'

'Splendid,' said Fox. 'I can see that I shall have to talk to him. In the meantime, I suggest that you go back to your cell and study the racing page. My informants tell me that *Condominium* in the two o'clock at Lingfield Park is a bit of a goer. Might be the only bit of luck you get this year. Or next, for that matter.'

'Well,' said Fox, when he was back in his office at New Scotland Yard, 'that all went very satisfactorily.' He beamed at Gilroy and Evans. 'And now, gentlemen,' he continued, 'I think that the time has come to nick Sliding Dawes.'

'What about this bloke Skinner, guv?' asked Gilroy.

'He'll keep, Jack. We'll deal with Sliding Dawes first.' Fox rubbed his hands together. 'What I want you to do, Denzil, is to take a team down to what Dawes thinks is his secret slaughter at Croydon and give it a spin. I'll give you an hour, by which time Jack and I will be talking to Dawes, who, Henry Findlater tells me, is at home, and let me know the result. If it's as I anticipate, we'll bring laughing Harry Dawes back to Charing Cross and pop him in with the rest. Then we'll see what Carmody has to say about that.'

Fox's Ford Granada, with Swann at the wheel, drew up outside Harry Dawes's house and stopped. For a good ten minutes, Fox sat in the passenger seat, watching. He had confirmed with one of Findlater's surveillance team, who was stationed at the bottom of Oxford Road, that Dawes hadn't moved since the last report that Fox had received.

During the time that Fox was waiting, the curtains of Harry Dawes's front-room window had been twitched aside and the nervous face of the old fence had peered out. Fox had waved, but had not seen Dawes pick up the telephone.

Minutes later, a white police car – its blue lights flashing – swept into the street from the Putney Bridge Road end and stopped so that its front bumper was almost touching the front bumper of Fox's car. Fox gazed out mildly at this latest example of fast police response.

Leaving his uniform cap in the car, the wireless operator

alighted and, hands in pockets, strolled in leisurely fashion to the window nearest Fox.

Fox wound down the window. 'Hallo,' he said.

'What's your bloody game?' asked the policeman.

'Well, I used to play squash in my younger days,' said Fox, 'but my doctor advised me to give it up. Contrary to popular opinion, it seems that it can actually induce a heart attack rather than preventing one. But if you want to talk about games, my driver Swann here is a dab hand at poker.' He glanced across at Swann. 'That's right, isn't it, Swann?'

'Yes, guv,' mumbled Swann.

'What are you doing hanging about here, apart from trying to make smart remarks? We've had a call about suspects loitering from—'

'From Harry Dawes, well-known, but alas unconvicted, handler of stolen property,' said Fox. 'That, however, is about to change,' he added and produced his warrant card. 'Now, constable, I suggest that you put your cap on and go away. You're making the place look untidy.'

The uniformed PC gulped, and would have saluted but for the absence of his headgear. 'I'm sorry, sir,' he said, 'I didn't know that you were—'

'Goodbye,' said Fox, 'and don't ever be tempted to apply for the Department, will you,' he added as the PC turned away. 'You haven't got what it takes.'

Waiting until the police car had left, Fox and Gilroy walked up the path of Dawes's house and rang the bell.

The frightened face of Harry Dawes peered round the half-opened door. 'Oh, it's you, Mr Fox,' he said.

'Yes,' said Fox. 'I'm responding to your call for police. Something to do with suspects loitering?' He placed a finger on Dawes's chest and propelled him slowly backwards. 'Shall we adjourn to your day room, Harry?'

'I didn't know it was you, Mr Fox. I just looked out and saw—'

'Don't tell me, Harry. You saw what you firmly believed to be someone of villainous intent hanging about, doubtless with the desire to do you some harm?'

'That's right, Mr Fox.' Dawes afforded himself a bleak smile.

'Well, you got that right, Harry,' said Fox.

'Would you like a cup of—' began Dawes but then the phone rang. 'It's for you, Mr Fox,' he said when he had answered it.

After a short conversation, Fox replaced the receiver and looked sorrowfully at Dawes. 'I'm afraid I've got some bad news for you, Harry, old son,' he said.

'Oh?' Dawes looked up at Fox from the recesses of his Rexine-covered armchair.

'I'm sorry to have to tell you,' began Fox, not looking at all sorry, 'that some of my officers have just turned over your slaughter down at Croydon and found all manner of bent gear. Almost the first name that your general manager uttered when he was nicked was yours, Harry. In fact, his exact words were, "This is all down to that bastard Harry Dawes".'

'I'll kill him,' said Dawes, clenching and unclenching his fists and then picking violently at the trim on the arms of his chair.

'You'll ruin the upholstery, Harry, if you do that,' said Fox. 'Am I to take it,' he went on, 'that your manager has not altogether pleased you by his desire to join your name with his on the indictment? He was called Pratt, by the way. Seemed eminently suitable, I thought. It even brought a smile to Detective Inspector Evans's face, and he doesn't laugh easily, I can tell you.'

'I don't know what this is all about, Mr Fox, honest. This bloke's trying to fit me up for some reason. It's bloody obvious, isn't it?' Dawes looked hopefully at Fox's smiling face but found no comfort there.

Fox nodded slowly. 'You may well be right, Harry,' he said. 'All the same, I'm arresting you for handling stolen property.' He stood up and then paused as if struck by a sudden, but long forgotten thought. 'And there's still the little question of the body we found in your lock-up at Lambeth to sort out.'

'Mr Skinner? This is Detective Chief Superintendent Thomas Fox . . . of the Flying Squad.' Fox purred down the telephone at his unctuous best.

'Oh, right. How can I help you, Chief Superintendent?'

'One of your employees has got into a bit of trouble, Mr Skinner. He claims to work at the Hayden Trust depot at Epsom, and I'm told that you're one of the trustees.' Fox knew that it was most unlikely that Skinner had got to hear of that morning's events. Police had been guarding the warehouses at both Epsom and Hounslow since the raids. And Ron Crozier had stayed there to answer any phones that may have rung.

'Yes, that's right. I am a trustee. Who is this fellow?'

'I don't think it would be a very good idea to discuss it on the phone, Mr Skinner—'

'No, perhaps not. Why don't you—'

'And I think it would be even less wise for me to call at your office,' said Fox, forestalling Skinner's next suggestion. 'You know how people talk and it's almost impossible to keep a secret in a big office building like yours. Supposing you meet me at Charing Cross Police Station and we can have a quiet word?'

'Ah, yes, I suppose so. Charing Cross Police Station, did you say?'

'Yes indeed.'

'Where is that exactly, Chief Superintendent?' asked Skinner.

'Charing Cross,' said Fox.

To his delight, Fox had discovered that the detective superintendent at Charing Cross Police Station only drank what Fox called proper coffee. And Fox was sitting in the superintendent's office drinking some of it when the station officer rang from the front counter.

'There's a Mr Skinner here to see you, sir.'

'Splendid,' said Fox. 'Pop him in the interview room and tell him I'll be with him shortly.' He replaced the receiver and took his time to finish both his coffee and his cigarette.

Peter Skinner was in his early forties and overweight. He had the look of a man who had a top-of-the-range company car and played golf and squash because he thought it was good for his image.

'I'm Thomas Fox . . . of the Flying Squad. We spoke on

191

the phone.' Fox seized Skinner's hand in a vice-like grip and was pleased to see that he winced.

'What's this problem you were telling me about?' asked Skinner.

'We arrested a man called Tinsley this morning,' said Fox, offering Skinner a cigarette.

Skinner shook his head. 'I don't, thank you. What was he arrested for?'

'Possession of stolen property.'

'Good grief! Just goes to show, doesn't it?'

'Just goes to show what, Mr Skinner?'

'Took that fellow on from the army. You'd think that a man who'd been a quartermaster could be trusted, wouldn't you?'

'Yes indeed,' said Fox, whose instincts told him that it would be most unwise to trust a quartermaster.

'What are the circumstances?' asked Skinner.

'The circumstances, Mr Skinner, are that police raided your depot at Epsom this morning and seized a substantial quantity of stolen property. Your Mr Tinsley, so I'm given to understand, manages the set-up there.'

'That's so.' Skinner gently teased his moustache and looked thoughtful as his brain moved into top gear.

'Mr Tinsley, however, seemed unaware that the property had, in fact, been stolen.' Fox gently rolled cigarette ash into the ashtray.

'Well, I don't understand that.' Skinner looked suitably baffled. 'If you don't mind my asking, Chief Superintendent, what caused you to look there in the first place?'

'Oh, that's easy,' said Fox. 'We'd been keeping the depot under observation and found that supplies were being regularly conveyed to it from a repository of stolen property in Hounslow which calls itself Carmody Trading Ltd. Vincent Carmody, who claims to be its managing director, is an old friend of police—'

'You mean he's an informant, or whatever you call them?'

'No, it means that we've nicked him many times before, Mr Skinner, for offences related to dishonesty,' said Fox. 'To say nothing of several convictions for crimes of violence.' He sat back in his chair and smiled.

'Good grief!' said Skinner again. 'And you mean to say that this man Tinsley has been running this racket under our very noses?'

'Not quite, Mr Skinner. He claims that it was masterminded by you.'

TWENTY TWO

FOX HAD PERUSED THAT MORNING'S edition of *The Times* while drinking a cup of coffee and was about to leave for Charing Cross Police Station when the phone rang. 'Fox,' he said.

'It's the Back Hall PC here, sir. There's a Mr Hayden to see you, with his lawyer.'

'How kind of him to call,' said Fox. 'I'll be down. By the way, is my car on the front?'

'One moment, sir.' The PC stood up and peered out of the window at Fox's Ford Granada, behind which was parked a chocolate-brown Rolls-Royce with a liveried chauffeur at the wheel. 'Yes, it is, sir,' he said.

When Fox arrived in Back Hall, as the main entrance to New Scotland Yard is perversely known, Hayden was reading the Roll of Honour. Next to him stood a man in a dark suit. 'Mr Hayden, good morning,' said Fox.

'Ah, Mr Fox.' Hayden shook hands. 'This is my solicitor,' he said, but did not furnish his lawyer's name.

'What can I do for you, Mr Hayden?' Fox gave a nod of brief acknowledgement to the solicitor.

Hayden looked around the crowded entrance hall. 'Is there somewhere we can talk in private?' he asked.

'Of course.' Fox led the two men into one of the suite of interview rooms near the Yard's Press Bureau and closed the door. 'I'm afraid the accommodation's a little meagre in here,' he said. He indicated a couple of chairs but Hayden and his lawyer remained standing.

'I'll get straight to the point, Mr Fox,' said Hayden. 'I've heard the distressing news about your raid on the charity's depot at Epsom yesterday when Tinsley was arrested—'

194

'I expect you have,' said Fox with a smile.

'I'm absolutely shocked at what I heard from Skinner, who, incidentally, is in overall charge of the operation. I need hardly say what a devastating effect this will have on the reputation of the Hayden Trust.'

'I imagine so,' murmured Fox.

Hayden appeared to deliberate. 'I was wondering, that is to say, we were wondering . . .' he began tentatively, indicating his solicitor with a gesture of the hand. 'We were wondering whether there was any chance of keeping it quiet . . . for the sake of the charity, of course.'

'Naturally,' said Fox. 'But your solicitor will tell you, I'm sure, that once Tinsley gets into the witness box, he can more or less say what he likes. And the evidence that will have to be adduced to secure a conviction must of necessity identify the Hayden Trust.' He smiled, first at Hayden and then at the solicitor.

'Supposing he were to plead guilty, Mr Fox?'

'In that case,' said Fox, 'only the brief facts need be given, I suppose. Rather depends on the judge. Some of them want it all dragged out, you know.'

'I see. Would you have any objection to my solicitor interviewing this awful man Tinsley? He'll be acting for him, you see. Not that I hold any brief for Tinsley, you'll understand, but purely for the sake of the charity.'

'No objection at all, Mr Hayden.'

'That's very kind of you.' Hayden moved closer to Fox, turning has back towards his solicitor. 'That letter I showed you, Mr Fox,' he said lowering his voice, 'from Number Ten. D'you remember?'

'Oh yes,' said Fox. 'I remember.'

'I'm told that it's to be announced in the Queen's Birthday Honours List in June. Only heard it unofficially, of course, but you'll understand that if this business about the depot at Epsom gets out, it could ruin everything.'

'Yes,' said Fox, 'I imagine it could.'

'Funny thing happened yesterday, Vince,' said Fox as he strolled into the interview room.

'Really?' said Carmody who failed to see any humour in

195

anything which had occurred in the preceding twenty-four hours.

'Oh yes.' Fox offered Carmody a cigarette. 'Quite by coincidence, we raided a slaughter down at Croydon and then arrested old Harry Dawes. Bang to rights. There, Vince, what d'you think of that?'

Carmody laughed. 'Serve him bloody right,' he said.

'I don't blame you for saying that, Vince,' said Fox. 'D'you know, he even had the audacity to try and put it all down to you?' Behind Fox, Gilroy stared at the ceiling.

'He did what?' Carmody was unable to control the fury in his voice. 'The bastard.'

'He's not you know. During the course of our enquiries, we examined his birth certificate and he definitely had a father. But I do understand the sentiments of your comment, Vince, dear boy.'

'You ain't heard nothing yet,' said Carmody. 'I want to make a statement.'

'What about?' Fox gave a convincing impression of being mildly surprised.

'About bloody Dawes. I know my name's on the door, but he's the one who was really running that outfit down at Hounslow.'

Fox scoffed. 'You don't expect me to believe that, surely?'

'Well, you'd better, copper, because I'm going to give you chapter and verse.'

'Oh well, if you insist.' Fox shrugged and turned to Gilroy. 'Better turn on the machine, Jack. Vincent here wishes to broadcast to the nation. In the meantime, I'll go and have another chat to the quartermaster. If he's finished talking to his brief.'

Alec Tinsley was slouched in a chair in the neighbouring interview room when Fox walked in. 'Did you manage to get a bet on that horse at Lingfield, Alec?' he asked. 'I see it came in at five-to-one.'

'What, in here? Some bloody hopes,' said Tinsley.

'Oh?' Fox sounded surprised. 'Obviously gaolers are clean-living young men these days,' he said. 'I understand that Mr Hayden's solicitor paid you a visit this morning.'

'Yes, he bloody did,' said Tinsley angrily. 'Saucy bastard

wants me to plead guilty. Even offered me two grand to do it.'

'Sounds reasonable,' said Fox. 'After all, you are guilty, aren't you?'

'Maybe, but so's that bloody Skinner.'

'Did you mention Skinner to your brief?'

'No. I thought I'd wait and mention him to you.'

'You did that yesterday,' said Fox, 'and I had a talk with him, here. Seemed quite a nice chap. Couldn't understand how a trustworthy fellow like you should suddenly go bent. Hotly denied his involvement, of course. I got the impression that he may sue you for slander.'

Tinsley leaned forward, an earnest expression on his face. 'I was in the army too long to put up with that sort of crap,' he said. 'And I'm not having some toffee-nosed bastard like Skinner trying to swing this lot on me.'

'So what did you have in mind, Alec, old son?'

'I'm going to tell you all about it,' said Tinsley, and sat back with a self-satisfied smile on his face.

When Fox got back to his office at New Scotland Yard, there was a message asking him to see Commander Myers.

'There's a file for you to see, Tommy,' said Myers as Fox entered the commander's office.

'Another one?' asked Fox gloomily. 'I've got them stacked up in my office.'

'Well, you will go marauding about the capital arresting people,' said Myers. 'You're supposed to stay in your office and deal with the paperwork, you know. Now that you're part of the management team.'

'The management team?' growled Fox. 'What d'you think I'm running, sir, a bloody department store or something? I joined this job to nick villains, not to push paper. And there's no management team in my set-up. I'm the guv'nor. I make the decisions and I take the can back when it all goes wrong.'

Myers shook his head wearily. He knew that he would never convince Fox. 'Talking of things going wrong, Tommy, how's the Dawn Sims murder enquiry going? The Commissioner's getting a bit anxious about it. Apparently the Home Secretary's been on to him as well.'

Fox shrugged. 'We are pursuing our enquiries with vigour, sir,' he said.

'You mean you're not getting anywhere?'

'You know how to be cruel, guv, don't you?' said Fox.

Myers grinned. 'This is the result of the complaint made against you by Stedman, Tommy,' he said, handing the file to Fox.

Fox glanced briefly at the last entry on the minute sheet and grinned before laying the file on Myers's desk. 'I should bloody think so too,' he said. 'But I'm surprised that Commander Willow managed to get all the way down to Parkhurst.'

'Oh, why's that?'

'Well, they call him the eternal flame at One Area Headquarters, guv.'

'Why?'

'He never goes out,' said Fox and strode back to his office.

'There was a call for you, sir,' said a DC who was just emerging from Fox's office. 'I've left a note on your desk. Would you telephone Lady Jane Sims.' The DC seemed impressed.

'Tommy, I'm so glad you could come. I hope I'm not making a nuisance of myself.' Jane Sims had invited Fox to her flat for supper. She had told him that she was feeling a bit low-spirited and needed cheering up.

'Not at all.'

'I was afraid that you might be tied up with some crime or another.' Jane poured out drinks and sat down opposite Fox.

'Good heavens no,' said Fox. 'Why should you think that?'

'Well, isn't that what happens? I'm always hearing about policemen who have to break appointments with their wife or girlfriend because something's cropped up. Supposing that Dawn's murderer had been arrested just as you were leaving? You'd've had to rush off and deal with it, wouldn't you?'

'Certainly not,' said Fox, taking a sip of his whisky. 'I'd have had him banged up in a cell and dealt with him in the morning. You've been watching too much television, my girl.'

Jane smiled. 'I've only prepared something simple,' she said. 'I'm afraid that I'm not a very good cook.'

Fox glanced across at the black glass-topped dining table and was glad to see that there were no candles on it. Staged, candle-lit suppers did not appeal to him. But the napery and glassware were obviously of good quality. 'I'm sure it'll be fine,' he said.

'I really enjoyed seeing *Starlight Express* the other night,' said Jane. 'It was kind of you to take me. I've felt down in the dumps what with Dawn being killed, and then Daddy dying. And now James has gone back to America, I feel rather lonely.'

'Go out and spend some money,' said Fox. 'Buy yourself some clothes. That's the way women cheer themselves up, isn't it?'

Jane looked at Fox with a pensive expression. Despite having asked Fox for supper, she was, once more, wearing jeans and a sweater. 'Does that mean that you don't like the clothes I wear, Tommy?' she asked.

Fox hadn't liked the way she had dressed for their evening out, but he didn't think that this was the time to say so. 'Whatever makes you think that?'

'When you picked me up to go to the theatre the other night, I got the distinct impression that you thought my outfit was dowdy.' Jane smiled at him and took a sip of whisky. 'Perhaps you'd open the white wine,' she said.

'Of course. In the fridge, is it?' Fox stood up and walked through to Jane's tiny kitchen.

'I can't really be bothered with clothes,' said Jane from the sitting-room as Fox searched around for a corkscrew.

'Well, you should.' Fox drew the cork from the Chardonnay. 'You've got the body and the colouring that deserve stylish clothes.'

In the sitting-room, Jane felt a frisson of excitement at the compliment, but did not respond to it. 'I never know where to go,' she said. 'I always seem to be too busy to bother.'

Fox placed the wine in the cooler on the dining table

and sat down opposite Jane. 'What d'you mean, too busy?'

'What I say. I'm a partner in a busy architectural practice, Tommy. I'm on the go most of the time.'

'Never let the job get on top of you, that's my policy and always has been.' Fox stood up and took Jane's glass. 'Get you another?'

Jane nodded. 'Yes, please.'

'Take a day off,' said Fox as he poured out more whisky, 'and spend it in Harvey Nichols or Harrods. Or in some of those boutiques in Kensington. Whatever you do, Jane, don't let yourself go, just because your father's died and Dawn has been murdered.' He grinned as he handed her her glass. 'And you can tell me to mind my own business if you like, but that's what I think.'

'You know, Tommy,' said Jane, smiling at him, 'there are times when you sound just like a policeman.'

The statements which Carmody and Tinsley had made were on Fox's desk, along with a cup of coffee, when he arrived at the Yard the following morning. Lighting his first cigarette of the day, he sipped slowly at his coffee and read through the statements. Carmody had put all the blame for his unfortunate predicament on Dawes, and Tinsley had done the same for Skinner. Only Skinner remained at large, but Fox decided that that situation would be remedied forthwith. He sent for Evans.

'Denzil, pop out and nick Peter Skinner, will you. Better get a warrant for conspiring with others to handle stolen property.'

Peter Skinner was one of those men who was full of bravado until the chips were down. Then he crumbled. He made none of the demands to see his solicitor that Fox's usual customers made, neither did he claim not to know what Fox was talking about. Nor did he decline to say anything. In fact, Skinner couldn't wait to unburden himself.

'I'm only a pawn in all this, Chief Superintendent,' began Skinner, the moment that Fox walked into the interview room.

200

Fox nodded. 'I imagine so,' he said. 'Who, then, is the king?'

'Hayden.' There was no hesitation in Skinner's response. No false honour-among-thieves that so many villains kidded themselves existed.

Fox gave Skinner a pitiful smile. 'You surely don't expect me to believe that a distinguished entrepreneur like Freddie Hayden is up to any sort of villainy, do you, Mr Skinner?'

Skinner shook his head and smiled, presumably at the thought that a policeman like Fox could be so easily taken in. But then he had only recently met Fox. 'Believe me, Mr Fox,' he said, 'the great Freddie Hayden is among the worst. I know that he's been to garden parties at the Palace, and it's an open secret that he's in the running for a knighthood, but he's the most immoral, unscrupulous bastard I've ever met.'

'If that's the case, and it's a big if, how did you get embroiled in his wrongdoing?' Fox lit a cigarette and gazed at the plump executive through a haze of smoke.

For a while, Skinner remained silent. 'You've met Hayden, I take it?' he said eventually.

'Yes, I have. Twice.'

'Then you'll have met his secretary, Toni.'

'Yes. Good-looking girl, I seem to recall.'

Skinner nodded. 'Very,' he said. 'Well, Toni and I have been having an affair. It's been going on for about two years now. The trouble is that if my wife gets to know about it, and it comes to a divorce, she'll take me for every penny I've got and—'

'Is this all relevant, Mr Skinner?'

'Very much so. Hayden found out about it. I don't know who told him, but I suspect Hooper, the chief security officer. He's always in and out of Hayden's office, so Toni has told me. Anyway, Hayden sent for me about a year ago. He told me he knew all about Toni and me, and threatened to tell my wife and to sack me. Trotted out some drivel about it being immoral and unacceptable for one of the charity's trustees to be conducting an extra-marital affair.' Skinner laughed bitterly at the thought. 'That was pretty rich, coming from him.'

'Meaning?'

'Meaning, Mr Fox, that he's well known for having a bit on the side. Toni said that he's always pawing her in the office and making indecent suggestions to her. Nothing would have given me greater satisfaction than to sort the bastard out, but that would have meant both Toni and I getting the sack. And frankly, we could neither of us afford for that to happen. Toni's a widow with a teenage daughter and she's the breadwinner. If I'd lost my job as well, I couldn't have helped her.'

'So what did Hayden say?'

'He more or less blackmailed me into doing some creative accounting for him.'

'In what way?'

'He obtained supplies for his charity from somewhere. I don't know where they came from and, although I suspected that they may have been stolen, I could never prove it. Tinsley handled that side of it, you see. My job was to lose it in the accounting. In short, Hayden would obtain the stuff, but the accounts of the charity would show that he'd paid full price for it on the open market. Very simply, he'd pocket the difference.' Skinner looked at Fox with a level gaze. 'As an accountant,' he said, 'I can tell you quite categorically that the Hayden empire is on the point of collapse.'

'Can you prove what you've been saying?' asked Fox.

Skinner grinned. 'You bet I can,' he said.

'How?'

'There are a number of tapes in my desk at home. The sort of micro-tapes that are used in dictating machines. I taped two or three of my conversations with him. Secretly, of course. After the first threatening interview, I thought that one day I might just finish up in a place like this.' Skinner glanced round the interview room. 'And I wanted to make sure that if that happened, I would be able to convince someone like you that I'd more or less been blackmailed into doing what I did.'

'Well, well,' said Fox. 'How very cunning of you. I think that the next thing we need to do, Mr Skinner, is to send

202

someone to your home to rescue those tapes, don't you?'

'The sooner the better,' said Skinner.

TWENTY THREE

THE TAPES, WHICH FOX HAD sent DI Evans to seize from Skinner's comfortable detached house in Wimbledon Park, had proved to Fox's satisfaction that Hayden had known exactly what was going on in the charity that he hoped was to earn him a knighthood. There was ample evidence, too, of Hayden's blackmailing threats, and Skinner had been telling the truth when he had said that Hayden had promised to expose his extra-marital fling with Toni Foster. And Hayden had been neither subtle nor lacking in crudity in the way in which he had delivered those threats.

The appropriate books of the charity had been seized and Detective Chief Superintendent Ray Probert of the Fraud Squad had assigned a detective inspector to examine them, with the help of Skinner, in the hope of proving what the accountant had alleged.

Fox and Gilroy strode across the entrance hall of Hayden's head office building and made straight for the bank of lifts.

' 'Ere, where d'you think you're going?' said the security guard, rising from his chair and reaching for the telephone.

'He's going to see your guv'nor,' said DC Tarling as one of his hands closed over the security guard's and the other laid his warrant card on the desk.

'Blimey, guv'nor, what's going on?' asked the security guard.

'Well, they haven't come to make a donation to Mr Hayden's charity, that's a dead cert,' said Tarling.

Fox and Gilroy alighted from the lift on the second floor

and made their way to Freddie Hayden's suite of offices. 'Good morning,' said Fox breezily to Hayden's secretary. 'We've come to see your boss.'

For a fleeting moment, the secretary looked puzzled. 'Ah,' she said, 'you're from the police, aren't you?'

'Indeed we are, Mrs Foster.'

Toni Foster looked surprised that Fox had known her name. 'I'm afraid Mr Hayden's engaged at the moment,' she said. 'He's got the chief security officer with him.'

'How very appropriate,' said Fox and pushed open the door leading to the inner office. Hayden was sitting in one of the leather settees, opposite John Hooper. 'Er, what—'

'Morning,' said Fox, and glancing at Hooper, added, 'Morning, John.'

'Hallo, guv,' said Hooper. He knew from years of experience that something was up. After Hayden had told him of Fox's raid at Epsom and the seizure of the charity's books, he had been expecting the arrival of the head of the Flying Squad. He knew Tommy Fox's style.

Hayden stood up. 'I was talking to my chief security officer,' he said, 'but if it's something urgent, I can—'

'Frederick Hayden, I have a warrant for your arrest on charges of securing gains by making unwarranted demands with menaces, and of conspiring with others to handle stolen property. Anything you say will be given in evidence. Want to put your coat on?'

Hayden stood in stunned silence, his face white. 'There must be some mistake,' he stuttered.

Fox smiled and shook his head. 'I don't make mistakes of that sort, Mr Hayden,' he said. 'Shall we go?'

'Er, I need to telephone my solicitor.' Hayden's hands flapped indecisively in front of him.

'By all means,' said Fox. 'When we get to the police station.' He turned to Hooper. 'See you around, John.'

As the two police officers and Hayden passed through Toni Foster's office, Fox glanced at her. 'I should cancel all Mr Hayden's appointments for today,' he said. 'He's just been arrested.'

'Of course, Mr Fox,' said the secretary and smiled. Vindictively.

In accordance with standard practice, Hayden's particulars were recorded by the custody sergeant at Charing Cross Police Station and his photograph and fingerprints were taken.

'Are you going to interview him, guv'nor?' asked Gilroy.

'I suppose so, Jack,' said Fox. 'It'll probably be a waste of time, but we might just glean something from what his brief says. Most lawyers I've met love the sound of their own voice.'

The distraught figure of Freddie Hayden was slumped in a chair next to his solicitor in the interview room.

Fox made a big thing of shaking hands with the solicitor. 'Didn't expect to meet you again so soon,' he said.

'What are these preposterous charges upon which you've arrested my client, Mr Fox?' asked the lawyer.

'He was told at the time, of course,' said Fox, 'but this is a copy of the charges which will be preferred against him.' He laid a flimsy sheet of paper on the table.

The solicitor scanned the charges with an expert eye. 'Making demands with menaces? Conspiring to handle stolen property?' He threw the paper on to the table. 'This is absolutely ludicrous,' he said. 'Are you seriously suggesting that a man of Mr Hayden's standing would trade in stolen property?'

'The facts of the matter,' said Fox, 'are that when we raided the depot at Epsom, stolen property was found. We have further substantial evidence from a number of witnesses connecting Mr Hayden with that property.'

'Who are these witnesses?'

'They are being considered as co-conspirators at the moment—' began Fox.

'That's not good enough,' said the lawyer. 'The evidence of one co-conspirator against—'

Fox held up his hand. 'I know all about that,' he said, 'but one of the witnesses may turn Queen's Evidence, and there is some technical evidence, namely tape-recorded conversations between Mr Hayden and that witness.'

'What is this evidence? The defence are entitled to—'

Again Fox interrupted. 'I know that too,' he said. 'But that is a matter between your counsel and counsel for the Crown.'

'I didn't know that any of that property was stolen.' Hayden suddenly sat up and joined in the conversation.

The solicitor leaned across and placed a hand on Hayden's arm. 'It would be most unwise of you to say anything at this stage, Freddie,' he said.

'Well, you're not just going to let this bloody man charge me, are you?'

'It's the only way, Freddie. We'll get the best counsel and I doubt that this will even get past the examining magistrate.'

'I didn't know that Dawes was dealing in stolen property,' blurted out Hayden.

'Who mentioned anything about Dawes?' asked Fox softly.

'My client declines to answer any questions,' said the solicitor.

'Don't blame him,' said Fox.

'This is Detective Chief Superintendent Thomas Fox . . . of the Flying Squad,' said Fox, when the assistant secretary in charge of the Police Department at the Home Office answered the phone.

'Good afternoon, Mr Fox. What can I do for you?'

'I have this day arrested a Mr Frederick Hayden, who is the head of the Hayden Trust charity, among other things,' said Fox airily.

'Oh, really?' said the Home Office official, wondering why a senior Scotland Yard detective was bothering him with this trivia.

'Yes indeed,' said Fox. 'For making demands with menaces and conspiring to handle stolen property.'

'Well I'm sure that's all very interesting, Mr Fox, but I have to say that I'm a little baffled as to why you should be telling me this.'

'You will be getting a full written report about it in due course, naturally,' continued Fox, 'but I have reason to believe that the Honours Office at 10 Downing Street will be passionately interested in this crumb of information.'

'Ah, I see,' said the assistant secretary, as the purpose of Fox's call started to become clear. 'Er, what made you think that they might wish to know, as a matter of interest?'

'I have very good informants,' said Fox.

An unshaven Harry Dawes shuffled into the interview room at Charing Cross Police Station. His night in the cells appeared to have aged him considerably, but Fox was in no mood to commiserate.

'Afternoon, Harry. Have a good lunch, did you?'

'This is all a stitch-up,' said Dawes. 'It's all because I made that complaint about you, isn't it? You're getting your own back.'

'What complaint was that, Harry?' asked Fox, flicking the seat of his chair with a clean handkerchief before sitting down.

'About you harassing me with all them coppers hanging about outside my house.'

'Oh that! Yes, I remember there was something about that. But you see, Harry, I explained that they were there to protect you. After we started arresting your little friends, I feared that someone might have tried to get at you. My superiors quite understood.'

Dawes looked at Fox with an expression of disgust on his face. 'A bleedin' whitewash, you mean?'

'Exactly so, Harry.' Fox smiled compassionately at the ageing fence. 'However, Harry, I haven't come all the way from Scotland Yard to discuss your welfare and safety.'

'Didn't think you bleedin' had,' muttered Dawes.

'We have a lot to talk about,' continued Fox. 'Not least of which is a number of robberies in diverse places and the disposal of the proceeds thereof by way of your various outlets.' Fox grinned. 'Among which were your slaughters at Lambeth, Croydon and Hounslow.'

'They was nothing to do with me.'

'The so-called managing director of the set-up at Hounslow, which had the impudence to call itself Carmody Trading Ltd, was one Vincent Carmody—'

'Never heard of him,' said Dawes automatically.

'Who, my surveillance officers tell me, visited your premises at Oxford Road on numerous occasions.' Fox thumbed the edge of the pile of files in front of him. 'I can give you dates and times, if you like. But there wouldn't be a great deal of point in that, would there, Harry. You were in every time he came to see you. Incidentally, he said that you serve bloody awful sherry.'

'There's nothing wrong with my sherry,' said Dawes with a flash of anger. 'It's just that Vince doesn't appreciate a good Manzanilla when he sees one. He's not an athlete, you see.'

'An athlete? What the hell's athletics got to do with sherry?'

'You know,' said Dawes. 'Someone what appreciates the finer things in life.'

'Ah!' said Fox, 'you mean an aesthete. However, Harry, we're not getting very far, are we? Having established, by your own admission, that you knew Vincent Carmody, I have to tell you that he's put everything down to you.'

'But I never—'

'He actually called you the mastermind, Harry. Great compliment that, don't you think?'

'He's trying to stitch me up, that's what he's trying to do.'

'Then we come to the question of the Hayden Trust.'

'What's that?' Dawes's head jerked up.

'Ah, I see you've heard of it.'

'No I ain't.'

Fox grinned. 'I can understand your saying that, Harry. It's a charity, and charity's not exactly your line of business, is it? On the other hand,' Fox went on, 'there have been some nasty allegations made about you in connection with the said charity.' He opened one of the files in front of him. 'In short, Mr Hayden has put it all down to you. He says that he didn't know that the gear was nicked. I got the impression that he thought you'd had him over.'

'The saucy bastard.' Dawes was clearly outraged by this latest piece of what he regarded as malicious testimony. 'Course he bloody knew it was bent.'

Fox shook his head slowly. 'Things aren't looking too

good, Harry,' he said. 'His mouthpiece is, at this very moment, on the trumpet drumming up the finest silk that money can buy to defend Mr Hayden, and knowing the ways of the criminal bar, I should say that he had a very good chance of succeeding.'

Dawes's head sunk onto his chest in an attitude of deep contemplation. 'You haven't got a fag, Mr Fox, have you?' he asked a moment later.

Fox slid his cigarette case across the bare Formica-topped table. 'Help yourself, Harry.'

Dawes took a cigarette and accepted a light. Then he leaned back in his chair and studied Fox for a while, as though assessing how far he could go. Making up his mind, he drew hard on his cigarette and leaned forward again. 'I've got something to tell you, Mr Fox,' he said. 'But I'd like to know what consideration I'll get for it.'

'Depends what it is, Harry. In short though, if you turn Queen's Evidence and they don't believe you, you'll go down for a fair old stretch.' It always grieved Fox to have to tell prisoners that. 'On the other hand, I can discuss it with the Crown Prosecution Service who might be prepared to come to some sort of arrangement. That's probably getting the best of both worlds, if you see what I mean.'

Dawes digested this crumb of not very encouraging information in silence. 'All right then,' he said at length. 'The murder of that girl is down to Hayden.'

'Really? Don't push your luck too far, Harry.'

'Stand on me, Mr Fox. It's the God's honest truth.'

'I'm afraid I'm going to need more than that, Harry.' Fox took a cigarette from his open case.

'That night, when it happened, I got a call from Hayden. He was in a blind panic. Screaming down the phone he was. Said he'd just topped this girl and that he had to get rid of the body, fast.'

'So you popped round to his drum, collected the body and banged it in your lock-up at Lambeth to await disposal, is that it?' Fox gazed at Dawes with a cynical expression of disbelief on his face. 'Why should I believe that out of the goodness of your heart, you helped him out? Why didn't you adopt your usual ploy of telling him to drop dead?'

'Because she was blackmailing him, the prat.'

'What had that got to do with you, Harry?'

'Well, I was in on it an' all, wasn't I?'

'In on what? The murder?'

'Nah! What happened was that he'd picked up with this bird. Reckoned he'd met her at some party. Anyhow, they starts having it off on a regular basis, see, and she wheedles it all out of him, don't she. . . about this charity. And he reckoned he'd told her about me an' all. Pillow talk, I s'pose.'

'And you believed this?' Fox was genuinely surprised that Dawes appeared to have been taken in by Hayden's tale.

'Not totally, no. But Hayden said that if I didn't help him out he'd grass me up. Said that he was very influential. Banged on about going to garden parties at Buckingham Palace and hob-nobbing with the Queen. He said that everybody'd believe him and that I'd finish up in stir, but if I done the business, he'd stay shtum.'

'Where did you collect Dawn Sims's body from, Harry?'

'One of them mews places down Pimlico,' said Dawes.

'Address?'

'Dunno.'

'How could you have collected a body from there if you don't know where it is?' Fox was beginning to doubt Dawes's story and wondered why he was telling it; it seemed a strange and unsuitable way for him to exact revenge on Hayden.

'Well, I did at the time like, but I've forgotten now. I could take you there, though, Mr Fox.'

'Go on, Harry.'

'Well, like I said, I got this phone call from Hayden. Must have been about eight o'clock on the Sunday evening. So I gave Vince a bell and he brought the transit round and we went down this mews place. It was dark and there wasn't no one about, so we banged the body in the van and took it down Lambeth. I thought it'd be all right there until we could do a proper job getting rid of it. But then you bleedin' lot turned up next morning.' Dawes sighed at the injustice of it all.

It was nearing eight o'clock in the evening and snowing steadily when Dawes led the police to a tiny mews in Pimlico. 'That's the one,' he said, pointing to a red door.

Swann, still grumbling, opened the door with the minimum of trouble and Fox led Gilroy and a team of scenes-of-crime officers into the small sitting-room on the first floor. It was comfortably furnished and the only indication of violent crime was an overturned table and a smashed lamp. It appeared that Hayden had not visited the place again since the night of the murder.

'Right, lads,' said Fox to the scenes-of-crime men, 'get to it.'

As a result of Dawes's statement to the police, Fox had decided not to charge Hayden with the other offences immediately, despite the protests of his solicitor, and had ordered that he be held in custody overnight.

The following day, Hayden's solicitor arrived early at Charing Cross Police Station so that he could be present when Hayden was charged and then taken to the nearby Bow Street magistrates court.

But Fox had been busier than the lawyer.

'What's going on?' asked the solicitor when Hayden was brought in to the interview room once again. 'You must either charge my client or release him.'

'I intend to ask him some questions,' said Fox. 'Well, one question actually.'

'But—'

'Don't presume to give me a lecture about what I may or may not ask a prisoner,' said Fox, and nodding to Gilroy to turn on the recording machine, administered the formal caution. 'Mr Hayden, are you the owner or lessee of a mews property in Pimlico known as—'

'My client declines to answer the question,' said the solicitor sharply.

'No I don't,' said Hayden. He looked to Fox, a pathetic expression on his face. 'Yes, I do own that property.'

'An examination of that property, carried out during the night, reveals that your fingerprints and those of Lady Dawn Sims were found there. We have also compared your fingerprints with certain marks found at her flat in Edgware Road and have identified them as yours, despite your having denied ever having been there.'

'I know,' said Hayden. Head bowed, his hands were linked together on the table in front of him, fingers fiercely intertwined. Then he looked up. 'I killed her,' he said.

'For God's sake, Freddie,' said the solicitor. 'Don't say any more.'

'Shut up,' said Hayden. 'I want to tell Mr Fox all about it.'

'I repeat that you are not obliged—' began Fox.

Hayden held up a hand. 'I know, I know,' he said, his voice croaking with strain. 'I was a fool. I was captivated by that girl. At first, she was so warm and understanding and I thought that I might get something out of life that has escaped me all these years. But I didn't know it would turn out the way it did. You see, Mr Fox, I was foolish enough to think that she loved me, and that if I divorced Tessa, Dawn would marry me. In the beginning, I was silly enough to think that she might be impressed by the title I was going to get. Then, of course, I found out that she was a lady in her own right, and that such things meant nothing to her. But she was only after my money.' He stared at Fox, willing him to understand the frailties of man. 'Then she started blackmailing me.'

'How?' asked Fox.

'Photographs.' Hayden hung his head.

'What sort of photographs?'

Hayden gave Fox a pathetic glance, as though the policeman should have known. 'Of Dawn and me . . . in bed together.'

Fox's eyes narrowed. 'Who took them, d'you know?'

'Her boyfriend. He appeared in the bedroom at Edgware Road one night. The first I knew was when a flash-bulb went off.'

'What was this man's name, My Hayden?'

'I've no idea. Dawn wouldn't tell me.'

'Mr Hayden,' said Fox, 'I don't understand why that

213

should have made you susceptible to blackmail? Just now, you said that you were contemplating divorcing Mrs Hayden in order to marry Dawn Sims. So why should the photographs have been a potential embarrassment?'

'Because she said that the other photographs would be sent to my wife as well.' Hayden suddenly seemed to be about ten years older. 'And not only to my wife, but to anyone who knew me for my charitable works.'

'What other photographs?'

'They were obscene pictures of Dawn,' said Hayden. 'The most disgusting poses I've ever seen. Quite graphic, I can assure you, Mr Fox.' He let out a great sigh as though relieved at having been able to tell someone about it at last. 'I kept paying until I couldn't afford any more, but still she pressed. That last night in Pimlico, she went too far. I got angry and grabbed hold of her.' He gave Fox a pleading look. 'I didn't mean to kill her,' he said. 'It just happened.'

'Christ! Aren't you ever going to leave me alone?' Jason Hope-Smith looked at Fox and Evans. 'I'm getting bloody fed up with this, I can tell you. It's nothing short of harassment.'

Fox pushed the door open and barged into Hope-Smith's flat. 'Get the photographs,' he said.

'You've got them, remember? You took them away the last time you came.'

'Not those. The photographs you took of Frederick Hayden in bed with Dawn Sims. And the others that you took of Barnes, the weaselly little civil servant, and all the others you and Dawn were blackmailing.'

'You must be imagining things,' said Hope-Smith. He appeared to be quite unmoved by Fox's allegation.

Fox shrugged. 'Please yourself,' he said, 'but I have ten officers downstairs who are just waiting for my signal to take this place apart. Then I shall obtain a crown court judge's warrant to examine your bank accounts and any safety deposit boxes you may have. But while all that's going on, Mr Hope-Smith, you'll be at the police station taking part in an identity parade. Mr Frederick Hayden is quite confident that he'll be able to pick out the nocturnal photographer who took pictures of him and Dawn in bed together.' There wasn't a hope of that; Hayden had said that he'd been blinded by the flash-bulb of the camera.'

But it was enough for Hope-Smith. He sank down into a chair and put his head between his hands. 'It was all Dawn's idea,' he said.

Fox nodded. 'A gentleman to the last,' he said.

Three months later, at the Old Bailey, Frederick Hayden pleaded diminished responsibility and was sentenced to fifteen years' imprisonment for the manslaughter of Lady Dawn Sims. The counts of making demands with menaces and that of conspiring to handle stolen property were left on the file, but the first year of his confinement was enlivened by frequent visits from representatives of the Serious Fraud Office. And at 10 Downing Street, an official rubbed out a pencilled question mark before scoring a line through Hayden's name.

The judge told Dawes that he would receive a lighter sentence than his crimes merited because he had assisted police enquiries into the death of Lady Dawn Sims, and then gave him ten years for being an accessory, conspiring to commit robbery and to handle stolen property.

Jason Hope-Smith went down for ten years too, but not before he had received a long lecture from the judge on the iniquities of demanding money with menaces.

Carmody received eight years on an indictment similar to that which Dawes had faced, and the other, smaller fry who had been arrested along the way, were sentenced to lesser periods of imprisonment.

Peter Skinner, Hayden's accountant and a trustee of his charity, was placed on probation for two years.

And Tommy Fox took Jane Sims out to dinner.

She was wearing an emerald green silk dress when Fox collected her from her flat near Knightsbridge. Her hair, long to her shoulders, was shining, and her high-heeled shoes set off her nylon-clad legs to perfection.

'Well, what d'you think, Tommy?' she asked, pirouetting in front of him.

215

'You've cracked it,' said Fox.

It was seven-thirty the next morning. Detective Sergeant Ernest Crabtree and Detective Constable Sean Tarling sat in a Flying Squad car in a street near Knightsbridge. They were acting on information received, as the police so often say. According to an informant of doubtful repute, there was going to be a robbery from a Post Office van. Other Flying Squad vehicles were in the area and DI Denzil Evans had his men deployed all over the place.

'Here,' said Crabtree, 'isn't that the guv'nor?' He pointed to a figure which had just emerged from a block of mansion flats. A figure wearing a light grey cashmere overcoat.

'Where?' asked Tarling. But at that moment a bus obscured his vision. And when it was gone the road was empty.

And the Post Office van didn't get robbed either.

Little, Brown now offers an exciting range of quality titles by both established and new authors. All of the books in this series are available by faxing, or posting your order to:

Little, Brown and Company (UK) Limited,
Mail order,
P.O. Box 11,
Falmouth,
Cornwall,
TR1O 9EN
Fax: 0326-376423

Payments can be made as follows: Cheque, postal order (payable to Little, Brown Cash Sales) or by credit cards, Visa/Access/Mastercard. Do not send cash or currency. U.K. customers and B.F.P.O.; Allow £1.00 for postage and packing for the first book, plus 50p for the second book, plus 30p for each additional book up to a maximum charge of £3.00 (7 books plus). U.K. orders over £75 free postage and packing.

Overseas customers including Ireland, please allow £2.00 for postage and packing for the first book, plus £1.00 for the second book, plus 50p for each additional book.

NAME (Block Letters) ....

ADDRESS ....

....

....

☐ I enclose my remittance for ....

☐ I wish to pay by Visa/Access/Mastercard

Number ☐☐☐☐☐☐☐☐☐☐☐☐☐☐☐☐

Card Expiry Date ☐☐☐☐